AF479884

Contents

Through Frozen Eyes

A Hood River Mystery Book 2

Lana M. Fox

Ellana M. Fox

To my boys: Bob Fox, Randy Fox and David Fox

I love you more!

Prologue

She was crazy to go out in the middle of the night in a snowstorm, but she had to know if the rumors she'd heard were true. Hopefully, it was just a stupid rumor, but despair settled in her stomach, making her feel queasy, and she worried it was more than that. She'd drive by the house, make sure everything looked okay, then she'd go home and sleep for ten hours. Fatigue dragged at her after working a double shift, and the cold wasn't helping.

Her tires crunched on the snow-packed roads. It had snowed again that day—that was like six days in a row—and it was supposed to freeze tonight. She could see stars blinking in the night sky and figured that was true. She hoped her home would stay warm enough for her to sleep. If not, she'd have to sleep in her car again. At least she'd just gotten paid and filled up her gas tank. She could run the car off and on during the night if she had to.

A shiver crawled up her back, and she wished she was finished with college and working so she could rent an apartment and lead a more normal life. She was so tired of trying to survive and being miserable all the time. If her mother would ever come through with her promises, but that was something she knew better than to hope for. Lilly Larson never did what she said she was going to do.

A familiar black pickup pulled out of the street in front of her car, the backend fishtailing in the snow. She held back, watching to see where it *went. The driver acted drunk; the vehicle sliding all over the road. She followed it through town, the stores all closed for the night. No one was out walking around. Just her and the crazy person driving the pickup. She should go home and not worry about other people, but it wasn't in her to not worry, so she drove on through the snow-packed streets.*

Where was the driver going? She followed the pickup down State Street. Turning down the hill on 2nd Street. They were heading for the freeway. Why this time of night?

She stayed behind. Curious. Driving slowly. Then the pickup turned right onto the freeway on- ramp. Knowing she should probably give it up and go home, she followed. If Gram was there, she would have known what to do. Pain edged around her heart. If Gram were still alive, she'd have a warm place to live and enough food to keep her belly full.

The pickup eased onto the freeway and drove slowly towards the next off-ramp. A big truck came towards her in the oncoming lane, its lights blinded her for a moment. She blinked and followed the pickup off the ramp. It turned left towards the Hood River bridge that crossed the Columbia River and separated Oregon from Washington.

Were they going to cross the bridge? Should she continue to follow or go home? Probably home. But she wanted to see where they were going, so she could tell someone if she needed to. She didn't trust the person driving the pickup. Where were they headed?

The lights on the bridge were bright, and she didn't want to be noticed, so she pulled over and sat on the side of the road. She turned off her lights and watched as the pickup slowed down by the tollbooth, then moved on. She wished she could see who was in the truck.

She let the pickup get out of sight on the bridge, then she pulled up to the tollbooth. No one manned the booth this early in the morning. She'd heard that they took a picture of your license plate and sent you a bill. Great, just what she needed was another bill to pay.

She started across the bridge. It wasn't sturdy at the best of times. The steel grating threw her little Kia around. She slowed down to a crawl, hating to drive over the bridge on a sunny day, let alone a snowy night.

Deciding she could drive by the lights on the bridge, she turned off her lights. She didn't want to announce her presence to the person in the pickup. She just wanted to see where they were going and if it was who she thought it was. When she knew they were safely on the other side, she'd go home.

The pickup lights were out, and she almost hit it, coming up on it in the dark. She slammed on her brakes and her little car slid around until she could get it stopped. Her stomach jumped into her throat and her nerve endings tingled.

Her heart pounded, fast and furious, when she noticed someone leaning over the rail of the bridge. What were they doing? She strained to see and when she did, her heart stopped, then pounded in her chest. Grabbing her phone out of her pocket, she hit Bella Ellisen's name, praying Bella would answer. She needed to talk to Bella's mom, Detective Ellisen. There were things going on that scared her. Things she needed to talk to someone about. But she didn't want to call the sheriff's office and talk to anyone else. Only Bella's mom.

The phone went to voicemail. She left a message. "Bella, this is Renetta. I need to talk to your mom. Can you give her my number and have her call me? It's important."

She clicked off the phone. She glanced at the person standing by the bridge rail. Now they were leaning over. Were they going to jump?

"Oh no! Oh, dear Lord, please no!" she cried as she jumped from the car and hurried towards the other person, screaming, "No, no, no!"

The other person turned towards her and growled, "Stay back." In the person's arms was a baby blanket. Renetta recognized it.

"What have you done?" she cried. Everything she'd been worried about slid into place in her mind. Renetta felt herself shake from head to toe, and not from the cold. "Please don't do this. We'll work something out. I promise." Her cheeks were wet with tears. She could barely see, but she rushed forward and grabbed at the bundle in the other person's arms.

The other person laughed. An evil sound. "You're too late."

Chapter 1

Chapter 1—Liz

"There's been a murder." Mitch's voice greeted me the minute I walked into the Sheriff's department that morning. My heart sank. Someone had lost their life, and it was up to us to find out what happened. While I loved the challenge of my job, I hated the thought that it might be someone I knew, which happened often in our small county.

Mitchel Ellisen, the Hood River County Sheriff, and my soon to be ex-husband, stood in front of reception with his arms crossed over his chest and worry lines creasing his forehead. He stared at me, making me feel more unsure of myself than I had in ages. Why did I let him have that effect on me? He had no right to my feelings anymore.

"A young woman was found out on Westcliff Drive. You and Rodriguez need to get out there," Mitch said. His tone was all business, and I wondered what he was really thinking behind his slate blue eyes. He was trying hard not to give anything away.

No "Hello, good to have you back, or how are you, Liz?" I had been away from the job for eight months. We hadn't spoken in weeks, and he couldn't even say hello? I narrowed my eyes. So that's the way he planned to deal with our separation and me working for him? I wondered if we could work together. Only time would tell.

Enrique Rodriguez stumbled in, rubbing sleep from his eyes. He grinned when he saw me. "Liz! Am I glad to see you!" He grabbed me in a bear hug that squished the breath from my chest. Even though we'd been friends and co-workers for a long time, he'd never hugged me like that before. "This place has been a zoo without you."

"Hey, Enrique. Good to see you, too." I patted his back, then stepped away as Mitch's voice cut in, razor sharp.

"You need to get moving. I'll text you the address. Let me know if you need me." He looked at me and the longing in his eyes whipped through me like an electrical current. I told myself I hadn't missed him. So why did my heart ache? Maybe because I'd loved him most of my life? It amazed me how hard it was to turn off my feelings when he'd cheated on me with my best friend. I should hate him, and part of me did. But another part of me longed for the good years of our marriage when he was my partner, my lover, and friend.

I was a detective on his team, but I wondered if I could work for him and keep my sanity. I'd thought about changing jobs. Why did it have to be me, though? I'd given up my home and my life. What had he given up?

Enrique and I turned around and went outside to the department issued SUV. I shivered as I crawled in on the passenger side. It was one of the coldest January days on record, according to the weather report on television that morning. The roads were a sheet of ice and traffic was almost nonexistent. Even my black down jacket would not be enough for this kind of weather, and I wished I'd put on an extra layer underneath my uniform shirt.

According to that same weather report, both Portland and everything East had come to a standstill. The snow had started on Christmas day and the temperatures had gotten colder and colder. It was a good day to stay inside. I hoped most people would. The city police were responding to accidents on both ends of town and freeway exits. Our deputies were checking roads all over the county.

I let Enrique drive because I still felt a little fuzzy from jetlag. Normally, I would have driven. I'm the better driver in the snow. Enrique always drives like he's late to a fire. My fists tightened as he went around a corner, and I felt the vehicle slide.

"It would be nice if people waited to kill each other until the weather was warmer." Enrique shook his head. "This weather brings out the worst in people's ability to drive."

"That's for sure." I glanced out the window at the ice and snow everywhere. Even though Hood River had a low crime rate most of the time, it seemed to rise during bad weather and in the summer during hot weather.

"I heard your plane was delayed coming home from Europe," Enrique said. He had stuck a piece of gum in his mouth before we left the office, and now he chewed, his jaws working and the gum popping. I knew he'd been trying to quit chewing tobacco before his baby came, and I was proud of him. I was sure it wasn't easy to quit.

"Yeah, we didn't know if we'd make it home Monday or not. They were threatening to close the airport." We were so thankful when the plane landed, and we got off in Portland. I just wanted my own bed.

Now I looked out the window at the frozen ground. Lights from different businesses shone on the road, making it look like an ice rink. Town had come to a standstill. I couldn't remember the last time we'd had such cold temperatures. It was in the twenties and dipping down into the teens at night.

"Glad you made it in. So, how was your trip?" he asked, shooting me his big grin.

I glanced at him. Did he know that my ex-best friend had crashed our trip? "It would've been great if we hadn't had to deal with Jennifer Lockwood."

Enrique shook his head. "I heard she surprised you over there."

"Yeah, you could say that." Jenn had thought it would be great to have a girl's trip. She didn't think about me not wanting to see her, let alone spend time with her. "She did her best to ruin the trip for me." While my daughter, Bella, had been angry at her dad and Jenn for their affair, she was a lot more forgiving than me. By the end of our time with Jenn, Bella was treating her like nothing had happened.

"That's crazy. Why would she do that?" Enrique popped his gum. I thought about taking it away from him, but tried to be patient since I knew he needed it.

"Because she thinks the world revolves around her. I'm surprised Ray has stuck with her. Most men would've booted her out when they found out she'd been having affairs." Ray Lockwood was Jenn's long-suffering husband. He was also a State Senator and gone from home a lot. Maybe he didn't know that Jenn was playing around when he was out of town.

My daughter and I had dealt with Jenn showing up in Germany and trying to take over our plans. Then she went missing, and we used up some of our days in Germany looking for her. I'd tried to tell Bella that Jenn was fine. She'd find her way home. And of course, I was right, but it took a few days before Bella gave in and stopped worrying about her. "Luckily, we enjoyed the trip despite her."

"She's a piece of work."

"Tell me about it." I rolled my eyes. He didn't have to. I'd known Jenn a long time. She'd always been self-centered, but I never would've thought she'd try to ruin my marriage. Maybe you never really knew anyone. The two people, besides Bella, in my life that I trusted most, and they had not considered me at all when they had an affair. It made me sick to think about it.

"So, what did you guys do?" Enrique glanced at me, then back at the road. The SUV slid, and I held on to the door handle.

I pulled my mind back from the deep despair I felt every time I thought about Mitch and Jenn. "We did the touristy things; sight-seeing and lots of shopping. The markets in Germany were so fun. We had to mail some of our stuff home because we couldn't get it all into our suitcases."

My daughter Bella and I had spent Christmas in Europe. After her father's and my breakup last spring, and my father's murder, I hadn't wanted to deal with the holidays. So, I'd taken Bella to Europe for a month with some of the money from Dad's estate. Thoughts of my dad sent a sharp pain through my heart. I'd also lost my only sister to murder because of the Bread of Life cult and their leader, Jeremiah Swanson, who was rotting away in jail for having his wife and my sister murdered, child trafficking and endangering the lives of those in his care. I hoped he'd be there for a long time, but I knew the chances were that he'd get out and be able to ruin more lives.

Enrique grinned and nodded. "I'm glad you didn't take Jo with you. She probably would have needed to rent an extra airplane to bring all her shopping home. Man, that woman can shop." He shook his head. "You should see the baby's room."

"I would've loved taking Jolene with us, but you were worried we wouldn't make it home before the baby came and she still had two months to go." That I agreed with him flitted through my mind.

"I know, but I wouldn't have slept at all while you were gone, and the doc didn't think it was such a great idea."

"Probably not." I loved Enrique's wife, Jolene. We've become close in the last few months. I helped her paint and decorate the baby's room, and we shopped for baby things. It was fun and took my mind off my crappy life.

My phone pinged, and I took it out and read the text from Mitch, telling us where to go on Westcliff Drive. "It looks like the body was found on the bluff above the river." I turned my thoughts back to the work ahead of us. Maybe if I concentrated on work, I wouldn't lose my mind. Another maybe.

Enrique nodded. "I wonder who it is."

Working in a small town had its disadvantages. We knew a lot of the victims and perps. Mitch hadn't given us a lot of information on this body, which meant he didn't have it. We would be the first officers to the scene, so we'd take the lead. I felt excitement and dread curl in my stomach. Excitement for a fresh case to sink my teeth into, and sadness for the dead girl and her family.

It didn't take long to drive to the west side of Hood River, and soon Enrique was pulling up to the address Mitch had given us. A woman sat on a boulder, a small dog of uncertain origins, in her arms. She wore a puffy red coat and a black stocking cap. Grey curls sprang from the cap, and her dog wore a red puffy vest. He or she was grey too, with a grey beard. I chuckled and pointed it out to Enrique, who laughed.

Enrique and I stepped from our vehicle, and the woman jumped up and hurried over to meet us. Her eyes were wide and her skin too pale. She was probably in her late seventies, and I worried that she'd been out in the cold too long and she might fall over from the stress of finding the body. I took her arm. "Are you okay, ma'am?"

She nodded and took a deep breath. "Hi, yes, but thank heavens you're here. I'm Jaclyn Downs and this is Georgie." She held up the little dog.

"Detective Ellisen and Detective Rodriguez." I introduced us, then guided her back to the rock she'd been sitting on. "Sit down and tell us what happened."

"That poor girl." Jaclyn pointed behind her towards the river, then looked back at us. Her eyes were wide, her nose was shiny, and she wiped it with her glove.

I shivered in the frigid cold air, feeling the hair in my nostrils freeze. I took a black wool scarf out of my pocket and wrapped it around my neck. "Were you the one who found her?"

The woman nodded. Her teeth chattered, and I knew we had to get her out of the cold fast. "Yes, Georgie and I found her. Well, really, it was him. We went out for a walk and were heading back to the house, and he started barking and straining at his leash. I let him take me to the edge of the cliff and when I looked down, I saw her." Her breath came out in puffs of white. "Poor thing. Do you think she froze to death? I wonder if she fell and couldn't get up?" Jaclyn shook her head and cuddled her dog. "Or maybe someone murdered her. Who would do something like that?"

She didn't seem to expect an answer, so I asked, "Do you know who she is?" She probably would have told us if she knew, but it never hurt to ask.

Enrique was making his way towards the body. The area had wooded terrain that sloped down to the river. I could hear him talking to Mitch on his radio as his boots slid on the uneven, ice-covered ground. I watched him, hoping he didn't start sliding and end up at the bottom of the cliff.

"No, probably a runaway. There have been a lot of homeless people camping across the freeway about a half mile from here. I hope they all found shelters. I don't see how they could survive in this cold." She shivered again, and I knew I had to get her somewhere warm.

"The warming shelter isn't too far from here," I assured her. "Did you see anyone else around?" I still held her arm, and she leaned into me. She was so thin she felt like a fragile bird.

Jaclyn shook her head. "No, just Georgie and me. We rarely see people out here when we're walking. We walk early." She shivered again.

"Okay, thank you for calling us. You need to get inside and get warm. Someone from the Sheriff's Department will come talk to you when we're finished here, okay? Do you want me to walk you home?"

The woman shook her head. "No, I'm okay, just cold." She hurried towards her house. Her dog yipped a few times, but she didn't put him down. I hoped she'd be okay. I knew that finding a body had traumatized her. We'd offer a counselor. Hopefully, she'd agree to talk to one.

The cold was seeping into my skin through my warm winter coat and clothes. I pulled my scarf up over my chin, longing for warmer weather. I headed towards Enrique, hoping this would be quick. But I knew crime scenes were never quick.

Enrique stood staring down at the mound of snow and ice. I slipped and slid towards him. The body was over an embankment, but not far down the cliff. "Do you recognize her?"

He shook his head, but his face had grown still. I didn't know if it was from shock or the freezing temperatures. "This is unbelievable," he whispered, looking at the body of a young girl.

Enrique's face had turned as white as the snow on the ground, and I felt my morning coffee stirring around in my stomach, threatening to come back up. "Oh, no."

I moved closer and looked down, wondering if I'd recognize her. The young woman was lying up against a tree, her body curled in a fetal position. "What in the world?" I looked closer. Someone had built a berm out of snow around the body, encasing her in it.

Enrique walked around the body, staring at the rectangle of snow. "Someone went to a lot of work to do this."

I stared at the young woman. Her eyes were wide open, and her hands were up, fingers curled, making it look like she was trying to claw her way out of the ice. My heart pounded. I didn't want to admit to what I was seeing. "She looks familiar."

Enrique squatted down. "I don't think I've seen her before."

When I knelt next to him, my breath caught in my throat. I had. In fact, at one time, I'd known her well. I was looking into the frozen eyes of my daughter's childhood friend, Renetta Larson. "Oh, dear Lord," I whispered. "Please don't let it be her."

"Who?" Enrique moved closer to the body.

"Renetta Larson. She and Bella were best friends in elementary school. Then they went their separate ways in middle school. Bella was into sports and Renetta wasn't, so they drifted apart." I touched the ice on Renetta's hair with my gloved hand. It was an involuntary move. I knew I shouldn't do it, but I couldn't help myself. "She was such a sweetie, but she had a horrible home life. I'm sure it's her." My stomach clenched. *Oh, please dear God, not her. Not Bella's friend.*

Enrique glanced up at me. Snow landed on his face and in his eyelashes. He blinked it away. "When did you last see her?"

"I don't remember. It's been a while. We should have kept in touch with her." I rubbed tears from my eyes. "Maybe this wouldn't have happened." I stared down at Renetta with my heart aching. *I'll find out who did this, sweet girl. If it's the last thing I do, I'll find out who stole your life away from you.*

"You can't know that."

"Can't I?" I felt guilt eat me up inside. I'd known that Renetta had been on her own most of her life. Her mother went from one man to another. All she cared about was the next hit. The thought of what this poor, sweet young woman had experienced as a child made me shudder. I knew Lilly was a lousy mother. I should have done more.

"I hate to tell Bella. She's going to be so upset." I put my hands on the ground and pushed myself up.

My daughter, Bella, was a sophomore at Oregon State University. She'd just gone back to school from winter break a few days earlier. I knew Bella would take Renetta's death hard. They were such good friends when they were younger.

"We'll find out who did this," Enrique said. "It was obviously premeditated. If that woman and her dog hadn't come this way on their walk, the body could've laid here until spring."

"Probably what the killer was hoping for." I tried to forget this was someone I knew, a young girl who shouldn't have died so young. I studied her body. Renetta wore jeans and a thick blue sweater. She had boots on her feet. Her long dark hair lay on her shoulders in thick strands. And her eyes, her beautiful blue eyes, were murky, but wide open. "What did you see?" I asked her softly.

"Can you tell how she died?" Enrique asked.

"No." I looked her over. There were no visible signs. Had someone drugged her? I pushed up the sleeve of her sweater with my gloved hand. No signs of needle marks on her skin, but that didn't mean the marks weren't somewhere else on her body. "We'll have to wait until Dr. King gets a look at her." I named the county coroner. "I don't want to move her."

Enrique and I looked up at the road as sirens headed towards us. I was relieved that help was on the way.

Enrique said, "Looks like Mitch called in the calvary. He wants you and I to talk to the folks in the homeless camp. He said Garcia and Jones can start canvassing the nearby houses." Enrique named the two deputies and looked at me. "That is, if you're up for it? Since you knew her, you don't have to be involved."

"I thought you knew me better than that. There's no way I'm not helping with this case." I'd fight Mitch to a standstill if he tried to leave me out of the investigation. I started around the ice, looking for clues. "Let's look around quickly before the others get here. I don't want them stepping on evidence."

"Sure thing, Boss." He always called me boss when we worked together. It was his private joke. He'd told me many times that he knew I was the real boss, not Mitch.

I sighed. So many things had changed. "Enrique, do you think it will be weird, me working for Mitch now that we're getting divorced?" I walked carefully around the body, searching for clues to who had committed this horrendous crime. My mind skittered back and forth between my ruined marriage and the case we were given. I knew I had to focus on Renetta and her killer. I couldn't let my personal problems take me away from the investigation.

Enrique looked up from where he'd bent down to examine something on the ground. "We won't let it." He looked back down. "Come here and look at this."

My boots crunched across the ice. I bent down and peered at the plastic circle he held up. I reached out, and he handed it to me. "It looks like a plastic bracelet." It was made of small, bright red plastic flowers. "She must've dropped it."

"Maybe, but it's interesting that it's just lying here. The snow has covered everything else. It's like someone dropped it recently."

"Where did you find it?" I glanced around, looking for anything else that may have been left. Who had dropped the bracelet? Had the killer left it intentionally? The thought of it being left for us to find filled me with horror.

"Laying on top of the snow close to her body." Enrique took an evidence bag out of his pocket and dropped the bracelet inside.

We scanned the area around the body but didn't find anything else. The sirens were getting closer, and we waited for Mitch and the coroner to get there.

Soon, the area was full of vehicles with red and blue lights flashing. The ambulance headed our way, its white and red lights blinking a steady rhythm. The sirens stopped, and Mitch, along with a few deputies, were heading down to meet us. I noticed the city cops were pulling in behind the county vehicles.

Mitch barked orders as he headed our way. Steam rose around his mouth as he talked. His eyes took in the scene, and he shook his head. "What do you have?" he asked when he was close enough.

Enrique and I both pointed to the snow built up around the body. "Someone built a berm around her," Enrique said.

Mitch looked closer and shook his head. He took in the scene. "It looks like he's framing her. Like a piece of art." His voice was soft, and I had to strain to hear with all the noise from the rest of our team.

I nodded, feeling sick inside. "Does that mean what I think it means?"

"I don't know. I sure hope not." He looked at me, and I could see tension in the lines around his eyes.

I told him about the woman who'd called it in, and the plastic bracelet Enrique found. Enrique handed the evidence bag with the bracelet in it to him. Mitch looked it over, then turned to Anna Garcia,

who had walked up next to them. "You and Jones canvas the neighborhood. See if you can find anyone who might know the victim."

"Um, Mitch," I said, stopping him.

He looked at me and raised his eyebrows. "What?"

I motioned to the body. "It's Renetta. Bella's friend, Renetta Larson."

Mitch moved closer and looked down. He shook his head and
whispered, "Crap."

I watched him kneel next to the girl and remembered one reason I'd
once loved this man so much. Even though he was tough, he had such
a tender heart for victims. He always felt crimes against the innocent
personally.

My heart clinched. How could he have treated me the way he
did? How could he have claimed to love me and then betray me in
such a horrible way? I turned away, not able to control the anger and
heartache inside. I wanted to grab him and shake him. Beat him over
the head. Shove him into a snowbank and leave him to freeze to death.

I stumbled away from the body. Okay, I thought, this isn't the time
or the place. I had to get a grip, or I wouldn't be able to do my work.
And I needed work right now. I needed to put everything Mitch had
done out of my mind and concentrate on Renetta.

A familiar voice rose above all the other voices, and I cringed.
Deputy Megan Connolly came striding towards me. "Liz, when did
you get back to town?"

Just the sound of Megan Connolly's voice made me want to scream.
But it jarred my trembling nerves and brought me back to the job
better than a pep talk from anyone else. "A couple days ago. Why aren't
you in uniform?"

Megan looked down at her blue jeans and cuffed brown boots. She
wore a black jacket and a bright blue scarf around her neck. Megan had

her straight blonde hair pulled back into a ponytail, and she squinted at me through coke-bottle thick glasses. "It's my day off. But when I heard about the body, I figured Mitch would need me."

Of course she did. Megan thought she was the only deputy in the department who could solve a case. I pointed towards Mitch. "He's over there."

Megan nodded, looking somber. "Liz, do you really think it's going to work, you staying with the county?" She was a tall woman, big-boned, and she leaned over to talk to me.

"I guess we'll find out." My neck burned. I'd known this conversation would come up as soon as I returned to work, and I'd also known Connolly would be the one to bring it up. I pushed my damp hair out of my face. My hood wasn't keeping the snow away.

Megan Connolly had tried to undermine me from the moment Mitch hired her. I didn't know or really care why, but it was annoying to have her looking over my shoulder and second-guessing me all the time.

"You should probably try the city if you want to stay in law enforcement." Her eyes were enormous behind her glasses, and I wondered why she wasn't wearing contacts like she normally did. I looked closer. Her eyes were red rimmed, like she'd been crying or had a cold.

You'd like that, I thought. "You think so?" I hated feeling Connolly towering over me.

Megan nodded. "Everyone thinks so. Listen, I'm just trying to give you a heads up. The entire department is worried about this. Including the sheriff."

I snorted. "If he wants to get rid of me, he needs to tell me that himself." Mitch had told me over and over that he didn't want me to leave the Sheriff's office. I was pretty sure he hadn't told Connolly anything different.

Megan smirked. "Oh, I'm sure he will." She headed towards the crime scene, then turned back. "Don't say I didn't warn you."

"Yeah, right," I muttered. I wanted to wipe the smug smile off her face. She'd been a pain in my backside from the moment we'd met.

"Talking to yourself?" Enrique came up next to me without me noticing. His jaws moved, and he popped his gum.

I glowered, wishing he'd get rid of it. "I guess. Are you ready to go?" I needed to get my head in the investigation and quit thinking about whether I'd made the right decision by coming back to work. This case needed my undivided attention. I could worry about my career after we solved it.

He nodded. "Let's go check out the homeless camp. Although, I'd think most of them would be in shelters in this weather."

"I think we should talk to Jaclyn again." He nodded, and I hollered at Mitch. "Enrique and I are going to get a statement from the lady who found the body."

He nodded. "Okay, then why don't you check out the homeless camp? See if there's anyone there and if they know anything."

I gave him a thumbs up and followed Enrique to the SUV, and, without thinking, climbed into the driver's side.

"Tired of my driving already?" he asked.

"Nah, just want to get there in one piece." I grinned at him.

Enrique snorted and popped his gum. "So, what did Connolly want? I saw you talking to her."

I looked out the window and watched as Connolly spoke to Mitch, then turned and headed back to her car. I put on my seatbelt. When Enrique climbed in beside me, I said, "She wanted to tell me that the whole department wants me to quit and go to work for the city. Is that true?"

"Nope," he said, but he didn't look at me.

I felt heat sweep over my face. Not from the air coming out of the heater but knowing how my co-workers were thinking about me. I hit the steering wheel with my thick glove. "I was afraid of this."

Enrique rubbed the back of his neck and chewed his gum. "I think some people may be a little worried about how things are going to work, but no one wants you gone. Well, maybe Connolly. But Mitch sure doesn't. He's been a bear since you took your leave, and it got worse when you and Bella went to Europe." He shook his head. "But a couple days before you got home, he was all smiles again."

If that was meant to make me feel better, and I knew it was, it didn't. I knew Mitch wanted to get back together. He'd told me that over and over. But I just couldn't...at least, not yet. Maybe never. I didn't know. I hated my indecision. How could I even think about going back to him? And yet, I missed him. I missed our talks about the job. Suddenly, it occurred to me that was all we ever talked about. That and our daughter. Had I been so engulfed in the job and raising Bella that I didn't notice that Mitch and I no longer had anything else to talk about? That was unsettling, and I needed to think about it more.

I glanced at Enrique. "I wish I knew what to do."

He rolled down his window and, to my relief, spit out his gum. "Well, right now, let's go find a murderer."

Chapter 2

C hapter—2

Jaclyn Downs had a frown pulling at her lips when she opened the door to us. "That didn't take long," she murmured as she let us into her home. She'd taken off her vest and wore wool slippers on her feet. Georgie pranced around, his tags jingling.

"We'd like to get your statement, Ms. Downs," I said, as I followed her into her warm living room. Her house smelled like cinnamon and pine, and I noticed two candles burning on the coffee table. I took off my gloves and shoved them into my pocket. There was a fire in the fireplace and soft music coming from a speaker next to an overstuffed grey chair. The room was small and cozy.

She motioned to the sofa that matched her chair, and Enrique and I sat down. I took out my notebook, hoping she noticed something on her walk that would help us find the killer. "Please take us through your morning walk."

She raised her hand, and Georgie jumped into her lap. "Well, there isn't much I can tell you except what I already said. Georgie and I walk every morning. This morning on our way home, he started yipping and pulling on his leash." She looked down at the dog in her arms. "Didn't you, Sweetie?"

"I tried to get him to come with me, but he was insistent, so we went and looked." She shook her head, and I could tell the experience rattled her. "That poor girl. I'm glad I was curious to see what Georgie was yipping at." She kept her eyes on her dog while petting his fur.

"And there was no one else around?" Enrique asked.

"I told you there wasn't," she said. "I didn't see anyone. It was snowing like the dickens, and I just wanted to get home where it was warm. But Georgie kept pulling at his leash and I knew I had to look and see what it was he was smelling. I thought it was probably another animal." She gave a sharp shake of her head.

"Had you heard any traffic on the road earlier? Maybe before you started out for your walk?" I asked.

She looked up at me. "No. There was nothing."

I glanced at Enrique, and he raised his eyebrows. "Ms. Downs, anything you can remember is important to our investigation. I know you want to help us find out who did this."

She scooped Georgie into her arms and stood up. "That's all I know, Detectives. Now, my son is coming over and I really need to..." She grabbed the back of her chair, seemed to forget what she needed to do, and sat back down.

"Can I get you something to drink?" I asked, afraid she might pass out. "Do you want us to wait until your son gets here?"

She shook her head. "No, my son will be here soon. He'll take care of us." Her eyes were moist. "Please, that's all I know. Can you leave now?"

We stood up and headed for the door. We'd have to talk to her again when she calmed down. Maybe when she'd calmed down, she'd remember more. "Of course. If you think of anything else, please call us."

She nodded but didn't follow us to the door. We let ourselves out. As we walked to the SUV, I asked Enrique, "What do you think?"

"Poor old lady. I think this was hard on her. I hope her son gets there soon." Enrique went to the passenger side and got in. He took a pack of gum from his pocket and stuck a piece in his mouth. I grimaced but said nothing.

I got behind the wheel and started the vehicle. "We need to keep an eye on her. Maybe talk to her son later."

Enrique nodded. "It could be she's just upset. But she seemed different from when we saw her earlier."

"Yeah, she did." I wondered what was going on with her. "I hope she really has a son coming to take care of her. We need to get the fire department to send a chaplain over to talk to her."

"I'll call them."

We both knew that some people didn't want a chaplain, but we could still offer to have one stop by. I turned the SUV around and headed across the overpass to the homeless camp. It sat next to the freeway and looked deserted in the snow. There were a few old broken-down motorhomes, a white van, and some colorful tents scattered around. I pulled up next to one of the motorhomes and put the car in Park.

"Let's find out if anyone's around." I gazed up at the old motorhome. It looked like someone had been there recently. The snow had covered any footprints, but there was a shopping cart next to the door, and it wasn't completely full of snow. We got out and walked closer.

"Doesn't look like it." Enrique walked around the perimeter of the motorhome. I trailed behind him, taking in the junk spread around, most of it peeking out of the snow. I didn't understand how people could live like this. Some, I knew, did it out of necessity, but there were others that loved the life. They didn't want to be constrained.

I went to the motorhome and pounded on the door. "Sheriff's office. Open up."

We listened for a minute, but no one stirred inside. I pounded on the door and shouted again. Still nothing. I looked at Enrique. "I guess try the others?"

He nodded and headed towards an older, more decrepit motorhome. "These look like they've been abandoned for years, but I know they haven't sat here that long."

I knew the homeless population had increased in Hood River in the last few years, just like it had in other towns and cities in the US. I sure hoped the folks who lived in them were staying in shelters to stay warm during the cold months. But not everyone wanted that, so there might be someone around.

The other motorhomes were empty, too. We walked around them, announcing we were from the County Sheriff's Office, but no one poked their heads out. Nor did we see any signs of life.

Next, we headed to the tents, which appeared to be abandoned. I sighed in relief. "I don't think anyone is here. They must all be in warming shelters."

"We can only hope," Enrique said. Then he sniffed the air. "Do you smell propane?"

"Yeah, but I'm not sure where it's coming from." I looked around. There was an old van parked close to the camp. The windows were fogged over. "Looks like someone's in that van." I pointed, and Enrique started in that direction.

"Hope they didn't asphyxiate themselves." Enrique trudged through the snow to the van. He banged on the door. "Sheriff's Office. Open up."

Enrique grabbed the door, and it opened. The smell of propane was strong, and I covered my nose. We looked inside. The van was a mess. Clothes and trash piled everywhere. "Anyone in here?" Enrique asked.

No one answered.

"We'd better check. They may be dead." I started to climb inside, but a man's voice behind me stopped me in my tracks.

"Hey! What do you think you're doing? That's my van."

Enrique and I turned towards the voice. A tall, skinny, jeans-clad man walked up. He had on a torn, dark blue coat and work boots. On his head was an old green stocking cap, and his pock-marked face looked like he'd just woken up. He had the look of a heroin user, rotten teeth, dirty skin, bad breath...I stepped back.

"Sheriff's Detectives, Sir," I told him. "Just checking to make sure you're okay."

"Yeah, right. Stay away from my van. You ain't got no right snooping around here."

"We're looking for someone who might know about a missing girl," Enrique said. "Do you know of anyone who hasn't been around lately?"

The guy laughed and rubbed his nose. His skin was ruddy from living outside. "We don't count heads or nothin' ya know. People come and go."

"Do you know Renetta Larson?" I asked. Even though we didn't have a formal identity, I knew it was Renetta whose body we'd found.

He stepped back and glared at me. "Ren? She's missing? How do you know that?"

"We've found the body of a young girl. Might be her." I watched him closely to see if he knew anything about the murder.

His face turned white, and tears spurted from his eyes. "No, it can't be Ren." He shook his head. "You need to talk to her old lady. She's staying in that shelter in town. Ren's probably with her." He swiped a dirty hand across his eyes. "It can't be her, man."

"How well did you know her?" Enrique asked.

The guy shook his head. "She's my sister." Then he broke down in tears, his shoulders shaking.

"Your sister?" I'd never heard of Renetta having a brother.

"Yeah, my old man and her mom hooked up and had me. She didn't want me around, so they gave me up. I just found my dear old mom like six months ago. The old witch still won't admit I'm her son." He shook his head, sniffed, wiped his nose, and scratched his butt. "But Ren did. She was great about it." His eyes were wild, and he swung his gaze around. "Where is she? I need to see her."

"We can take you to see the body," I offered. Renetta had never mentioned a brother to me or Bella as far as I knew. Why did this guy show up now? Why hadn't Bella mentioned him? I'd have to ask her when I called her about Renetta.

"No way. I'll take myself. Just tell me where to find her." He shook his head and started towards his pickup.

"What's your name?" I asked.

He turned back towards me. He scratched his head through the thick stocking cap he wore. "Brad Thomas. And I ain't ever been in trouble with the cops, so don't think you can pin anything on me."

I looked at him until he squirmed. I didn't believe him for a second and wondered if he'd given us his real name.

"Follow us," Enrique said. He looked around the camp. "Anyone else staying here right now?"

Brad shook his head. "Don't think so. Too cold. I've got a little propane heater in the van. It keeps me warm enough. Never did like sleeping inside."

"You need to make sure the heater isn't close to anything. Detective Ellisen and I smelled propane when we walked up." Enrique stomped his feet in the snow, scuffling it around.

Brad muttered something and went inside the van for a couple of minutes. When he came back out, he shook his head. "Good thing you said something. Someone dropped a sweatshirt on the heater. Could've caused a fire."

Exactly what Enrique and I had been afraid of.

There was an old pickup parked close to the van. Brad headed for it, and we followed him. When we got closer, I realized there was a little car parked next to it. The car was an older model white Kia, but it looked like it had been taken care of. Snow had piled up on top of it, showing that it had been sitting there for a while.

"Whose car is that?" I asked Brad. I wondered if it was Renetta's.

"That's Ren's."

"So, you knew she was missing?" I narrowed my eyes at him. Why wasn't he telling us everything he knew?

He shook his head. "I thought she was staying with her friend. She does that sometimes."

"Who's her friend?" I took a notebook out and prepared to write the name down. "Did her friend pick her up?"

He shrugged. "I don't know. She must have. I don't know her name. Somebody she met at work. Ren works at that coffee shop up on the heights. She was saving money to go to school." He sounded proud, then his eyes filled again. "Oh, man..." He jumped in the pickup and slammed the door.

I worried that he'd take off, and we'd have to chase him, but he followed us to the crime scene and parked behind the SUV. I held my breath as we headed towards the body, hoping he'd say it wasn't

Renetta. But when we got close, a guttural cry came from deep within Brad and he fell to his knees next to her.

Chapter 3

Chapter 3—Mitch

Sheriff Mitch Ellisen stood up when he saw his wife heading his way down the snowy slope. She was holding onto a young man who looked like he might keel over at any minute. When the guy fell to his knees and keened, Mitch knew they had a positive ID of the body.

Mitch's heart fell. He knew exactly how the young guy felt. That deep aching loss. It was the same feeling he'd had since Liz had walked out on him. That it was his fault she'd left made it worse. He hated himself for hurting her and destroying the best thing that had ever happened to him. They'd been together since high school, when he'd been the star quarterback on the football team, and she was the head cheerleader. He had to get her back. He'd been thinking about it and knew he needed to do something big to show her he still loved her. Telling her wasn't getting the job done. He had something he was working on. It was a huge surprise for Liz. He hoped it would work out.

But first, he had a murder to solve. He was glad Liz was back at work. She was his best investigator, and he knew he'd need her skills to find the killer.

Liz looked at him. "This is Brad Thomas. He said he's the victim's brother." Her tone was cool, but professional, and he wondered how they could work together. Before, they'd had an easy working partnership, but then Jenn and his stupidity had ruined all that. If she could just put that behind them and move on, he could show her how much she meant to him. His gut hurt. He had to make her want to give him another chance.

"Mr. Thomas, I'm Sheriff Ellisen. Do you recognize the victim?" Mitch stared at Brad, who was crying and rubbing his face. He obviously recognized Renetta. Did he know her well? Or was this an act?

Brad nodded and struggled to his feet. Tears ran in streams down his face. "Who did this? WHO FREAKIN' DID THIS TO MY SISTER?" He clenched his fists and looked around like he was going to take a swing at someone.

Enrique grabbed one arm and Mitch the other and the guy crumbled back to the ground. "Renetta is really his sister?" Mitch asked Liz.

She nodded. "He says Lilly gave him up when he was born. He just found her again."

Mitch stared at the young man. He saw nothing about him that looked like Lilly or Renetta, but maybe he looked like his father.

"Why don't you guys take him to the office and get him warmed up? We need to find out what he knows about our victim. I want to stay and talk to Doc King when she gets here." He looked at his watch. "She should be here soon."

Liz nodded and reached down to help Brad Thomas to his feet. He'd calmed down, but Mitch knew they needed to keep an eye on him. He stumbled when he stood, and Liz squeezed his arm. "You okay, Mr. Thomas?"

He nodded, then shrugged. "This is crazy." He put his head down and pinched the skin between his eyes with his thumb and forefinger. "I can't believe Ren's dead." He put his arm up and sobbed into his sleeve.

Mitch eyed him, then turned to Liz and Enrique. "I've got Garcia and Jones out canvasing the neighborhood. After you finish with him, go to the warming shelter, and talk to the people who are staying there. If Renetta was living in the shelter, someone there may know what happened to her."

Liz spoke to him, causing his heart to leap. "Mitch, can we talk a minute?"

"Of course." He nodded to Enrique, who turned and hurried Brad out of there. Brad cried out, threatening to kill whoever killed his sister. Mitch didn't blame him, but he didn't need some guy with a gun going around taking shots at everyone he suspected. They'd have to watch Brad Thomas.

"What's up?" he asked Liz.

"Does Brad Thomas look familiar? Have we arrested him before?"

Mitch thought about it for a second. "I don't think so. Does he look familiar to you?"

She nodded. "There's something about him. I can't put my finger on what it is. I thought maybe you'd remember."

He shook his head. "Let me think about it. I'll have Garcia run his priors. Maybe we've had a run in with him." He trusted Liz's hunches. If she thought she'd seen Brad before, she probably had.

"Thanks." She turned to go, and he said her name, stopping her, not wanting her to leave, but knowing he needed her out there searching for the killer.

"Liz." When she turned back to him, he said. "Be careful."

She nodded and walked towards Enrique and Brad Thomas. Mitch watched her go. He had a sinking feeling in the pit of his stomach. Something was not right. Something he couldn't put his finger on. He'd run the gauntlet of emotions in the last few months. Anger, despair, loneliness, but this felt different. He felt the small hairs on the back of his neck stand up. His stomach clenched. He felt like they were up against an evil that would stretch their department to the limits. He just hoped he could keep everyone safe.

He heard the department SUV start up and looked up as Liz pulled out onto the road. She had good instincts. So did Enrique. Between them and others in the department, they'd find the killer.

Mitch looked at the body. While he waited for the crime scene team to get there, he searched every inch around it. He didn't know what to make of it. Someone had put a snow berm around her. Why?

Mitch had seen a lot of crime scenes in his career, but not any like this. Sometimes the perp would cover the body, leave it naked, and pose it. He'd seen all kinds of things. But building a snow berm around it? He wondered if the killer wanted to display the kill.

He felt an icy tremor down his back. He sure hoped not. That could mean things were going on that he didn't want to think about. But of course, as Sheriff, he had to think about everything.

He noticed Connolly pull up and stop behind his pickup. She climbed out of her rig with two paper cups of coffee in her hands. Mitch had sent her to get coffee, hoping it would warm them up while they waited for the crime scene techs to get there.

"How long do you think she's been here?" Connolly asked, handing Mitch a cup of coffee, then taking a sip of hers.

Mitch shook his head. "We'll see what Doc King says. I wonder if someone killed her and left her body here, or if someone drugged her and left her here to freeze. Either way, this guy wants to make a statement."

"What statement?"

"I don't know. If we figure that out, we'll probably find the killer." He looked around. There were deputies parked on the side of the road while they canvassed the nearby houses. He knew his team would do everything in their power to solve the case as fast as possible.

Mitch's heart felt heavy as he studied the ground around the body. His team would have to put in long hours. They needed to find the killer fast before things became crazy in town. To his knowledge, there hadn't been a lot of murders in Hood River. There had only been a couple since he'd been in law enforcement in the valley. But things were changing. The valley was growing, people coming in and changing the dynamics. And bringing in more crime.

Mitch squatted down next to the body and made himself look closer. Renetta had been a beautiful girl when she and Bella were friends. She was still beautiful, but how long before life would have sucked the beauty out of her? Had she gotten into something that caused her death? Drugs? Prostitution? There were a dozen things he could think of that could've gone wrong with either scenario. Had her mother tried to get Renetta into prostitution? Mitch wouldn't bet against it. Lilly Larson would do anything for the next hit. He felt sick. What had happened to this poor young girl?

He moved her hair away from her neck with his gloved hand and checked for marks on her skin, which had now turned a light blue. There was a tiny drop of blood on her lips. That was it as far as he could see without moving the body.

"What happened to you?" he whispered to Renetta.

He didn't mean to say it out loud, but he must have because Connolly said, "Some crazy-ass idiot killed her, that's what happened."

"Yes, but there's more to it than that. Why kill an innocent young girl? Why this girl?"

"Maybe she wasn't so innocent." Connolly squatted down next to him. "She might've been into some crazy stuff like her mother."

"I don't think so," Mitch kept Connolly around because of her persistent efforts in searching for suspects. But she wasn't an intuitive detective. She never seemed to understand the motives for the crimes. She just wouldn't stop until she found the criminal. But Mitch knew that sometimes you had to figure out the why before you could figure out the who, and this might be one of those times.

Connolly cleared her throat. "Uh, boss, there's something I need to talk to you about." She swiped at her nose with her gloved hand. "This might not be the right time, but since it's just you and me here..." she broke off and stood.

"What's that?" Mitch got up and frowned at the worried look on her face.

"Well, it's about Detective Ellisen."

"Liz? What about her? Have you heard something I should know?" Mitch felt his heart thud. Was this the moment he'd been dreading for months? Was Connolly going to tell him that Liz was leaving the job permanently? He felt cold inside and for a couple of seconds, he couldn't breathe.

"I've been talking to several of the deputies. We all think she should leave."

Mitch stared at her. "Leave?"

Connolly's thick glasses were clouded, and she took them off and wiped them on her scarf. "The job. She should try to get on with the city or maybe the state. We don't think her staying, with everything that has gone on, is a good idea."

Mitch narrowed his eyes and gave her a pointed glare. "As long as I'm sheriff, Liz has a place on my team. If you hear anyone saying otherwise, send them to me."

Chapter 4

Chapter 4—Liz

I started the SUV and headed towards the office. Brad Thomas sat in back mumbling about Renetta and Lilly. I listened closely. He rambled on about what a horrible mother Lilly had been to Renetta. How she didn't deserve to be alive and Renetta dead. He was sure Lilly had done something that had caused Renetta's murder. Then he shut up and sat back with his eyes closed and tears running down his face.

It was snowing again, and I turned up the heat. I hated to because of the stench coming off Brad Thomas in waves. He smelled of booze, urine, and body odor. I wanted to roll my window down, but I knew that would freeze us all.

As we traveled down State Street, passed the stately old homes still lit with Christmas lights, I noticed several cars pulled over on the side of the road. Some were trying to get back on the road and others were trying to stop from sliding around. People were out in their warm winter coats, shoveling sidewalks.

My nose twitched from the smells coming from the back seat. Brad Thomas smelled like he hadn't bathed in years. I hoped his odor didn't linger in the SUV once he got out.

Enrique was quiet until we got to the office and led Brad into an interview room. We gave him a cup of coffee to warm him up, then sat with him to ask a few questions.

"When was the last time you saw Renetta?" I started the questioning.

Brad drank down half the coffee, made a face and put the cup down. "I don't know. Couple of days ago, I guess. She was staying with a friend from work because it was so cold, and she didn't want to stay in the shelter with her crazy mother." He sniffed and rubbed his nose, a string of snot landing on his coat sleeve.

"Why wouldn't she want to stay with her mother?" I asked. I wasn't sure about the relationship between mother and daughter except that Renetta had always seemed protective of Lilly. It should've been the other way around.

He picked up the cup and drained the rest of the coffee. He raised an eyebrow. "I'm sure you've run into Lilly. She's crazy like a lunatic. She's never been much of a mother to Renetta. But Ren, you know, she won't believe that." He shook his head. "I don't get it."

"How long have they been living in the camp?" Enrique asked.

Brad shrugged. "Since last summer, I think. Lilly kept saying she was going to get them a house, but she never did. She was too busy drinking and shooting up any money she could come up with."

"Does she hold a job?" I asked.

"Not really." He picked up his coffee cup and tipped it up, trying to get the last drop. "She gets money from people who feel sorry for her, and some from men." He winked. "If you know what I mean."

"Did Renetta...?" I started to ask. I didn't want to believe that of her, but I knew that when someone was desperate, they did things they never would ordinarily do.

Brad cut in. "No. Never. She hated that her mom would sell herself to some fat city official. Ren would never do that."

"City official?" I asked. "Like whom?"

He held the cup out. "I don't know. She never said names. Just mentioned she had clients with lots of money in Hood River." He shook the cup at her. "Do you think I could have more coffee and maybe somethin' to eat?"

Enrique stood and headed for the door. "I'll get you some more coffee."

"Thanks, man."

"Then how did she expect to get enough money for somewhere to live?" I watched him think that over. His face was long and lean and his eyes buggy. He was so skinny, he looked malnourished, and I wondered when he'd last eaten.

"She said she was coming into some money soon." He wiped his finger under his nose, which had been running since we came inside. "'Course I didn't believe her."

"Why not?" I didn't believe her either. We heard the same thing over and over from people down on their luck. Unless she was blackmailing someone she'd slept with. I made a mental note to question Lilly about her men when we talked to her.

"She's always jabbering. Thinks she's better than she is. She told us she comes from a lot of money. But when we asked her who her family is, she shuts up fast." He shook his head and picked at a scab on his hand. "Probably comes from a bunch of losers."

"You don't know her family?" He must not have looked far into his family tree. Of course, finding out Lilly Larson was his biological mother might've caused him to stop looking for fear of what else he might discover about his background.

"Nah, she never would say. Ren didn't even know who they were."

"What's Lilly's last name?" I wondered if he knew her by a different name than Larson.

Brad shrugged. "She goes by Larson, same as Ren. Not sure that's her legal name."

"Is there anything else you can tell me about your sister? Do you have any idea who would do this to her?" I knew Brad was convinced Renetta's death had something to do with Lilly. What had she gotten herself and her daughter into?

Brad shook his head, and his eyes filled with tears. "No," he said, softly. "Ren was the sweetest girl in the world. She wouldn't hurt nobody. She was always helping people."

Enrique came back carrying a cup of coffee, a sandwich, and a package of chips. He put them in front of Brad, whose eyes lit up at the sight of the food. "Thanks, man. I'm starving."

Enrique nodded, and we watched Brad eat. He was so skinny; I was sure he'd missed a lot of meals. "Did Renetta stay in the van with you?" I asked.

He shook his head and swallowed. Then he took a swig of coffee. "Nah, she and Lil stayed in that old motorhome next to me. Well, sometimes Lil stayed there. Mostly it was just Ren."

"Where was Lilly?" I wanted to know if she spent time with Renetta. Or had she dumped her in the motorhome and gone to stay somewhere else?

He grimaced, burped, and shrugged. "She'd stay out in a tent with one of the men, or she'd stay in a hotel room. She wasn't too particular where she stayed."

I made a mental note to check out the motorhome, then after Brad had finished his food, we decided we'd gotten all we were going to get from him, and Enrique and I drove him back to his pickup.

"I have a feeling that Renetta's mother may know something," Enrique said as I turned the SUV around and headed back to town. "Should we head to the shelter next?"

I nodded. "I think you're right. Let's see if we can find her. Then we need to search that motorhome." I wanted to let Lilly know of Renetta's death before she heard it somewhere else.

"We could send a deputy over to search it."

"No, I want to be there." I needed to see what was in there with my own eyes, not just hear about it.

The Hood River Warming Shelter opened eleven years ago in response to a homeless person dying from exposure that winter in Hood River. Several valley people came together to make sure that never happened again.

Since then, it had moved around a lot, but ended up on Oak Street on a property donated by a Hood River resident. There were several small structures, one where medical people could help the residents and one with a shower facility.

Mitch and I had volunteered to stay overnight a few times during the winters since it opened, checking people in, and giving them warm clothes and food. Several area restaurants and the Senior Center provided meals. Many volunteered their time, money, or clothing, which gave me a sense of pride in our community.

A preacher from one of the churches in the area greeted us when we stopped in front of the shelter. He introduced himself as Pastor Gregg Banks. He was tall and slim, with black hair and a dark beard. His eyes were dark brown, and he had a long nose. I'd seen him around town, but I hadn't met him. "What can I do for you officers?"

"We're looking for a woman named Lilly Larson," I said. We stood outside our rig, and I stomped my feet to keep warm.

"Come into the office," Gregg said, opening the door and motioning us inside. "We'll all freeze out here."

We walked in and I felt the warmth pervade my stiff limbs. The preacher motioned us to a table and chairs which sat in one corner. The room was big enough for a couple of easy chairs, the dining room set and a television. I noticed a coffeemaker and a small refrigerator on another small table. Someone had turned on the television to a game show, but the volume was down. The room smelled of coffee, old food, and body odor.

We sat around the table, and Gregg pulled a clipboard closer and looked at the list of names he'd written down. "I don't think Lilly has come in yet." He looked up at us. "Most people don't start showing up until later in the day."

"We were just at the homeless camp down by the freeway and she wasn't there. Do you know where she might've gone?" I asked, hoping he'd have a bead on where she might be.

He shrugged and played with the clipboard, opening and closing the clip until I wanted to scream at him to stop. "Could be anywhere. As you know, most of these folks like to hang out around Walmart or down by the bridge."

"Seems like a chilly day to be hanging around outside," Enrique said, giving his big smile.

"I know, but they still do." He set the clipboard aside, and I didn't have to scream after all.

Enrique and I both nodded. We often stopped and tried to get them inside. "What can you tell us about Lilly?" I asked.

Gregg pursed his lips. "She in some kind of trouble?"

"We need to let her know her daughter is dead," I said, dreading it, but wanting to get it over with.

He raised his head and stared at me. "Renetta?"

"Yes, I'm sorry. I should have realized that you knew her, too." I watched him closely to see how well he knew Renetta. He was upset by her death, but anyone would've been.

"What happened?" Gregg demanded. He leaned back in his chair.

"She was murdered," I said, watching him for a reaction. Did he know anything about her murder?

His face turned white, and he stood up and walked around in a circle while running his hands through his hair. "That poor little girl. How was she killed?"

"We're not sure. She was found on the West cliffs above the river." I watched him.

He sank back into his chair, looking sick. Then he said, softly, "She was such a great kid. She had plans to go to school, make something of herself. She didn't deserve this."

"No one does," Enrique said.

Gregg looked up at us. "No, I know. It just seems worse when it's someone like Renetta."

"What can you tell us about her home life?" I asked, wondering if he knew what Renetta had been through in the last few months. "Did you notice anything going on that would lead to her death?"

"She didn't have a home life. Not really. Her mom...Lilly...kept it together, sort of, until Renetta was about ten. Then she started spending all her money on drinking and drugs. She's been in and out of rehab a dozen times."

I hadn't known that and wondered if Bella had. She hadn't talked about Renetta once they were in high school, but Bella saw her now and then. She'd mentioned it a few months ago.

"Where did Renetta go while her mom was in rehab?" Enrique asked. "Does she have other family around?"

"There was a grandmother," he said, softly. "She was a wonderful lady. She kept Renetta as often as Lilly would let her, but she died suddenly when Renetta was about fourteen, I think. Broke the poor girl's heart. Grandma Sandi was her only security. The church ladies tried to keep in touch with Ren, but Lilly moved her around so much." He shook his head. "It was hard." He glanced up at them. "I feel like we let her down."

I felt the same way. Too many people slip through the cracks of society, I thought, my heart aching for Renetta and others like her. "What was her grandmother's last name?"

"Larson. She was Renetta's dad's mother. He died in a car accident when Ren was little. Sandi loved Ren. If she had lived, Ren would have always had a home."

Guilt put its hands around my heart and squeezed. I should've paid more attention. I should have known Bella's friend was in trouble. How was I going to tell my daughter that her friend was dead, when I felt partially to blame?

Chapter 5

Enrique and I left the shelter and headed towards the Hood River bridge. Since the freeway was closed in both directions, traffic was non-existent. Under the overpass was a popular place for the homeless to hang out with their signs, begging passersby for money. But no one stood at the bottom of the exit ramp today. I couldn't imagine anyone hanging out there in the cold temperatures, but sure enough, when we pulled up, there were a few people tucked under the freeway standing around a fire.

They looked up when we climbed from the SUV. We headed towards them and stopped close to the fire but tried not to seem threatening. Fear appeared on some of the younger faces, and resignation on others. I held up my hands.

"We're not here to give you smack. We're looking for Lilly, Renetta Larson's mom." I stood with my feet apart, using my loud voice so it would carry to everyone standing around the fire.

The crowd shifted and parted. A woman wearing a bright purple coat that was at least two sizes too big for her looked up at us. "What's going on with Ren? She in some kind of trouble?" She laughed, and I noticed she was missing one of her front teeth. One sign of a crackhead. She was also thin to the point of being gaunt. Another sign.

I looked closer. Sure enough, it was Lilly, and I squinted, trying to recognize Renetta's mom from when the girls were young. Back then, Lilly had been slender, with full breasts and long dark hair. She'd had big dark brown eyes and reminded me of the actress Salma Hayek. She'd always acted like she was better than everyone.

I'd seen her many times over the years. I'd arrested her for soliciting and stealing. Her looks had changed, but she still had the attitude. Must've been born with it.

"Hello Lilly," I said, trying to figure out if she'd heard about Renetta yet. I didn't think by her demeanor that she had.

Lilly frowned. "You Bella's mom? The cop?" She spit out the word, cop. "What do you want with me? Just leave me alone. I haven't done nothing."

I reached out to her, but Lilly jerked away, giving me an icy glare. "Whatta ya want? Don't touch me."

"Lilly, Renetta is dead." I said the words softly, trying to keep tears from forming in my eyes. I couldn't imagine someone saying those words to me. It would kill me if something happened to Bella.

"Dead?" Lilly frowned. "What you saying? Renetta isn't dead. She's working today."

"When was the last time you saw your daughter?" Enrique asked, stepping closer to me. His voice was kind and Lilly smiled, but it slid from her face and a look of pain took its place.

Lilly stared at him. Several of the other people shuffled away and looked everywhere except at Lilly. "Yesterday. She brought me a coffee when she got off work."

A young woman standing across the fire from us shook her head. Her frizzy blonde hair bounced against her shoulders. "It wasn't yesterday. It was a week ago."

"No! Quit lying. It was yesterday." Lilly looked at the others for confirmation, but several shook their heads.

"Remember, Lilly," the girl said, "You were upset because you hadn't seen her for several days."

Lilly frowned. "She usually brings me coffee when she works at the coffee shop." She glanced up at me in confusion. "What happened to my daughter?"

"We found her body by Westcliff Drive. Do you know why she'd be there? Did she know someone in the area?" I asked.

"How you know it was her?" She spit the words at me.

"I know Renetta, Lilly. She and Bella were friends. And Brad Thomas identified her." My heart ached for the shadow of the woman Lilly had been. What had made her make the choices that brought her here? Had she gone off the deep end when her husband died?

"That Brad don't have a brain in his head. He's a complete idiot, and you'd be smart to remember that." She pointed a finger at me.

"Okay, I'll remember. I'm sorry about Renetta, Lilly." I stared at her. With no makeup and her hair stringy and sticking out of her stocking cap, I could see a resemblance to Brad Thomas. That's why he looked familiar.

Lilly shook her head and backed away. "No, that's not right. Not my Rennie. Why would someone do that to my girl?"

She continued to shake her head. Then she fell into a heap on the ground. I was afraid she would go into shock. Enrique and I started towards her, but before we got there, a man bent down and picked her up.

"Did she faint?" A woman hurried over. She was large, and she wore purple pajama pants with a black hoodie under her huge green coat. She had a stocking cap pulled over her hair and a large mole on her chin, with black hair growing out of it.

"She's okay," the man holding Lilly said. "Probably lightheaded, huh Lil?"

Lilly's eyes opened, and she whispered something I couldn't hear. I moved closer. "What did she say?"

The man, a burly guy in a faded grey hoodie and a brown Carhartt jacket that had seen better days, looked up at me. "She said she knows who killed Renetta."

The crowd, who had been muttering amongst themselves, stood still. Everything grew quiet. Enrique and I got down on our knees in the snow next to Lilly. "Who?" I asked. "Who killed Renetta, Lilly?"

Lilly shook her head. The man holding her sat her on a lawn chair next to the fire.

"Tell me who, Lilly," I said, standing up and putting my hand on Lilly's arm. I wanted to shake it out of her.

Lilly shook me off. She stared at the fire. "You won't believe me."

"Try me. Please Lilly, if you know who did this, tell me who it is so I can put them away for hurting Renetta." I looked closely at her face. Did she know anything, or was she just making it up? I couldn't tell. I'd never been able to read Lilly Larson.

Lilly shook her head. "I'm not sayin' nothin' more." She crossed her arms and stared at the fire.

"Brad Thomas said you mentioned you might come into some money. Where was it coming from? Would that have anything to do with what happened to Renetta?" Was she really coming into money, I wondered, or was she just saying that to make herself look better?

Lilly jumped up. "Brad's lying. I never said nothin' like that. You can't believe nothin' that scumbag says." She backed away from us, shaking her head.

"I want to find out who did this to Renetta, Lilly. Anything you can tell me might help. Was she doing drugs? Could she have taken an overdose?"

"Of course not. Ren wouldn't touch no drugs." Lilly looked at the people standing around, and they all shook their heads.

No matter how hard we tried, we couldn't get anything else out of her. We talked to the other people there, but no one seemed to have any idea what had happened to Renetta. All we heard was what a good girl she was. If they knew anything, they weren't saying, which was normal for how they lived and interacted with law enforcement, but I wanted to haul them all into the office and grill them. The only thing that stopped me was I knew it wouldn't do any good. They would be closed-mouthed there as well.

"Lilly, is it okay if we search your motorhome? We need to see if there's anything there that will help us find out who killed Renetta." I looked down at her.

Lilly sniffed and opened one eye, staring at me. "You got a search warrant?"

"No, but you know I can easily get one." I kept my voice firm, knowing she'd try to fight me on this.

Lilly nodded, surprising me. She raised her head and pushed back the hood of her coat. "Go ahead. I want you to find the SOB that killed my girl." She got up and walked towards me with her hand outstretched.

Enrique started towards me, but I put up my hand to keep him away.

I shook her hand. "I will, Lilly. I'll find him. Please, if you know anything that will help me, let me know."

Back in the SUV, I gripped the steering wheel, then turned and looked at Enrique. He was fiddling with the heat controls. "Do you think she knows something?"

"Who knows?" He turned the heat up and buckled his seatbelt. "She's so high all the time. It's amazing she remembers she had a daughter."

"I know, but still..." I let the sentence drop. Lilly was a drug addict, a prostitute, a mess, and yet she was a mother. Maybe she knew, or thought she knew, who killed Renetta. I had to figure out a way to get through to her.

"Still, we should keep an eye on her in case she knows something. Do you want to go to the coffee shop first, or back to the camp and look through the motorhome?"

"Let's check out the motorhome first."

Enrique nodded, and I headed towards the homeless camp once again. He called Mitch to let him know what we had planned. Enrique had him on speaker, and I heard Mitch say he'd meet us there. "There's something I need to run by you."

"What's going on?" Enrique asked.

"I'll talk to you when we get there. I'm still at the crime scene. As soon as the doc takes the body away, I'll come straight there."

Enrique pushed a button on his phone, and it went silent. "Wonder what that's all about."

"Maybe he found something at the scene and doesn't want to let it out yet." Worry nagged at me. What had Mitch found that was worse than what we already suspected?

"Maybe."

The camp still looked deserted when I pulled the SUV in and stopped next to Brad's van. His pickup wasn't there.

"Wonder where Brad went," I said as I put the SUV in Park and turned off the motor. I looked around the area, thinking he may have parked somewhere else. But the place looked undisturbed. No traffic had been in or out since we were there earlier.

"Hard telling. He probably has a route he does every day. I think many of these folks do. They have their routines just like everyone else." Enrique opened his door and got out.

I stepped out on my side and stood looking around, taking in the silence. It was cold, and I shivered. I couldn't imagine not having a home where I could go to get warm. What would it be like to live like this? "It breaks my heart that Renetta lived here. Her life must've been so difficult."

Enrique nodded, his jaws working his gum.

"I know she didn't want to be here. She wanted a warm place to sleep and a mother who came home at night." I walked towards the motorhome. "I wonder if it's locked."

"We'll soon find out."

We trudged through the snow to the steps of the broken-down motorhome. It was several feet from Brad's van and when we got close, I realized the door was hanging open. I turned to Enrique and put my finger up to my lips. Then I pointed at the open door. Was someone inside?

Enrique nodded and took his service revolver out and pointed it at the ground. I did the same, then we moved closer to the door. I stopped on one side and listened. I thought I heard rustling around in the back of the home and jerked my head towards the sound.

Enrique moved towards the back door. It was closed, and he stopped to wait for me.

I pointed my gun inside and shouted. "Sheriff's department! Come out with your hands up."

More rustling sounds came from inside, but no one came into view. I wondered if an animal had gotten in and was foraging for food. I yelled again. "Sheriff's department. Come out now with your hands in the air."

A man appeared in the doorway. He was about five feet tall and as round as a barrel. "Whas' all the yelling about? I'm coming."

I kept my gun trained on him. "Put your hands in the air and come out slowly."

He held up his hands, and I saw he had a dirty cloth bag clutched in one. "Put the bag down."

He stared at me for a second. "Thas' my stuff. I ain't leavin' it here."

"Come out slowly." I demanded.

He teetered a second on the top step, then he bumbled his way down to the ground.

"Now, slowly lower your bag to the ground next to you," I said in a commanding voice. I assumed he was taking advantage of no one being there and helping himself to whatever he could find.

Enrique walked up behind him, and the little man jumped and did as I asked.

"What's in the bag?" Enrique asked.

"Jus' some food. I was hungry." He shook his grizzled head and looked up at Enrique. "I wasn't goin' to take nothin' else."

Enrique leaned down and picked up the bag. He looked inside and nodded. I lowered my gun, and Enrique patted the man down.

"Lil lets me have food if she's around. But she hasn't been here today. If you see her, you ask her if I'm not tellin' the truth." His eyes were wide, and his hands shook.

Enrique picked up the bag and handed it to him. "You live here, too?"

The man nodded to a tent across the narrow road. "Over there."

"What's your name?" I asked. He looked like a cross between Santa Claus and a dwarf in Snow White. A not very clean dwarf. If the smell coming off him in waves was anything to go by, I knew it had been a long time since his last bath. He smelled of campfire and coffee, with body odor mixed in.

"Jolly Weathers."

"How well do you know Lilly?" I asked.

He shrugged. "We ain't best buds, but Lil's okay. Ren's the one who makes sure I have somethin' to eat. She's always bringin' me food or coffee. She's a real sweet little gal."

Enrique glanced at me. I took a deep breath. "Mr. Weathers, I'm sorry to inform you, but we found the body of a young woman this morning and we're pretty sure it's Renetta Larson."

The little man's eyes were enormous. "No!" Tears rolled down his face and into his scraggily beard. Then he picked up his bag and scurried towards his tent.

Enrique started to follow him, but I shook my head. "Let him go. He probably just needs time to process it. We'll check on him before we leave."

We watched as the little man weaved a path to his tent. I was afraid he might trip over his own feet.

Chapter 6

C hapter 6

I stepped up into the motorhome. It was freezing cold, but clean inside. Probably Renetta's doing. I moved further inside, and Enrique stepped in behind me. It was dim in the living area, and I reached up to turn on a light, surprised when it worked.

"Wow. I didn't think about them having power. Must charge it with a generator." Enrique put his hands on his hips and glanced around the small room.

I followed his gaze. The front, which consisted of captain's chairs and the dashboard, was curtained off, making the living area cozy. There was a small built-in booth, a short sofa, and a cooking area. A hallway led to the back of the motorhome. It was cold, and I noticed the windows had frost on the inside.

"Looks like Renetta used the table for a desk." I looked at the papers strewn across the flat surface. I bent over and picked up a stack of bills, rifling through them, finding a credit card statement, a bill for gas at the local Texaco, and a cell phone bill. "I wonder where her cell phone is. Did anyone mention seeing it at the scene?"

Enrique shook his head. "No one said anything. We can ask Mitch when he gets here. Meanwhile, I'll look around here for it."

"Probably should ask Brad Thomas if we don't find it." I slipped the credit card bill out of its envelope. "Wow, Renetta was carrying quite a big balance. I wonder…" I looked down at the list of purchases. "Looks like she was going to school at the community college. This lists books and tuition for the new quarter." I rubbed my forehead with my gloved hand. I hated she would not finish school, get a job, and have a life. Anger burned inside me at the person responsible for her murder.

Enrique looked over my shoulder. "Poor kid. She was trying to make a life for herself."

"Yeah." I stuffed the bill back in its envelope. I felt nauseated and my teeth chattered. "Let's look around and get out of here. I'm freezing."

"You got it." Enrique opened cupboards over the sink, and I headed to the back, where the bedroom was.

Someone made the bed with a pink comforter. A blue teddy bear sat on the top near the pillows. The sight of the bear broke my heart and tears filled my eyes. I made myself look through the tiny closet, picking up old bags that Renetta had stored at the bottom and going through them. The room was so tiny, and Renetta didn't have a lot of stuff, so it didn't take long.

I wondered where Lilly kept her things. There wasn't room in the bedroom for two closets and I hadn't seen anything that looked like it might belong to Lilly in with Renetta's clothes. I also didn't see a cell phone.

Enrique came to the door. "Did you look through the bathroom?"

"Not yet." I patted the clothes in the closet to see if Renetta had left anything in the pockets.

Enrique stepped into the tiny bedroom next to me and looked around. His expression was grim as he reached out and picked up the bear. "What monster would kill an innocent young girl?"

I glanced up at him and shook my head. I looked at the bear, which seemed like a symbol of Renetta's innocence. Something caught my eye. "What's that?"

The back of the bear's neck had something attached to it. Enrique turned the stuffed animal around. It looked like someone had put a ball into a piece of fabric and tied it together. Then they'd put a rubber band around it and attached it to the bear. "Looks like a wad of cash." He held up the money for me to see.

"How much is there?" I looked over his shoulder.

Enrique unrolled the money. His eyes grew big. "Looks like it's mostly hundreds. Without counting, I'd say at least a thousand dollars." He frowned at the bills in his hands. "She didn't get this working at a coffee shop."

"We'd better bag the money and the bear. Mitch will kill us if we don't." Where had she gotten the money? Had she been saving for a long time? If she was, why would she max out her credit cards?

Enrique nodded and took out an evidence bag, placing the bear and money inside. "Have you found anything else?"

"Not really. The odd thing is, I don't see any sign of Lilly living here. Do you?" The room looked like a young woman lived there. There was no sign of Lilly.

"Nope. It's clean. The cupboards are organized and color-coded. Either Renetta was super-anal about things, or someone came in and cleaned the house."

"She must've been organized. Can you see Lilly leaving that wad of cash? She'd be on that in a heartbeat." How had Renetta hid it from Lilly? She must've kept it a secret so her mother couldn't steal it from her.

"We'll have to ask her about it. See if she knows where Renetta got it."

"And we need to find out where she was staying. I have a hard time thinking she slept on the street in this weather."

The outside door opened, letting in more cold air. We both got up and drew our guns, but Mitch stepped in, and we sheathed them.

"Find anything?" he asked.

"Not much. This place is so clean, I doubt we will find anything. Except this." Enrique held up the plastic bag with the bear in it.

"A teddy bear?" Mitch asked. He took it out of Enrique's hand and looked it over. His face had a greyish cast to it. What was he thinking?

Enrique nodded. "With a bunch of cash attached to it."

Mitch glanced at me. "What do you make of that?"

"We don't know what to think. I just looked at her visa bill and it's almost to the limit. It looks like she's been living off that. I don't know why she'd have that much cash. We'll talk to her mom again. See if she knows anything. Although we didn't get much out of her last time we tried." I leaned over and pulled the covers off the bed. "Did you find a cell phone next to her body? We found her cell phone bill." I felt around under her pillows and inside the pillowcases.

Mitch shook his head. "No cell phone. You might want to ask Lilly. Did someone go through Renetta's car?"

"Not yet." I made a mental note to do that before we left the camp.

"I'm worried about this case." Mitch scratched the back of his neck. "There's something nagging at me. I want you all to be extra careful while trying to track this guy down."

We both nodded. "What are you thinking?" I asked.

"I don't think it was a simple murder. There are other things going on. I know you're both skilled investigators but be even more attentive. We don't need more young girls murdered."

A chill ran up my spine. In all the years I'd worked law enforcement with Mitch, I'd never seen him this concerned. "You think the killer will strike again?"

"I don't know. Like I said, it's nothing concrete, just a feeling. The hair on the back of my neck has been standing straight up since we found Renetta. Maybe it's because she was a friend of Bella's. Maybe it's something else. I just want to solve this as soon as possible."

"Easy pickings," I whispered. "Renetta was an easy target for a murderer." I thought about all the young girls who had no one to look out for them. They were easy prey.

"But why?" Enrique asked. "Why would anyone want to kill her?"

"Maybe she knew something about the killer that he didn't want to get out," I suggested. "We have to look back over her life and see what we can find." I wasn't telling Enrique anything he didn't know. But I felt like Lilly was the reason for Renetta's death.

Enrique nodded. "Maybe she owed him or her money and couldn't pay it back."

"Another thing." Mitch rubbed the back of his head. "Dr. King found a bullet hole in Renetta's stomach. That's probably how she died. We didn't see it because the killer cleaned her up and put different clothes on her."

I shivered, knowing too well what we could be looking at. "If he was showcasing his kill, he likely will do it again."

"Why would he do that?" Enrique asked.

"Because he enjoyed it. I don't like it. He dressed her in different clothes and left her in a snow berm." Mitch led the way out of the motorhome. "We've got to find out what happened. People will remain on edge until we find the killer. I'm already getting phone calls telling me to solve this fast."

As if we could snap our fingers and have the killer's name, "We'll find him," I said. *If it's the last thing I do.*

Mitch took off and Enrique and I went to check out Renetta's car. It was locked. We scraped snow off the windshield, but even though we shined our high-powered flashlights in the car, we didn't see a cell phone sitting out in the open.

"Come to think of it, I didn't see a laptop in the motorhome either. If Renetta was going to school, she would have had a laptop or some kind of computer, wouldn't she?"

"You would think so." I frowned and headed back to the motorhome. It was such a rookie mistake not to have looked for it when we were in there. My only excuse was that I was upset about Renetta.

Enrique followed me in, and we searched the motorhome again, but we didn't find either. "Maybe it's in the trunk of her car," Enrique suggested.

I nodded. "We need to get a locksmith out here to open the car." I glanced around the small area. "Why don't you call him? I'm going to look around some more." I started opening cupboards, looking under the table, and going through closets again, hoping Renetta's laptop was there somewhere. I didn't find it.

Enrique made the call, and we waited in the SUV until the locksmith arrived. His name was Danny White, and he was a year ahead of me in school. I'd always liked him. He was one of those guys that was always nice to be around. We went out to meet him.

"Hey Danny."

He grinned. "Nice to see you, Liz. You too, Enrique." Danny was slim and had a beak nose with a tiny mustache under it. His eyes were close together, and he had big ears, but he was such a nice guy. After you got to know him, you forgot how homely he was.

"You, too. Sorry to drag you out in this cold," I said.

He shrugged and pulled a black case out of his pickup. "No problem. What's going on?"

We told him that Renetta had been killed, and that we were looking for her cell phone and computer, if she owned them. "This won't take long," Danny said. He brought out a tool and in a couple of minutes had the car open. He hit the lever to pop the trunk, and it popped open.

The three of us stared down at two little pink suitcases.

Chapter 7

C hapter 7
Enrique and I stared at each other. My heart dropped and I felt nauseated. These couldn't belong to Renetta. For one thing, they were so tiny, she wouldn't have been able to get anything in them. And for the second, they had white kittens and ladybugs on them. They looked like they belonged to little girls who were going to grandma's house for the weekend. I cringed. They looked like suitcases Bella had when she was little.

I pulled gloves out of my pocket and put them on. Danny stepped back away from the trunk, giving me a quizzical look. "Not what you expected to find?"

"No." My stomach lurched, and I couldn't help thinking about last spring and the Bread of Life Cult. They had been trafficking children. My sister died trying to save some of the littlest ones. Was this another case like that? There was big money in trafficking. Depression kicked me in the chest. I didn't want to go through that again. It had gutted me the last time.

I reached into the trunk and took the suitcases out one at a time. I laid them on the ground and opened first one and then the other. There were tiny clothes probably belonging to an infant and a toddler in them. "Why would Renetta have baby clothes in her car?"

"Maybe she was babysitting and planned to take the babies some-where," Danny suggested.

"So, where are the children?" I looked around at the two men. "Have there been children reported missing?" I asked Enrique. There could've been some missing while I was gone, and I hadn't had time to hear about it.

"Not that I've heard. She must've been interrupted before she got wherever she was taking them," Enrique said, his voice cracking. I knew he was thinking of his little baby, who was on the way.

I could barely breathe. Had whoever killed Renetta killed two little girls? Or were they safe with their parents and I was reading more into this than was here? I looked at Enrique. "We need to find out if anyone has reported missing children."

"If they had, there would be a manhunt going on. She must've had the clothes in the car and forgot to give them to the mom after she babysat."

Maybe, but that didn't feel right to me. "I still think we need to call Mitch and get him back here."

I went through the suitcases a second time while Enrique made the call. I looked for a name tucked into the side pockets. Nothing. Then I looked through the small clothing and still found nothing, except memories of Bella as a toddler with her soft blonde hair and big blue eyes. I had to get a grip on myself. I couldn't solve this case if I thought about my daughter every time something came up.

I zipped the cases and held them up to look the outside over, hoping for some kind of identification. Nothing. I didn't like this. Surely if two little girls had gone missing in the county, we would have heard of it.

"Mitch is on his way back."

I nodded. Danny stirred beside me, and I turned to him. "You can head home, Danny. Please don't tell anyone what we found."

"I won't."

He knew the drill, and I trusted him to keep his mouth shut. After he left, Enrique and I stared at each other, neither one of us wanting to voice what we were thinking. I felt sick inside and knew Enrique did, too. What had happened to the little owners of the pink suitcases?

We stood next to Renetta's car until Mitch arrived. He got out of his county pickup and came towards us. "What's going on?"

I gestured to the trunk of Renetta's car. "Look what we found in the trunk. We were looking for her cell phone or laptop." I shook my head.

Mitch stared down at the suitcases. He bent down and riffled through the clothes. "We need to know who these belong to and why they're in Renetta's car."

"We thought you should see them. Have there been any children missing lately?"

"Not that I know of. Not in this area anyway. I'll have Garcia check it out, see if there are missing kids anywhere around us."

I poked around in the trunk. Anger surged through me. I hated people who preyed on innocent children. "I don't see her computer or cell. I wonder if the killer took them?"

"Probably." Mitch opened the driver's door and looked around inside, sticking his hands down between the seats, doing all the things Enrique and I had already done.

I looked over his shoulder as he searched. He finally gave up and moved back out of the car. He was just about to close the door when something caught my eye. Next to the driver's seat something glinted in the light.

"Wait, don't shut the door."

Mitch turned to watch as I bent down and pulled up a pink cased cell phone. "It was here all along."

I hit the button to try and turn it on, but of course, it was dead.

Mitch held out his hand. "I'll take it back to the office and get one of the techs to see if they can open it." He opened the back door. "I'm sure you guys looked back here for her laptop?"

Renetta's stuff filled the backseat. There was a sleeping bag with blankets and a pillow. And there were bags filled with snacks, plus bottles of water. One bag held two large sweatshirts, one grey and one navy blue.

"I don't see a laptop, but it looks like she was living in her car part time." I put everything back the way I'd found it and closed the door.

"You guys go talk to the people at the coffee shop. Maybe they know where she kept her laptop." Mitch looked at the small white car. "I'll have this towed, and our techs can look it over."

We nodded, and when I started past him, Mitch touched my arm. "Are you okay?"

I knew he felt my anger. "I will be once we find the SOB that did this."

He started to say something else, but the dispatcher was on the mic trying to reach him, so he squeezed my arm, nodded at Enrique, and walked away. I heard the dispatcher telling him he was needed back at the scene and wondered what they had found.

I swallowed my anger and watched Mitch climb in his pickup. There was something about this case that he wasn't telling us. I knew him well enough to know that something big was bothering him. Did he have an idea who killed Renetta and he didn't want to tell us until he was sure? That wasn't like him. He needed to keep us informed of his thoughts, so we'd know where to look. Enrique and I headed to our SUV.

The locals called the hill going up Twelfth Street, Hospital Hill, and no one liked to drive it in bad weather. It was steep and slick in the ice. Unfortunately for Hood River drivers it was the best route to take from the lower part of town to the upper, which was aptly called, The Heights. The coffee shop where Renetta worked was on the left a few blocks after the road flatened out.

I pulled up and stopped in front of the coffee shop, my thoughts in turmoil. The parking spots in front of the store were empty. "Not many people out for coffee this morning."

Enrique opened his door, spit out his gum and hopped out. "Hope the manager made it in."

We walked to the door and saw the closed sign. I tried the door and found it locked. "Great, now we'll have to come back."

"Looks like there's someone in there." Enrique moved closer to the door. The top half of it was a window. "It's Gina." He knocked, and the woman looked up and pointed to the closed sign. "We need to talk to you," Enrique yelled through the glass.

She nodded and walked over to let us in. "Hey, what's up? You're lucky to catch me here. It's so nasty out, I decided to close for the day."

"We need to talk to you about one of your employees." Enrique said, stepping into the warm building. I followed, shivering and longing for a hot cup of coffee.

"Hey Liz." Gina smiled. She was about the same height as me, slender with dark hair pulled back in a ponytail. She wore blue framed glasses and had freckles across her nose. "What has Lori done now?"

"Lori?" Enrique asked.

"This isn't about Lori? She's the one that's always in trouble. Not usually with you, but she likes to skip out paying her rent, plays music so loud I'm surprised you haven't been called, and fights with her boyfriend." She placed her hands on her slim hips. "If not Lori, who?"

"Does Renetta Larson work here?" I asked.

"Renetta? Renetta can't be in any trouble. She's the sweetest kid in the world." Gina's brown eyes grew large behind her glasses.

"We found Renetta's body this morning down on Westcliff Drive," Enrique told her, his voice gentle.

Gina stared at him. "No. What happened?" She blinked tears from her eyes.

"You might want to sit down," he said, taking her arm and helping her to a chair. Once she was seated, he said, "She was murdered."

"Oh no. That poor kid." Tears fell unchecked from Gina's eyes and she took off her glasses and swiped them away. "Have you talked to her mother? If she's responsible for this..." Gina broke off, shaking her head.

"What makes you think that?" I asked, sitting down next to her. Everything led to Lilly, which didn't surprise me. What had she done?

"She's a worthless excuse for a human being, that's why. She has never taken care of Ren. It has been the other way around. Ren's had to work since she was old enough to take care of Lilly." She gestured around the empty room. "We've all helped when we could."

"Do you have any other ideas of who may have done this to her?" I asked, hopeful she could give us something.

Gina shook her head. "No, she was such a love. But I was afraid something like this might happen." She rubbed her hands together then jumped up and headed for the industrial sized coffee maker behind the counter. "Let me make you a cup of coffee. It will only take a second."

"You don't have to do that," I said, but I was glad Gina insisted.

"I need one, too." She busied herself measuring out coffee beans and putting them into a grinder.

"Why were you afraid for Renetta?" I pulled a notebook and pen from my pocket. I needed to write down everything she said so I wouldn't forget.

"Because she lived in that homeless camp with Lilly and that guy who said he was her brother. There's something about those two." She turned on the grinder and a few seconds later, turned it off. The smell of fresh coffee grounds filled the air. She put them in the coffeemaker and hit a button. "He claimed he was her brother, but he looks nothing like Ren, and I wouldn't be surprised if he and Lilly were sleeping together."

Enrique coughed. "What makes you say that?"

"The way they acted when they came in here. He's young enough to be her son. Not that it would bother Lilly. She'd sell her own mother for a hit." She brushed more tears from her eyes and took mugs down from the shelf above her head. "And that Brad was all over her. It was sickening."

I nodded. "Did Renetta have a computer?"

Gina looked up. "Yeah, she had an old laptop. I know because she'd come in here sometimes in the afternoon and do her schoolwork. I let her use the Wi-Fi and gave her hot chocolate."

"That was nice of you. Do you have any idea where it could be? We haven't been able to locate it."

Gina shook her head. "No, I'm sorry. She always took it with her when she left."

"Was Renetta close to anyone else who works here? We'd like to talk to them." I made a note about the laptop. I'm still old-fashioned enough to do this the old way. Some of the younger deputies type notes on their phones faster than I can write in my notebook.

Gina nodded. "Everyone liked her, but she was closest to Kari. She babysat for her sometimes."

I perked up. Maybe the little suitcases we found belonged to Kari's children. "Can you give us an address?" I asked.

Gina nodded and told us where Kari Young lived. There were a couple of other girls who worked there, too, and she gave us their addresses and cell phone numbers. I jotted them down.

By then the coffee was ready, and Gina grabbed to-go cups. "I don't know what I was thinking. You probably want your coffee to go." She poured us each a cup and handed it to us.

We thanked her and offered to pay, but she waved our offer away. "It's not necessary. I'll catch you next time."

"If you can think of anything else, please let one of us know," I said, holding the warm cup in my hand. It was the good people, like Gina, who made me love my job. There were a lot of them in town and I had sworn to protect them. I felt the heavy weight of that on my conscience as we walked to the door.

Gina followed us.

"I just remembered. There was this guy. He came in here for coffee a lot, especially when Ren was working. He tried to get her to go out with him. When she said no, he was upset."

"Do you know his name?" I asked.

She nodded. "Blake Peters."

I'd heard that name before. "Isn't he a new dentist here in town?" I'd been looking for a dentist when mine retired and someone had suggested Blake Peters.

Gina nodded. "Yeah, he works over on May Street. Seemed like a nice guy at first, but he got obsessed with Ren." She shook her head. "I wasn't comfortable with how he acted, and we never left Ren in the store by herself after that."

Chapter 8

Chapter 8—Bella

Bella's phone alarm went off at 10 a.m. She struggled up from a deep sleep and picked the phone up off the bedside table, silencing the alarm. She'd studied until 3 a.m. and she was the type that needed a full ten hours of sleep every night.

She yawned, climbed out of bed, and headed for the bathroom, taking her cell phone with her. Her roommate had already left for her morning class. Bella sighed. She'd need to jump in the shower and head out in about a half hour if she wanted to make her eleven o'clock class.

The phone in her hand buzzed with a text, but Bella had to pee in the worst sort of way, and she sat on the toilet before looking down at the phone. She had a text and a phone call from her friend back home, Renetta Larson.

The text was simple, **Call me ASAP.** Bella frowned and hit the voicemail button to see what was going on. Renetta's voice shook as she said, "Bella, this is Renetta. I need to talk to your mom. Can you give her my number and have her call me? It's important."

Bella found that odd and scrolled through all the missed calls that were left on her phone during the last few hours. Most were from friends at college, but she noticed that Renetta had called several times. Something was up and Bella hoped her friend was okay.

She tried calling her back, but it went straight to voicemail. She left a message telling Ren to call her. Then she sent her a text. **What's up? Call me.** She also texted her mom's cell number to Renetta. Her friend had told her a secret last time they'd been together. It was a crazy secret and Bella didn't really understand why Renetta didn't want anyone to know, but she felt like she couldn't tell anyone, not even her mom, even though she really wanted to. Now she wondered if Renetta's phone call was about that.

Bella got up from the toilet and tugged her pj's off and jumped in the shower. Her mind was already on the test she had in Economics. She didn't want to follow her parents into law enforcement. While in high school she decided she wanted to go into Hotel Management. The trip she took with her mom to Europe over Christmas only made that longing stronger. Languages came easy for her, and she was taking German and French in college. She'd taken Spanish in high school. German wasn't so easy, but she loved French and even though she probably would not use it that much, she wanted to speak it.

She quickly washed her hair, soaped herself and rinsed, then turned off the water and stepped from the shower. She dressed in skinny jeans and a large navy-blue sweater and blow-dried her long blonde hair. Then she pulled on warm socks and stuck her feet into knee-high boots. It was cold in Corvallis, but nothing like the weather at home. Her mom and dad had both called her the night before, while she was studying—insert eye roll—and told her Hood River was having the biggest snowstorm of the century.

In a way, Bella wanted to go home. She would love to go skiing with friends or sledding down the hill on her granddad's property. But another part of her—the part that hated her parents' separation and probable divorce—didn't want to be home anymore. It was too hard to be around everyone who knew that her dad had cheated on her mom. And almost everyone knew.

Grabbing her heavy winter coat, she put it on, and picked up her phone. She was about to drop it into her backpack when she looked to see if Renetta had called or texted. She hadn't, so Bella headed out the door to her class.

She tucked her hair into the hood of her coat and walked to the bus stop, thinking about Renetta. Her friend had such a hard life. Her mom was a mess and Ren didn't really have anyone to turn to when she needed help except for a few friends. Britney was good to her, but Bella thought Kari took advantage of Ren's kindness. She was always asking Ren to keep her two kids. Bella knew Ren loved the children, but she had a life of her own, too, and she needed to do things and go places besides working and studying all the time.

The bus pulled up and Bella got on. She hurried down the center aisle and sat in a seat that had an empty one next to it. A good place for her backpack. She unzipped the top of the backpack and reached in for her phone, hoping Ren had texted her back. But there still wasn't a text or a call from her.

Bella started to text her mom, but Ben Howard had gotten on the bus at the last second and he stood next to her seat, smiling down at her. Bella felt a tingle in her stomach and smiled up at him.

"Got room for me?" he asked, giving her his gorgeous smile. He was tall and had dark blond hair and the whitest teeth she'd ever seen outside the movies.

"Sure." She moved her backpack to the floor and smiled back at him. They'd been flirting a little in Econ, and texting for weeks. She hoped it might lead to a date. Ben was nice and as far as she knew he didn't do drugs or drink excessively. Those were both important to her. She knew that most of the kids in college did both, but she didn't do drugs at all and only drank socially—please don't tell her mom—and she didn't want the boy she dated to be hooked on anything either.

Ben sat next to her, leaning his shoulder into hers and Bella completely forgot to text her mom.

Chapter 9

Chapter 9—Mitch

When Mitch got back to the scene, he dismissed the deputy he'd left to keep an eye on things, telling him to go help canvass the neighborhood. Then he turned to Connolly. She was in full detective mode, looking at every inch of snow around where Renetta had lain. She made him think of Velma on Scooby Doo and if they hadn't been standing at the crime scene, he might have laughed.

Mitch heard Connolly huff as she walked around, looking closely at the ground. He watched her, wondering why she'd called him back to the scene. He'd planned to return, anyway. The Medical Examiner had taken Renetta away, but they needed to comb the area.

"Does this crime scene look staged to you?" Connolly asked, breaking in on his thoughts.

Mitch nodded. "Yeah, she wasn't just dropped here. The killer thought about it before leaving her." Mitch took a roll of antacids out of his pocket and put two in his mouth. The coffee was rolling about in his stomach, causing heartburn.

Connolly leaned closer to the berm the killer had built. "I was almost home and came back to take another look. This is bad, Sheriff."

"I know." Why had the killer framed her? And what else would they discover during this investigation?

"She looked like Lilly, didn't she?" Connolly squinted and moved some snow around with her foot.

Mitch nodded. "Lilly was once as pretty as Renetta." An errant thought, one of him flirting with Lilly at a bar one night several years ago, flitted through his mind. At the time she was sexy and knew it. No, she didn't just know it, she flaunted it.

Connolly continued talking about Lilly. "Hard to believe now. Have you seen her recently? She's missing a front tooth, skinny as a scarecrow and looks like your typical druggie."

"She didn't look great last time I saw her. Poor Renetta, she didn't have a chance."

Connolly stared down the cliff at the snow. Mitch watched her, wondering what she was thinking. She backed away, a thoughtful look on her face.

"Did you know her father or grandmother?" he asked.

"No, her father died before I moved to Hood River, and I never met her grandmother." Connolly stepped back and surveyed the area again.

Mitch glanced up at the road, then back at Connolly. "You don't have to stay here. It's your day off."

"I need to help if I can. I can take another day off. What can I do to help you?" She pushed her glasses back up on her nose.

Mitch thought for a second. "Why don't you go talk to the woman who found her. Liz and Enrique talked to her, but she didn't give them a lot of information. Maybe she will to you."

"Sure, do you know which house she lives in?"

Mitch gave her the address and told her the woman's name. Connolly nodded and wrote the name down, then took off. "I'll be back as soon as I know everything she knows."

Mitch didn't doubt that in the slightest. Connolly would stay on her until the woman spilled her guts or filed a complaint. He walked back up the hill to his pickup and climbed in, turning the engine on to get warm. He needed to wait there until the crime scene investigators showed up.

He took a notepad out of his center console and grabbed a pen he kept in the cup holder and started writing everything he could think of about the scene. The one thing that kept sticking in his mind was why had the killer framed her body?

After he had made a note of everything he could think of, he let himself check his emails hoping he had one from the last investigator he'd hired to find Liz's mom. Since Liz's dad's murder, Mitch had been looking for her mother.

Melanie Scott had left her husband and girls and disappeared from their lives. Liz had told him that as far as she knew, Melanie had never been in touch again. Her dad would only say that she had to go, and that he loved the girls and would never leave them. Liz blamed her mother for Rose joining a cult and eventually being murdered by a man in the cult.

Mitch hoped that he'd be able to find Melanie and discover why she left like she did. Maybe it would bring Liz some comfort. If he found her and she wasn't the sort of person Liz would want to know, he didn't have to tell her. But he needed something to make Liz realize he still loved her, and he hoped that finding her mother would do that for him. If she was still alive.

He looked through his emails and saw nothing, so he sent off a quick message to the private investigator. It felt like the woman wasn't doing anything. He'd ask for an accounting of her last couple of weeks and if she hadn't done anything, he'd fire her and try someone else.

He heard a vehicle drive up and looked up to see the crime scene van. He clicked out of his iPad and laid it on the seat. Then he went to meet them.

Chapter 10

Snow came down in big flakes as we walked outside. We headed for the county SUV. My feet slid, even with my heavy winter boots, and I grabbed the door handle to stop myself from falling.

After we were back in our vehicle, Enrique put his cup in the coffee holder and turned to me. "A dentist who kills. I mean, is that even a thing? What, is he tired of sticking his fingers in people's mouths and getting bit?"

Enrique always made me laugh. That was one reason I liked to work with him. The other was that he's an outstanding detective. "I'm glad he's not my dentist. I almost went to see him."

Enrique shook his head. "I'm sure it has happened before, but that gives me the creeps."

"We need to talk to him. Mitch will be interested in that little bit of info. But why would he kill Renetta? So, he tried to pick her up, and that didn't work. That really doesn't give him a motive."

"No, but he's someone to look at just because he's older and was obsessed with her." Enrique took a sip of his coffee.

"I agree we need to talk to him." I knew we needed more than just the fact that he was obsessed with Renetta. Lots of men became obsessed with young women. It didn't mean they killed them.

Enrique shook his head. "This case is giving me the heebie-jeebies."

"Heebie-jeebies? I've never heard you use that expression before." I gave him a surprised look.

He shrugged, his expression turning serious. "There's something..." he broke off and shook his head. "We know this town. We know these people. I can't believe there's a killer walking our streets."

I turned on the car and pulled out onto the street. "It seems weird because we don't get many murders here. I hope we're not wasting time talking to all of Renetta's acquaintances only to find out it's some guy who wandered in from Des Moines."

"Des Moines?" Enrique asked.

"It sounded good."

"Okay," he drew the word out. "We've got a couple leads. Which one do you want to talk to first?"

I turned from 12th onto C Street and drove a block over to 13th. "I want to talk to the dentist first, and then the girls who worked with Renetta. But first can we go get some lunch? I'm starving." My stomach growled. I could not live on coffee alone.

"Sure, if we can find anything open." Enrique looked up and down the street. "Most of the businesses are closed today."

I drove to a small Mexican Restaurant and pulled up in front, thankful to see the open sign. My stomach growled again. We got out and went inside. "I'll beg them to feed us."

The lingering smell of spices and melted cheese filled the air when we walked in. The owner, a short dark complected man in his sixties, greeted us. "Come in. We were just thinking we should close today. Nobody's out in this weather." He shook his head and showed us to a booth.

"Hey Miguel, how's it going?" Enrique asked, sliding into the booth.

Miguel answered in Spanish, then asked Enrique a question. He had a sparkle in his eyes and patted Enrique on the back. I wasn't fluent in Spanish, but I could follow their conversation enough to realize Miguel was asking about Jolene and the baby.

"One more month, then I'm taking paternity leave. Liz here will have to keep everyone safe without my help for a while." Enrique grinned at me.

My heart sank. I knew he planned to take time off work when the baby came, but I'd hoped he wouldn't be gone too long. I needed his detective skills on this case. I hoped Jolene wouldn't give birth until we solved it.

"We're starving. I'm glad you're open." I took the menu Miguel offered me and looked at it.

We had just ordered when the door opened, and a couple of women walked in. I recognized Kari Young from the coffee shop. She was with a woman I didn't know. I nodded to Enrique, and he glanced over at them.

"Eat first, questions later?" he asked.

I nodded and watched as Miguel greeted the women, then came back to put a cup of hot coffee in front of each of us. "You wan' to order now?"

We put our orders in, and we were sipping coffee when Kari Young got up and walked over to our table. "Oh, my gosh. Is it true about Renetta? I just heard she was killed."

She slid into a chair at the table next to us. She'd taken off her coat and scarf, but she wore gloves. Her hands must feel like ice, I thought. Kari was a pretty young woman with short dark hair and brown eyes. I had seen her in the coffee shop, and even though Kari was friendly enough, her expression always remained closed, almost expressionless. Today, though, her eyes were shimmering with tears.

"Yes, it's true," I said, gently. "When did you last see her?" I stared at her hands. She rubbed her gloved fingers together.

Kari wiped a tear from her face. "A couple days ago. She was such a nice kid. Who would do this to her?"

"That's what we're trying to find out. In fact, we need to talk to you and the other people who worked with her at the coffee shop." I looked her in the eyes and saw pain written there. She must've loved Renetta too.

Kari nodded. "All I know is she lived in that homeless camp. I felt so sorry for her."

"Gina said she babysat for you a few times?" Enrique asked.

A shadow passed over her face "Yes, she spent the night with the kids a couple of times when I needed to go out of town. She was wonderful with them."

"She didn't mention anyone stalking her or threatening her in any way?" I asked, hoping she'd give us something to go on.

"No." Kari frowned and shook her head. "I don't think so."

"What about Dr. Peters?" I asked. "According to Gina he came into the shop a lot and seemed interested in Renetta."

Kari's eyes widened. "Oh, yeah, him. He was always hitting on her, and she was creeped out because he was so much older." She shrugged. "Several of the other girls thought he was hot, so they didn't pay any attention to her." She glanced out the window, then back at them. "Do you think he did it? I mean, he was always wanting to talk to her. And I heard him ask her out a few times."

"Did he ask any of the other girls out?" Enrique asked.

Kari shook her head. "No, I don't think so. A couple of them were falling all over themselves trying to get his attention, but now that I think of it, he only had eyes for Ren." She rubbed her hands down her arms as though trying to get warm. "There was something about him I didn't like."

"Can you be more specific?" I asked, watching her closely for signs that she knew something that would help us.

She shook her head. "No, it's probably nothing, but he just...I don't know, kind of gives me the creeps. He comes across as nice, and he's handsome, but...I don't trust him. There's something in his eyes." She shook her head again.

"Can you think of anyone else she hung around with?" I asked, noticing that she was shaking. Poor girl, I thought. How awful to have your friend murdered.

"Renetta didn't have many friends, because she was so focused on working and trying to survive. She wanted to save enough money to get an apartment. I paid her to keep my kids and recommended her to my friends. She got a lot of babysitting jobs because she was great with kids."

I took my notebook out and handed it to Kari. "Could you write the names and phone numbers of the friends who had Renetta babysit for them?"

"Sure." She jotted down a couple names and numbers and handed the notepad and pen back. Then she stood up. "It's hard to believe that something like this would happen in Hood River, especially to someone I know." She swiped the tears from under her eyes.

I nodded and thanked her. "We may need to talk to you again." People always said they were surprised when something happened in Hood River because it was a small town, but I knew crime could happen anywhere. Just because Hood River had a population of only 8300 didn't mean we didn't get our share of crimes.

Miguel arrived with our food, and Kari walked back to her table. I glanced at the woman with her and got the impression of someone about the same age as Kari, maybe a little older. She was on the heavy side and wore her blonde hair in a braid that fell to the middle of her back.

I leaned closer to Enrique. "Do you recognize the woman with Kari?"

Enrique looked at the two women. "Doesn't she work at the hospital?"

"Maybe." I thought I'd seen her before but couldn't place her. "Our next stop should be a visit to this dentist. What do you think?" I dug into my food and noticed Enrique was devouring his.

Enrique finished the enchiladas on his plate and wiped his mouth with a napkin. "Yup. This guy sounds bad to me. What's he doing stalking a nineteen-year-old?"

I finished my meal and took money out to pay for our lunch. Enrique started to argue, but I waved him off. "It's my turn."

After I paid Miguel, we headed out the door. "I wonder if the dentist office is open today."

It was still snowing when we stepped out onto the sidewalk. "Won't be for much longer if it is," Enrique said.

We walked through a couple feet of snow, and I heard it crunch under our feet as we walked to the SUV and got in. "I'm already tired of winter," I said, starting the SUV and moving into the road.

We could've walked to the dentist's office but decided to drive the two blocks. Once I pulled up outside, we saw it was closed. I hit the steering wheel. "Man! This weather is not helping our investigation. Almost everything in Hood River is closed today."

"Yeah, I'll see if I can get an address for the doc's home." Enrique searched and soon had the address. "Looks like he's living on Eugene. Want to head over there?"

"Yup." I turned the SUV around and headed towards the address Enrique gave me. I was eager to talk to the dentist and find out his side of the story.

We pulled up outside a modest home that sat back from the road. It had a big front yard, and the house looked like it had been painted not too long before. Smoke curled from the chimney. I pointed it out. "Looks like the doctor is home."

We trudged through the snow to the front door. Enrique rang the doorbell and a couple minutes later the door opened. Dr. Blake Peters was not what I'd expected. I thought he'd wear glasses and have a receding hairline. The man who came to the door was drop dead gorgeous. He had thick brown hair and hazel eyes. He was tall and muscular, dressed in faded jeans and a blue sweatshirt. I could understand why the girls at the coffee shop were falling over him. What I didn't understand was why he had targeted Renetta.

We introduced ourselves and Dr. Peters invited us in. We walked through a tiled entryway into a great room. There was a fire in the fireplace and soft music played in the background. On one side of the room, there was a baby-grand piano. Lovely place, I thought.

Dr. Peters invited us to sit on the brown leather sectional that had been situated so you could see the Columbia River and Mount Adams. "You have a gorgeous view," I said, looking out the window. I turned back towards him and noticed a row of pictures on the mantel. The pictures were of two preteen boys. "Your kids?" I asked.

He nodded, a shadow passing over his face. "Unfortunately, they're living with their mother right now."

"That's hard."

"Yes. What can I do for you? I'm a little confused why you're here. Is there something going on at my office?" He sat on the edge of the matching ottoman, an anxious look in his eyes.

"We're looking into the murder of a young woman, and your name came up. We're just trying to find out what happened and why." He looked calm, and I realized right away he was either a great actor or he had nothing to do with Renetta's murder.

"Who?" Dr. Peters sat up a little straighter. A frown formed between his eyes. I noticed he gripped his hands together. Was more going on than I realized?

"Renetta Larson," Enrique said.

It took him a minute, then he must've realized who we were talking about. "Renetta? The girl from the coffee shop near my office?"

"Yes." I kept my eyes on him looking for any sign that he was keeping something from us.

"Oh, that's too bad. I'm sorry to hear that." He shook his head. "I can't believe she was murdered, but what does that have to do with me?"

"That's what we're trying to find out," I said. "We heard that you had quite a crush on her and asked her out more than once."

He let the question hang in the air for a couple minutes. "Yes, but I didn't realize how young she was when I asked her out. As soon as one of the other girls told me, I stopped." He shrugged. "I'm new in town and Renetta was nice...I wanted to get to know her. I figured she was in her mid-twenties, but I found out she was still in her teens. Way too young for me. But it wasn't really an issue."

"Why is that?" Enrique asked.

He spread his hands, then dropped them to his lap. "Every time I asked her out, she said no."

"It was our understanding that you didn't want to take no for an answer," I said, looking him in the eye.

He met my gaze then looked away. "Not at first. If a guy gave up the first time he asks a girl out and she says no, there wouldn't be as many happy couples out there. Sometimes it takes some convincing. But I never pushed her, no matter what you heard. I'm not that kind of guy."

"Did you notice any other guys hanging around her?" Enrique asked.

"Not really. I only ever saw her at the coffee shop. If there were other guys flirting with her, and I'm sure there were, I didn't notice." He stood and walked to the door and opened it.

We followed. "Thank you for your time, Doctor. If you think of anything that might help us find Renetta's killer, please get in touch." I handed him my card. I had a feeling that no matter what, the doctor would not reach out to us.

"Of course."

After we got back in the car, I turned to Enrique. "Well, what do you think?"

"I don't know. He seemed shocked when we told him about Renetta." Enrique took a piece of gum out of his pocket and after unwrapping it, shoved it into his mouth. "He seemed kind of fidgety to me. Wonder what he's hiding."

I started the vehicle. "Yeah, me too. We need to keep an eye on him." There was something there. He was too quick to assure us he'd left Renetta alone when he realized she was too young. I had a hunch that Blake Peters wasn't all he was cracked up to be. But was he our killer?

Chapter 11

C hapter 11

I put the car in reverse and backed out of the driveway. Across the road, a couple of kids bundled up in bright colored down jackets and snow boots were building a snowman. I smiled. "Soon, your little one will be out building snowmen." I said to Enrique and pointed to the children.

"Yeah, if he ever gets here." Enrique twisted in his seat to look at the kids playing in the snow.

"One more month." I thought back to when I carried Bella. By the eighth month, I'd been as big as a house. Mitch and I had been so excited. After three miscarriages, I'd finally carried a baby to term. She was a miracle.

Then I thought about Renetta, and depression hit hard, almost drowning me in sorrow. I felt every child should be welcomed with love and excitement. What kind of life had Renetta had? I knew it hadn't been good, and I ached for her. If only I'd tried harder to spend time with her. Maybe I could've helped.

Enrique's phone rang as I drove towards the address on Pine Street where one of the girls Renetta worked with lived. "It's Jo. I'd better take it."

I nodded, eager to know that Jo and the baby were okay.

"Hey babe, what's up?" His voice was soft, and it made me smile. Then his voice changed, and I could hear the stress. "Okay, I'll be right there. It's going to be okay, honey. I love you, too."

I glanced over at him, my heart racing. "Everything okay?"

Enrique shook his head. "You'd better take me back to my truck. Jo's having contractions. I need to get her to the hospital." Sweat broke out across his forehead. "It's too early."

I reached over and touched his arm trying to calm him down. "It's probably Braxton-Hicks, which are false labor pains. Most women get them the last month before the baby's born. He'll be fine. Maybe a little smaller than if she carries him full term."

"I hope so." He sat forward in his seat as though he could get to Jo faster that way.

I drove as fast as I dared, smiling to myself. It was unusual to see the normally easy-going Enrique wound up like a clock. A couple minutes later, we pulled up in front of the sheriff's office, which was in the county courthouse. "Let me know, okay?" I was worried, but I had a feeling everything would work out just fine.

"Yeah." Enrique jumped out of the SUV, slammed the door shut, slapped the roof, and took off for his pickup.

I turned the county SUV around and headed back up the hill to Pine Street and the address I had for Amy Bryne, one of the other girls who worked at the coffee shop. I hated it that Enrique wasn't with me. It was always better to interview people in pairs because you both came up with different impressions, but I knew Enrique needed to be with Jolene and their baby.

The roads were getting worse as the day wore on. There were snowplows out, but I knew they couldn't keep up with all the snow coming down. I drove up Hospital Hill and at the top continued South to Pine

Street. The house I was looking for was on the left, not far off the main road.

It was a one-level white house with an attached garage. Someone had built a snowman, and I wondered if Renetta had babysat for Amy, too. I parked behind a small white SUV in the driveway and made my way to the front door.

I could hear canned laughter inside the house and assumed Amy or someone was watching a sitcom. I knocked on the door and waited a few minutes. When no one came to the door, I knocked louder.

After another couple of minutes, a young woman wearing black sweats and a grey sweatshirt opened the door. Her hair was short and looked greasy, like she hadn't washed it in a few days. It was a dark blonde, and she'd tucked it behind her ears. "Yes?"

"Hi, I'm Detective Liz Ellisen. I'd like to talk to you about Renetta Larson. Are you Amy Bryne?"

The young woman's eyes grew enormous in her pale face. She nodded.

"May I come in?" Behind her, I could see that her house was a mess. Maybe she was a terrible housekeeper, or she was moving. There were boxes stacked up in the hall, some falling over with clothes spilling out of them. An older coffee maker sat on a bench with a crockpot.

Amy stepped back to let me inside. "I'm sorry the house is such a mess. I'm getting ready to move, so I'm going through things."

"No problem." I stepped into the small living room. Boxes and piles of stuff filled every surface. There was a large screen TV hanging on the wall. The cord dangled down to a plugin. "What's going on?"

"I'm moving in with a friend of mine. The rent has gone up again and I can't afford this place anymore."

"I'm sorry." I knew that the high rent in Hood River was a burden for most people. Sometimes they took in roommates just to make ends meet. "Were you living alone?"

She shook her head. "No, I have two kids. They're with their dad this week. My other roommate moved out a few weeks ago. She moved in with her boyfriend."

I nodded. "Is it okay if I ask you a few questions about Renetta Larson?" I looked for some place for us to sit, but her stuff covered every surface.

Amy looked like she'd rather be anywhere but there answering questions. "I heard she was killed. I just can't believe it." She opened the door wider. "Come into the kitchen. At least we can sit down."

She led the way down a tiny hall to the kitchen. It was small, but a lot neater than the living room. She motioned to the chairs next to the table. "Have a seat."

I rounded the table and sat down. Amy stood leaning against the counter. "Don't you want to sit?" I asked.

Amy walked over and sat on the edge of a chair. "I don't know what I can tell you. Of course, I'm really sad about Ren. She didn't deserve that. But no one does, do they?"

"No, they don't. When was the last time you saw Renetta?" There was something in her voice that caught my attention. She didn't seem all that sorry about Renetta. Had they had a falling out?

Amy cleared her throat. "Um…I don't know. About a week ago? I haven't been working at the coffee shop a lot lately. My other job is cleaning rentals and I've been busy with that. I just go into the shop when Gina needs someone, and I have a day off."

"Oh, okay." I took my notebook and a pen out of my vest pocket. "Did you notice anything unusual about her? Did she say anything that made you think she might be in trouble?"

"Mmm, no, I can't think of anything. She came in to get coffee for herself and her mom. You know about her mom, right?"

I knew what was coming, but I acted like I didn't, to see what she'd say. "What about her?"

Amy picked at a hangnail on her thumb. "She's a prostitute. She hangs out down by the bridge and I hear she has lots of clients. If I were going to look at someone who might hurt Ren, I'd start there."

"You think her mom killed her?"

"No! Not her mom, but she might know who did it. She hangs out with the dregs of society."

That wasn't what I'd heard. I'd heard that Lilly was servicing some of the most important guys in town. Interesting, though, that Amy said Lilly might know who killed Renetta and Lilly said the same thing. "We'll certainly look into that, thanks. Is there anything else you can think of that would help?"

She shook her head. Her hair swung free, and she pushed it back behind her ears. "I can't think of anything."

"Do you know if Renetta had a boyfriend?" Had they fought over a guy? There was an age difference, but Amy wasn't that much older than Renetta. Maybe that's why she acted unconcerned about Renetta's murder. Did she think it gave her a better chance?

Amy narrowed her eyes. "Maybe? I'm not sure. She was so busy with school and trying to survive. I don't know if she had time for guys." She thought for a minute. "There was some guy who kept trying to get her to go out with him. He came into the coffee shop every day for a while and Ren was getting upset. Then he quit coming in. I'm not sure what happened. Maybe he found someone else to pester."

"Do you know his name?" I expected her to say Blake Peters. But Amy surprised me.

"Yeah, Brad Thomas. He used to live with another gal who works at the coffee shop."

"Brad? He said he was her brother."

Amy shrugged. "Her brother? I didn't know that. He acted like he wanted to get into her pants all the time. It made his girlfriend so mad I heard she kicked him out and he's living at that homeless place down by the freeway."

"Who is the other girl?" I looked at her closely to see if her expression would tell me anything.

"Kari Young."

That was a surprise. Kari hadn't mentioned it when I'd talked to her earlier. "Are you sure?"

Amy ran her finger over the table. "That's the rumor. Kari's living with another friend now." She looked worried. "I haven't seen Brad for quite a while."

"Did they split up because of Renetta?" I made a mental note to call Kari and ask her about Brad.

Amy shook her head. "No, I heard he was beating her up. Kari told him to get out and he left. I haven't heard anything about him in a long time."

I jotted down his name and wrote Kari next to it. "Okay, thanks. Can you think of anything else?"

"No." Amy looked down at her hands, tugging at the hangnail again.

I took my phone out of my pocket and clicked on the picture of the pink suitcases we'd found in the back of Renetta's car. I showed her the picture. "Do you recognize these suitcases?"

She looked at the picture. Her face turned red, but she shook her head. "No, they don't belong to my kids."

"Do you know who they belong to?" Did I see shock on her face? Recognition? I was having difficulty reading her. What was going on behind her blue eyes?

"No." She stood up. "If that's all? I really need to finish packing."

I watched her for a couple minutes. Did she seem relieved that she didn't recognize the suitcases? I wasn't sure. I took a business card out of my vest and handed it to her. Then I stood. "If you think of anything that might help us find out who did this, please call me."

Amy headed for the front door. "I will. I hope you find the killer."

I nodded and walked through the snow to the SUV. There was something Amy wasn't telling me. I knew the signs. Amy hadn't wanted to meet my eyes. She was totally focused on her hangnails. What was she hiding?

Chapter 12

Chapter 12

Back in the SUV, I called the number I had for Kari Young. She didn't answer so I left a message for her to call me back. I wanted to find out if Brad had lied about being Renetta's brother. Had he tried to date her? If he got rough with Kari, maybe he had also gotten rough with Renetta. Had his anger, because she wanted nothing to do with him, pushed him to hurt her, possibly kill her?

I needed to have another talk with Brad Thomas.

Britney Fraizer lived on Highline Drive on the Eastside of Hood River. She was the other girl who worked part time for Gina at the coffee shop. Gina had said she thought Renetta and Britney had been close.

I drove over to see Britney before I went home for the day. I had an hour before my shift ended and knew that by the time I drove to Highline Drive, and talked to Britney, it would be time to head home.

I drove the SUV back to 12th Street and turned right. Then I followed a snowplow down to State Street. The temperature was dropping, and the streets were getting slicker by the second. I knew the county was sanding the roads, but they probably had trouble keeping up with the snow.

The plow turned left at the intersection of 12th and State, and I turned right, heading East to Hwy 35. I drove slowly, glad for the studded snow tires on my department vehicle. My radio was squawking, but I could hear the crunch of my tires on the snow. I drove out of town and turned South onto Hwy 35 heading up to the turnoff to Eastside Road which would take me to Highline Drive.

The North end of the road sat above Highway 35 and had gorgeous views of the Columbia River. The address I was looking for sat on a point and had a view of both the river and Mt. Hood to the South. I whistled and wondered why Britney worked in a coffee shop if she could afford to live on a million-dollar piece of property.

Their driveway was narrow, but someone had plowed them out, so I didn't have any trouble getting to the house. It was a large grey house with a circular driveway, an attached garage and two outbuildings.

There were lights on inside. I parked and got out, then walked up to the front porch. The house had two stories with a wraparound porch. There was a Christmas wreath on the front door even though Christmas had come and gone three weeks ago.

I rang the doorbell. A couple minutes later the door opened, and a little girl stood there with her thumb in her mouth and a stuffed penguin in her arms. She looked to be about three.

"Hello," I said, giving her a smile. "Is your mommy home?"

A young woman came rushing from another part of the house. "Kennedy, I told you to wait for me." She looked up at me and smiled. "She loves visitors."

I smiled again at the little girl. "That's a nice penguin. What's her name?"

Kennedy kissed the stuffed penguin and said, "Booger."

The woman, whom I assumed was Britney, shrugged, then picked up the little girl and stood in front of the door. She frowned. "Is everything okay?"

I held out my hand. "I'm Detective Liz Ellisen."

The woman shook my hand. "Britney Fraizer."

"I want to talk to you about one of your co-workers, Renetta Larson." I wondered how she would take the news of Renetta's murder.

Alarm flickered across her face. "Is she okay?"

I shook my head. "I'm sorry."

"What happened?" Tears formed in the woman's eyes.

"Can we go in where it's warm?" I could tell the little girl was starting to shake from the cold and I didn't want to keep them out in the freezing temperatures longer than I had to.

"Oh, of course. I'm sorry." She set the child down and said, "Run in and check on Barney, honey." She turned back to me. "Barney's our long-suffering cat."

I smiled as Kennedy hurried down the hall. Bella had loved cats as a little girl. We'd always had a couple around the house until she got older and decided she wanted a horse. We went through a horse phase, and when she grew out of that, we were without pets until my dad died and I inherited his yellow Labrador, Bailey.

Britney opened the door wider and put a trembling hand to her face. "Please come in."

I nodded and followed her into a bright, cheerful kitchen. The cabinets were all painted white, and the appliances were stainless steel. The granite counters were grey with white marbling. It was a large room, with a round wooden table on one side. There were drawings of penguins and cats on the refrigerator. Kennedy was quite the little artist. The room was warm and welcoming. I could tell it was where the family gathered from the comfy chairs around the table and the bar stools next to the island. Britney had what smelled like tortilla soup cooking on the stove and my stomach gurgled.

She motioned me to the table. "Have a seat." She sank into a chair.

"I'm sorry to have to tell you about Renetta, but we are talking to everyone who worked at the coffee shop with her. Gina told us you and Renetta were friends."

"Yes, we..." she looked up. "What happened to her?" Her mouth trembled.

"We found her body on Westcliff Drive. We're pretty sure she was murdered."

Britney cried out, then covered her mouth. "Oh, no!" She sobbed, and I handed her a paper towel off the roll on the counter.

When she'd gotten hold of herself, she said, "She was such a sweet girl. We, my husband and I, loved her like a sister. We had her over for meals a lot." She held her hands palms up. "I love to cook. I tried to get her to move in with us. I hated for her to live in that motorhome, but she wouldn't. She said she wanted to take care of herself."

I nodded, happy to hear that Renetta got a home cooked meal now and then. "I heard she was going to college?"

Britney nodded. "Yes, she wanted to be a teacher. She was so good with the kids. She'd stay overnight if we wanted to get away for a while. The kids love her. I have a little boy, also. He's one and a half." Tears streamed down the young woman's face. "I can't believe this. Who would do this to her?"

"That's what we're trying to find out. Do you know of anyone who would want to harm her?"

Britney's eyes grew round, and I was sure she was going to give me a name, but she shook her head, her eyes downcast. "No, Ren was just the sweetest girl in the world. I can't imagine anyone wanting to kill her." She took another piece of paper towel off the roll and blew her nose. "It must've been something to do with her mother. You know she's a mess, right?"

I nodded. "Do you think her mother would've hurt her?" The timer on the oven dinged and Britney got up and took a loaf of homemade bread out and set it on the counter. I didn't think I'd ever smelled anything so amazing.

"No, but she was always doing things that Ren had to take care of." She brushed the top of the bread with butter. Then she came over and sat back down.

"Such as?" I made myself quit thinking about the great smells coming from her cooking and baking. I wondered if I should hire a cook. As if I could afford one.

"Charging things at the store, then spending all her money on drugs and booze. And Ren would have to pay her mom's bills, or they wouldn't be able to get food and gas. She was sick of paying for Lilly. She told me she just wanted to get out of Hood River and away from her. I wish she would have. Maybe she'd still be alive." She wiped tears from her eyes. "We tried to give her money, just to help, you know?"

"Did you give her some recently?" Was that where the thousand dollars came from? I wondered.

Britney nodded. "I just hated to see her struggle. She was trying so hard. My folks gave us some money for Christmas, and I told my husband I wanted Renetta to have it. It wasn't much, but I hoped it would take some of the stress off her."

I nodded. "That was good of you. We found a thousand dollars in cash in her motorhome. Is that the amount you gave her?"

Tears fell from Britney's eyes. "Yes. She didn't have time to spend any of it."

"I hate to ask, but did Renetta take drugs?"

Britney gave a sharp shake of her head. "No, absolutely not. But I wouldn't put it past Lilly to owe some drug dealer a bunch of money and expect Ren to pay for it."

My phone rang. I took it out and looked at the screen and saw it was Connolly. I hit end. The last thing I wanted to do in the middle of an investigation was talk to Connolly. Instead, I went to my pictures and brought up one of the pink suitcases. "Do you recognize these suitcases?"

Her eyes widened. "Yes, those are Kennedy's. She uses them when she goes to spend the night at Grandma's. We thought we left them last time we went. Where did you get this picture?" Deep lines formed on her forehead.

"I took it. The suitcases were in the back of Renetta's car."

Britney's face turned white, and she looked like she might throw up. "But...how...why...where would Renetta get them?"

"That's what we'd like to know. When was the last time you saw them?" Could this beautiful woman who seemed to love her kids be a killer?

She shook her head as though trying to clear it. "I don't know. A week ago, I guess." Her frown deepened. "My husband picked the kids up from his mom's after they spent the weekend with her. He didn't bring the suitcases inside when he got home. He said he'd get them the next day. Then, when he went out to get them from his pickup, they were gone. It was so weird. He thought maybe he forgot to pick them up when he got the kids."

"Did you call his mother and ask about them?"

"No, we were going to, but we didn't. There wasn't anything in them that Kennedy needed right away. We just thought we'd get them next time we were down there."

"And you're sure these belong to your daughter?" I held out my phone for her to get another look.

"I think so. If not, they're just like the ones she had. I bought them at Walmart. I guess anyone could've bought some like them." She chewed on her thumb for a second, then said, "Do you want me to text my mother-in-law and ask if Kennedy's are there?"

"Sure. That would be great." If these weren't Kennedy's, whose were they?

She pulled her phone out of her back pocket and thumbed a text faster than I could say the words. A couple minutes later her phone dinged. She looked down at it. "Hmm, apparently, she's not home. Said she'll look when she gets back."

"Okay. Let me know. Is there anyone else you can think of that might know something? I talked to Amy Bryne, and she said that Brad Thomas was harassing Renetta. Trying to get her to date him."

Britney's head snapped up. "Brad? He's Ren's brother. Amy's probably just trying to make Ren look bad. She dated Amy's ex a few times and Amy was furious."

"Her ex? Who is he?"

"Colin Symons. He and Amy were married for a while, but it didn't work out. Colin is harmless. He goes from girl to girl, but he doesn't have a mean bone in his body."

She seemed protective of Colin, and I wondered what he was to her. Twin spots of red colored her cheeks.

I filed that away to think about later. "How about Dr. Blake Peters?"

"The dentist?" Britney grimaced.

"Yes. I heard he'd been harassing Ren, too. Asking her out and not wanting to take no for an answer."

Britney stared out the window for a few seconds. Then she shook her head. "I just can't see him as a killer. He liked Ren, but as soon as he found out how old she was, he backed off."

But did he really? I wondered.

My phone rang again, and I frowned, took it out of my pocket and looked at it. It was Mitch. "Excuse me, I need to take this."

"Of course. I'll go check on Kennedy."

Britney left the room, and I answered my phone. "This is Liz. What's going on?" I wanted to go home and eat something. My stomach felt like I'd missed too many meals.

"There's been a fight at the warming center. Lilly Larson got beat up."

"Oh, no." Great. Now I'd have to deal with that. Maybe I had a candy bar in my pack.

"And there's a wreck down on Cascade. A semi-truck slid off the road and plowed into a house. There are injuries. I'm headed there. I need you and Connolly to go to the warming shelter and see if you can find out what's going on."

Ugh, I thought. Not Connolly. So, that's why she was calling. "Okay, I'm about finished here, I'll head up there."

"And Liz, be careful. The roads are horrible."

"I will." He knew I could drive in any weather, and I knew he was just letting me know he was concerned, but it rankled. He needed to back off and stop worrying about me.

He started to say something else but stopped himself. "Okay, let me know what's going on."

"I will." I stood up and headed back towards the front of the house to look for Britney.

Chapter 13

C hapter 13

I heard Britney's voice and followed the sound into the great room. She was talking into her phone in a low voice. "Of course, I won't." She glanced up and saw me. "I have to go." After she hung up, she said, "Sorry, that was my husband. I told him you found Kennedy's suitcases in Renetta's car."

What else had she told him before I walked into the room? She had guilt written all over her face. Why was everyone I'd come into contact with in this case acting guilty?

"I need to leave. If you hear anything, or remember anything, please call me." I held out my card.

Britney walked over and took it. "Okay, but I don't know anything. I wish I did."

I looked around the room. "Where is your husband? Is he working today?"

Britney nodded. "He had a meeting with a client in Portland yesterday. I told him to reschedule it because of the weather, but he went anyway. He's an architect. He just started his own business here, and he didn't feel like he could put this client off." She shrugged. "Then he got caught in the storm and couldn't get home. I hope the freeway opens soon."

"If they can open it, they will. It's hardly ever closed more than a couple of days." But this was the snowstorm that beat most of them in recorded snowfall. When I was a kid, we got five feet of snow one year, but that was a long time ago.

Britney nodded. "He got a motel room, and he's got his laptop, so he's able to work. He'll be home soon, I'm sure."

I smiled, said goodbye to Britney and Kennedy, and let myself out. The lawn and parking area looked like a winter wonderland. Snow had piled up to the top of the fence that enclosed their yard. I hoped they didn't lose electricity, since I wasn't sure if Britney and the children could stay warm if it went off.

The roads from the East side of Hood River into town were slick, and I took my time. Luckily, there wasn't a lot of traffic. Most people were staying home during the storm. I drove up Oak Street to the warming shelter.

Connolly was already there when I pulled in. I stopped next to the other county SUV and climbed out. Immediately, I saw Connolly struggling with Lilly and went over to help. Nothing was ever easy when dealing with Lilly. It was as though she did everything she could to make our life more difficult.

"About time you got here," Connolly said, wrestling with Lilly who struggled to get away. Connolly wheezed from the effort.

I didn't bother to answer her. I knew from experience that it wouldn't do any good. She was as bad as Lilly at making my life difficult. "Where's Brad?"

Connolly looked up and swore. "He was just here." She must've slacked off her tight hold on Lilly because Lilly squealed and broke free. She headed for the road with Connolly yelling at her to stop. I ran after her and tackled Lilly, throwing her into a snowbank.

"Get off me!" Lilly screamed. She flailed her arms and kicked out, catching me in the ribs and then giving me a solid headbutt. I saw stars, then everything went black for an instant. When I came to, Connolly was chasing Lilly through the snow. I ran after them, holding my side as I ran.

Connolly reached out to grab Lilly's coat and the woman darted to the right. I hurtled myself through the air and tackled her again, bringing her down. The pain in my side felt like I'd been bit by a rabid dog.

Lilly squirmed and screamed. "It's not my fault. That slimeball stole my money. Ren left it for me, and he took it. You need to get him!" Lilly struggled to free herself, but I grabbed a zip tie from my pocket and locked her hands together.

"Hold still," I said as I hauled Lilly to her feet. She had the beginnings of two black eyes. I figured the money Enrique found earlier at Ren's motorhome was what Lilly was talking about. "I was told that money was a gift to Renetta from a friend."

Lilly snorted. "She'd still want me to have it, not that shit for brains."

I shook my head. Lilly only thought about Lilly.

As we walked back to the warming shelter, Connolly huffed and puffed beside us, but didn't talk. This surprised me. Usually, she wouldn't shut up. I glanced up at her and noticed she was paler than normal. She bent over for a couple of minutes, holding her stomach.

"You okay, Connolly?"

"I'm fine," she snapped, and I gave her a sharp look wondering why I'd bothered to ask. Connolly had been trying to undermine me for years. Mitch hadn't let her, but what would happen now that he no longer had my back?

Lilly mumbled something that didn't make sense. Once we made it back to the shelter, I noticed she had blood all over her face and hands. "Better call medical and have her checked out," I told Connolly.

Brad stumbled out of the shelter wearing a stocking cap pulled away from his ear. A woman I didn't recognize was behind him. He pointed a finger at Lilly. "You keep that crazy witch away from me. She tried to bite my ear off." He rubbed his ear, and his hand came away covered in blood.

Connolly looked up at the sound of his voice and squinted at him. "What?" She clutched her side and bent over.

"You okay?" I asked her. "Do you know this guy?"

She glanced up at him and shook her head. "No..." she gasped and turned away.

Brad moved up next to the volunteer, holding a washcloth to his torn ear.

The woman stepped forward. She wore jeans and a heavy sweater. She wore black work boots on her feet. "Hello Deputies, I'm Sheryl Kline. I told Brad I'd talk to you. I saw Lilly attack him."

I didn't correct her by saying I was a detective, not a deputy. I heard Connolly snort. I didn't know if Sheryl was a volunteer or a person seeking shelter. "Okay, thank you. Why don't you go back inside, and we'll come in and talk to you in a minute?"

The woman nodded and stepped back into the shelter.

Brad walked closer and Lilly spit on him. He jumped back. "She's certifiable! You gonna let her get away with spitting on people?"

"I want my money, you slimeball. You stole it. I had lots of cash at my place, and you took it."

She struggled to get out of my hold, and I pushed her towards the county car.

"Let's get you to the office and then we'll sort this out. It's too cold to talk out here." She was stronger than I gave her credit for, and I struggled to hold onto her. I wasn't about to tell her that Enrique and I had taken Renetta's money as evidence. I didn't want my ear bit off.

Just then a quick responder vehicle drove in, lights flashing. "Looks like we'll get you looked at first."

The truck pulled up and stopped. Brad hurried over to the responders who stepped out. "Can you put some antiseptic on my ear? That crazy old witch bit it and she probably has rabies."

I knew the two first responders, Nick Wilson and Brenda Miller. I raised my hand. "Hi guys."

Brenda grabbed a first aid kit and motioned Brad closer. Nick Wilson came towards me. He was probably in his thirties with light brown hair and a scruffy beard. He was plain until you noticed his eyes. They were a bright blue and crinkled in the corners. "Hey Liz, welcome back. What's going on?"

"Thanks. It seems these two got in a fight over money and Brad's ear got the worst end of the deal. But Lilly has blood all over her. Not sure if she's hurt or if it's Brad's blood."

"Okay, we'll check it out." He walked over to help his partner.

"Thanks," I said. "I need to talk to the woman inside. Connolly will stay with you."

Connolly had pushed Lilly up against the building. Lilly tried to kick her and as I walked into the building, I heard her scream obscenities along with, "I hate you and I'm going to sue you for everything you've got!"

Inside, I found Sheryl Kline. She was a soft-spoken woman with greying brown hair and kind eyes behind her glasses.

"Can you tell me what happened?" I asked, pointing towards the door. My head hurt, and my ribs hurt, and I knew I needed to get them taped, but that would have to wait.

The woman nodded. "Brad came in to visit with me. He does anytime I'm here. He's real social and visits with all us volunteers. We were sitting here talking and Lilly stormed in. She went right up to Brad and motioned him to lean over so she could tell him something, then she bit his ear." She shook her head. "It was awful. Blood everywhere. I went to get a cloth to put on it to stop the bleeding, and when I came back, they'd taken the fight outside."

I took a notebook and pen out of my pocket and jotted down Sheryl's name and what she'd said, knowing I'd never remember the details if I didn't. "And then what happened?"

"I tried to tell them to stop, but they were going for each other like crazy. It seems like they have quite a history. So, I came back in and called the police."

And the police called us, I thought, but I didn't say anything. I knew we'd been called in because City was busy with wrecks all over town. "Did Brad tell you anything while we were chasing Lilly?" Like what he'd done to make her bite him.

The woman shrugged. "Just that Lilly is crazy, and he didn't take her money."

I nodded and wrote that down. "Okay, thank you. I may have more questions later."

"Sure. There's just one thing."

I glanced up at the worried tone in her voice. "What's that?"

Sheryl said, "Before they went outside and started throwing punches Lilly said, 'you know who killed Renetta. I know you do. You'd better give me my money back or I'll tell them cops.'"

"What did Brad say?" Maybe we were going to get a break in the case. My heart sped up. At least it was a lead.

"He didn't say anything. But he looked really frightened." She shook her head and shoved her hair behind her ear. "I thought you should know that."

I stood up. "Thank you. Can you think of anything else?"

"No, except I think if Brad knew who killed his sister, I'm sure he'd tell you."

I wasn't so sure, but I nodded anyway. I was just about to head to the door when it crashed open, and Nick Wilson stuck his head in. "You'd better come, Liz. Deputy Connolly just passed out."

Chapter 14

Chapter 14

I followed Nick outside. My side was killing me, but I knew I'd have to wait to get it looked at. Lilly was sitting in the back of Connolly's SUV, screaming obscenities. Brad stood up against the building and watched as one of the EMTs, Brenda Miller, knelt in the snow, trying to get Connolly to respond. "What happened?" I asked, kneeling next to Miller.

She looked up. "She put the perp in the back of her car, shut the door and turned around and fell. I ran over to see what was going on. It looks like she was stabbed."

Miller pointed to Connolly's side. "It's hard to tell with her dark coat, but her left side is bleeding. I put a compression bandage on her, but we've got to get her to the hospital so they can see how bad it is. She was in so much pain, I gave her a shot of painkiller until we can get her to the hospital."

"Lilly had a knife?" Unbelievable. If she'd had one, why hadn't she stabbed Brad instead of biting him?

The woman shook her head. "I don't know. I didn't see one and I didn't see her stab the Deputy."

We could hear Lilly screaming with the doors closed. "Do you know if Deputy Connolly checked Lilly for a weapon?"

Miller shook her head. "She didn't say anything about a weapon. She told us to check her out, then she put her in the back of her vehicle."

I walked over to Connolly's vehicle and opened the back door. Lilly turned to look at me and started screaming again. She cussed like a pro.

I got down close to her face. Later I would think about how dangerous it was to get that close to Lilly's teeth, but at the time I wanted to make sure she heard what I had to say. "Shut up and listen to me. This will go easier on you if you tell the truth. Did you stab Deputy Connolly?"

"With what? I ain't got no knife. Ask her. She searched me before she stuck me in the back of this stupid car."

I dragged her out and searched her again. Then I made her stand up next to the SUV while I went through it. No knife. I put Lilly back in the SUV and walked over to where Connolly lay on her side in the snow. I knelt. "Can you hear me, Deputy?"

She moaned and grabbed her side.

"Who stabbed you? Was it Lilly or Brad?" I looked her over, trying to figure out what had happened. She was in pain. I could tell from the squished look on her face.

She shook her head. "No, it wasn't them." She tried to sit up, but passed out again before she could.

Why hadn't Connolly said anything when she'd first arrived? She must've been hurting like crazy. I glanced up at the first responders. "How far out is the ambulance?"

"They're sending one from Odell," Nick said, naming the small town South of Hood River. "Both Hood River and West Side ambulances are busy with the wreck."

"Lots of folks hurt?" A Semi-truck plowing into a home was bad.

Nick nodded. "I just talked to Dispatch. The operator said it's a mess over there. Apparently, there were several people living in the house the semi slammed into. I'm not sure if there are any deaths, but several people were hurt."

I shook my head; glad I'd been needed here. Being involved in the chaos of a wreck like that was not fun. It would take forever to clear it up. "Can we move Connolly into the shelter until the ambulance comes? I'll drive Lilly down to the office and put her in a room. Maybe if she has time to think, she'll stop screaming."

"Nah, she won't," Brad said. "Probably needs a hit."

I had forgotten he was standing there. "Are you okay? Do you need to go to the hospital?"

He reached up and gingerly touched his ear. "Nah, I'm good. Doc said I don't need no stitches." He motioned to Miller.

"I'm not a doctor, sir. I'm a paramedic. You probably need to be seen just in case infection sets in."

"Let's get Connolly into the shelter. Nick, can you call Odell Fire Department and see what their ETA is? I don't want her freezing to death on top of being stabbed." She glanced at Brad. "Did you see Lilly stab the officer? "I didn't trust Connolly's claim that she had been stabbed before arriving at the shelter.

He shook his head. "No, but I wouldn't be surprised. She's crazy at the best of times, and she really goes berserk when she needs a hit."

With the help of Nick and Brenda, we moved Connolly into the shelter. When we laid her on the sofa in the main room, she started to wake up.

"What happened? Where am I?" She tried to sit up, but I put my hand on her shoulder and eased her back down.

"It looks like someone stabbed you. Did Lilly do that to you?"

Connolly's eyes rolled back in her head. Then she moved and groaned. "Hurts."

I leaned over her. "I'm sure it does. Did you get the knife from Lilly?"

Connolly groaned again. "Not Lilly." Then she closed her eyes and went out again.

Nick and I looked at each other. "Did she say it wasn't Lilly who stabbed her?" Nick asked.

"Yeah." I turned to Brad. "Do you know what happened to Deputy Connolly?" This didn't make sense. If Lilly or Brad didn't stab her, who did? I couldn't imagine the volunteer doing it. I glanced at her, and she raised her hands.

"It wasn't me; I promise. I don't have a knife or any reason to stab her."

I nodded. I didn't really think it was her, but someone stabbed the deputy.

Brad shook his head. "I didn't see Lil stab her. If she'd had a knife, she would've come after me."

"Medical is almost here," Nick announced.

"Can you take Brad to the hospital?" Connolly had a death grip on my hand. I knew she'd be horrified if she came to and realized what she was doing.

"Yes, we can," Nick said.

"Okay, good." I turned to Brad. "I want you to go to the emergency room and have them look at your ear."

He nodded and turned to leave, but I put out my hand and stopped him. "Are you really Renetta's brother?"

"Yes. Why? Is that old bat saying I'm not? She'd like to pretend she never had me, but I have proof." His eyes were wild, and I wondered what he was on.

"I need to talk to you again, but you need to get that ear taken care of."

He raised his hand and nodded again.

After Connolly and Brad were taken to the hospital, I drove Connolly's SUV to the office. I'd have to have someone take me back to my vehicle once I got Lilly settled.

The trip to the sheriff's office didn't take long, but it seemed longer because Lilly wouldn't shut up. I wanted to gag her, but I took her inside and booked her for assault.

I tried to question her, but Lilly shouted more obscenities, and I gave up. I left her in the interview room with Deputy Walsh trying to get her to the jail in The Dalles. Norcor, or Northern Oregon Regional Correctional Facility, was the closest jail, but with the freeway closed, I wasn't sure how we'd get her up there.

I thought about it and decided we needed to get hold of ODOT, or Oregon Department of Transportation and see if they could help us. "Call ODOT and see if you can follow a plow up to Norcor," I told Walsh. Then I went back to the front office to see if there was anyone who could take me to get my vehicle.

Alissa Sanchez ran the front office most weekdays. She stood up when I asked if there was anyone around who could take me to my car. "I'm through for the day. I can run you up."

"Are you sure? I hate for you to have to go out of your way." I knew Alissa lived on the Eastside of town.

"No, it's okay. I need to run to the grocery store anyway. Rosauers is just up the hill."

"Thank you, that will be great."

Alissa dropped me off at the warming shelter and I drove the county issued SUV back to the office and got my Jeep. I called Mitch to see if they needed any help before I headed home.

"No, go on home. We've just about got this mess cleared." He sounded exhausted. "I need to meet with you and Connolly in the morning."

"Oh, crap."

"What's the matter?"

"I forgot to tell you about Connolly. Have you heard from her?" I turned my car back towards town. The last thing I wanted to do after a long day was to go to the hospital and check on Megan Connolly. I crossed my fingers, hoping Mitch would say the woman was home.

"No, what's going on?"

My heart sank. I told him everything I knew.

"Someone knifed her?"

"Apparently, or she knifed herself. She's at the hospital." I sighed. "I'll go check on her." Even though I didn't want to drive back to town, it wouldn't hurt to have a nurse tape my ribs, and I wanted to know what had happened to Connolly. It didn't make sense that someone would stab her, and she wouldn't tell us who did it.

"Thanks, that will help. We've probably got another few hours here."

"It must've been quite a mess. Sorry I missed it." Not really. Actually, I was glad I didn't have to sort through the damage of the wreck.

He snorted out a laugh. "No, you aren't. It's been a hell of a day. I'll be glad to go home."

I smiled. Talking to Mitch like this felt like old times. I wished...but I wasn't sure what I wished. *If wishes were horses...* I'd heard my mother's voice saying that so many times in my head, even though I'd been really young when my mom had left. Was it because I'd lost both my dad and sister last spring? Had their deaths brought back to me the fact that I had a mother out there somewhere?

What had my mother wished for? A more exciting life? No children to take care of? If that was what she wanted, she'd certainly gotten it. What did I wish for? That Mitch had never cheated. That he'd loved me enough to stay faithful. That...there were so many things. But wishing didn't make things right and I pushed it all to the back of my mind.

"Okay, I'm almost at the hospital. I'll call and give you an update after I've seen Megan."

"Sounds great. Oh, Doctor King called. She's done with Renetta's autopsy."

"That poor little girl." My heart ached for her. "We have to find out who did this to her and put them away."

"We will."

I hung up as I pulled into the hospital parking lot. Of all people, it should not have been me checking on Connolly. The woman had had it in for me since she'd joined the force five years earlier. At first, I'd thought Connolly didn't like that I was the sheriff's wife. She'd made some derogatory comments over the years about me getting preferential treatment, but now I wondered if it was something else. I just couldn't put my finger on what.

Once inside, I made my way to the emergency room. I knew how long it usually took to be seen and released or admitted—at least four hours—and Connolly had only been there for just over an hour.

The receptionist looked up when I walked in. She was an older woman with dark hair pulled up into a bun on top of her head. She'd stuck a pencil in it and was using another one to write something down. I wondered how many pencils she took out of her hair when she got home each day.

"Hey, Nita."

"Liz, nice to see you. What's going on? You bring someone in?"

I shook my head. "No, I need the nurse to tape my ribs." I held my hand up to my side.

Nita nodded and picked up her phone and called into the ER for a nurse.

"I'm checking on Deputy Connolly. Is she still in emergency?" I pointed towards the double doors next to the reception area.

Nita shook her head. "Didn't the doctor call you? Deputy Connolly was taken into surgery about ten minutes ago. She was bleeding profusely. They had to get her in and stop it before she bled out."

Chapter 15

C hapter 15

I stared at Nita. "Did she say what happened to her?"

Nita shook her head. "I probably shouldn't say anything." She leaned closer, and I knew she was dying to tell me something. Nita always said that before she told everything she knew. "But I overheard Dr. Jenson say it looks like she was in a fight. Bruising across her chest and stomach, like she was down, and someone kicked her. And then took a knife to her."

"Whoa, that's crazy. Did the doctor ask her what happened?"

"Yup, but Deputy Connolly was too far out of it by the time she got here." She looked around to see if anyone was in earshot. Then she lowered her voice. "It looks like domestic abuse."

That would have been Liz's first thought, too. But to her knowledge, Connolly didn't have a boyfriend. What was going on with her? Had she been in a bar fight? If she had, the bartender would have reported it, wouldn't they?

"How about Brad Thomas? Did he get seen?"

Nita nodded, a thoughtful look on her face. "The doctor gave him some antibiotic cream to put on his ear. He wasn't here long."

"Have they brought many people in from the semi-truck accident?"

Nita nodded. "A couple of people were seen, then released. I heard they haven't found one woman living there. They don't know if she's still under the rubble or if she was somewhere else when it happened." She looked out the emergency room door. "We keep waiting for medical to bring more people in. Of course, you can hear anything, but we heard there were twenty people in that house."

"He couldn't slide into an empty house."

Nita shook her head. "Nope. Poor guy. He's pretty shook up. Although he wasn't injured, he's very upset. He kept saying he couldn't get the semi to turn. It just kept sliding down the hill."

"He should've parked it. The freeway is closed. Why was he out tonight anyway?" I couldn't believe how stupid some people could be.

"Apparently, he came around the mountain and thought he'd be able to go East from here. You'd think he would've heard that the freeway was closed. Maybe he was just trying to get as close as he could, so he'd have less time to travel tomorrow or whenever they open the freeway."

I shook my head. "It's scary that people like that are out driving semis around. I'm sure the sheriff will call for updates about Deputy Connolly. After I get checked out, I'm going home." I was beat. It had been a busy, emotional first day back at work.

A nurse came out of the ER and motioned for me to follow her. I did, and she taped my ribs, giving me a lecture about taking care when I chase perps. She laughed, and I did, too, which hurt, so I held my side.

I went back into the reception area and Nita looked up and smiled. "You didn't ask about Detective Rodriguez's wife."

"How is she?"

"Jolene's in labor. The baby is early, but the doctor thinks they'll both be fine."

"Oh, that's great. It has been such a crazy day, I forgot to call Enrique. I'll call him on the way home."

Nita shrugged. "Or you could run up to maternity and say hello."

I hadn't thought about that. "They'll let me in?"

Nita gave her a knowing smile. "Sure, unless Enrique and Jolene have said no visitors. But I'm sure they'd be happy to see you."

I grinned, thanked her, and headed up to the second-floor maternity department. I was so excited about the baby and happy for my friends.

Once there, I hit the buzzer and asked the nurse on duty for Detective Rodriguez. It wasn't long before he came out and motioned for me to follow him. He put his finger to his lips, and we walked down the hall to Jolene's room.

Once we were there, Enrique turned to me. "Most of the nurses wouldn't say anything, but there's this one cranky old lady."

I laughed and walked over to the bed and smiled at Jolene. She looked tired, but happy. "How are you doing?"

Jolene reached out and took my hand. "I'm okay. And the doctor assures me that the baby is too."

"He has to be," I said, squeezing her hand.

"I heard you had quite a day after I left you," Enrique said, giving me his big grin.

I sighed. "Yeah, I'm beat. I'm going home and falling into bed." We talked a few more minutes while I filled Enrique in on what had happened after he left, then I headed to the door. "Let me know about baby boy."

Enrique followed me out of Jolene's room. "I will. It will probably be a few more hours." He opened the double doors for me. "I heard Connolly's in surgery. What happened?"

I filled him in as best as I could. "She couldn't tell me what happened."

"Another mystery," Enrique said. "I sure hope tomorrow isn't as crazy for you guys as today was."

"This was quite a day. Let me know if you hear anything." Enrique would probably know before I did if anything came up.

"Same." He gave me a quick salute, making me laugh, and went back to his wife.

I wasn't looking forward to the next three months with Enrique off on paternity leave. And with Connolly out of commission, we'd really be shorthanded.

I pulled the hood up on my coat and trudged through the snow to my Jeep. I knew I should check in with the accident scene, but I was bone-tired and took Mitch's word for it they would finish soon.

Then my heart sank. I'd forgotten to tell Mitch about Connolly. I climbed into my Jeep and started it. As I pulled out of the hospital parking lot, I hit Mitch's name on my screen.

He answered immediately. "Liz, go home. We're about to finish up here."

I felt my Jeep slide and gripped the wheel as I made it up the hill onto the heights. "I'm headed there, but I thought you should know about Connolly."

Mitch sighed. "How is she?"

"She's in surgery. This is weird, Mitch. The doctor thinks it's domestic abuse." What had Connolly gotten herself into? Was she in an abusive relationship? I couldn't imagine her putting up with someone beating her up. She was the type who would beat up anyone who tried to hurt her.

"Connolly doesn't even have a boyfriend, does she?"

I snorted. "Not that I know of. What man in his right mind would want to date her?"

"That's not fair, and you know it. You two are going to have to work things out. I can't have the department on edge all the time because you can't get along."

I saw red. I'd been nothing but nice to Connolly. Connolly was the one who picked fights all the time. I could recite about a million things she had done and said over the past five years to undermine me. But I didn't. Instead, in a cold voice, I said, "I don't know any more than that. They rushed her into surgery to stop the bleeding."

"Crap. Okay, I'll check on her before I head home. I can't imagine why she'd go to a crime scene when she'd been stabbed. Are you sure Lilly didn't do it?"

"That was my first thought, but Connolly came to enough to tell me it wasn't Lilly."

"I guess we'll have to wait until she wakes up." His tone was gentle. "Any news on Rodriquez's baby?"

I told him.

"That's good. Okay, you drive safe, and I'll talk to you tomorrow."

I started to hang up when he said, "And Liz, I'm sorry I said what I did about you and Connolly. I'm just exhausted, and I thought..."

"Yeah...I know what you thought." I pushed the button to disconnect. My face burned with anger.

I drove home, grinding my teeth the whole way. I wasn't sure why I let Mitch get to me. He'd lost all rights to my feelings. And Connolly, too. There was no reason for the way the woman treated me, and Mitch had never seen my side of it. He thought we had some kind of cat fight going on and ignored it. Argh! I wished I could walk away from it all.

Why can't you? A voice in my head said. What's keeping you here? I'd asked myself that a million times in the months since I found out about Mitch and Jenn. And I knew why I didn't want to leave. My job. I really loved my job and didn't want to walk away from it.

I drove home through the snow, thinking about Renetta and Connolly. Were the two incidents connected? I noticed when I pulled into my driveway that someone had plowed it. I knew it was my neighbor, Travis. I hadn't seen him since before Bella and I left for Europe, but it was exactly the kind of thing he would do.

The kitchen light was on, and I didn't remember leaving it on. Was Travis still there? I hoped not. I was having enough trouble figuring out my life without adding my sexy neighbor into the mix. He'd made it clear in the months following my split with Mitch that he was interested in more than just friendship.

But I wasn't sure how I felt. It was too soon. I was very, okay extremely, attracted to him. What woman wouldn't be? He was tall, dark and handsome with curly hair and the most amazing smile. But I felt conflicted. I'd thought I'd love Mitch for the rest of my life. I'd loved him for almost twenty-five years. How did you turn that off? He certainly didn't deserve my love after the way he and my ex-best friend had treated me. And to be honest, I didn't know if I still loved him or if it had become a habit. Not that I planned to forgive Mitch or Jenn, but I didn't know how to move on. That was the hard part.

I parked my Jeep in the garage and started into the house feeling so tired; I thought I could sleep for a week. I stepped up on the deck and the first thing I noticed was the kitchen door was ajar.

I looked around for Travis's pickup. It wasn't there. In my haste to leave that morning, had I forgotten to close the door? And where was Bailey? The yellow Labrador I'd inherited, along with my dad's home and orchard, should've come to greet me.

The hair on the back of my neck stood up. I pulled my handgun out and eased open the door. The first thing I noticed was the smell of something cooking. "Travis?" I called.

Bailey came bounding across the kitchen with Travis right behind her. I took a deep breath. "You scared me."

"I'm sorry. I let Bailey out the back and didn't hear you drive in. The snow must've muffled the sound of your Jeep."

My heart was still knocking against my chest. "How come the front door was open?"

Travis frowned. "It was? I didn't open it."

I turned back towards the door. I opened it and walked outside with Travis right behind me. I took the flashlight from my belt and shined it on the ground around the door. There were no footprints, but the snow had been falling so hard it would've covered up any.

I shined the light around the yard. Had someone been to my house? How did they get the door unlocked? Did Travis interrupt them?

"How long have you been here?" I turned off the flashlight and looked at him.

"I brought Bailey over about a half-hour ago. I thought you might want her here when you got home. I heard you were busy, so I brought some soup over for you."

I nodded. "Thank you, Travis. The soup smells wonderful."

I felt uneasy as we walked back into the house. Bailey pushed her way past us and grabbed her ball, trying to get Travis to throw it for her. He rubbed her head. He'd kept her for me while I was in Europe. Then he offered to keep her during the day while I worked. I honestly didn't know what I'd do without him.

I examined the doorknob to see if someone had tampered with it but didn't see anything obvious. We went in and I closed the door. "Was the alarm on when you got here?"

Travis shook his head. "I came in through the backdoor. I didn't think you had remembered to set the alarm."

I always set the alarm. Had I forgotten that morning? Had I also forgotten to close and lock the front door? I didn't think so. Had someone come into my house? Bella, Travis, and I were the only ones who knew the code. Unless Bella had given it to one of her friends? But why would they come to my house and leave the door open? It didn't make sense.

Travis went to the stove to stir the soup. "I have bread heating in the oven. Why don't you change, and we'll eat." He had a worried frown between his eyes, and I knew he was concerned, too.

I nodded. "Thanks, I will." I walked back to my room, looking around a second time as I went. I still didn't see that anything was missing, but I didn't like the idea of someone being in my house. I felt violated.

In my room, I changed into a long sweatshirt and leggings. I looked around my bedroom. My haven. I'd decorated it in soft grey, white, and pink. It was peaceful. I headed to the safe my dad had installed. Had the intruder wanted money? Had they broken in and stole the cash I kept in the safe?

A quick search showed that it was still closed and locked. I let myself out of the bedroom, knowing I'd have to search every inch of the house before I felt safe enough to sleep.

Chapter 16

C hapter 16

I went back into the kitchen, where Travis was setting the table for dinner. My phone rang just as I was about to sit down. I sighed, took it out of my pocket and saw that it was Mitch. "I'd better take this."

Travis nodded and turned the burner down under the soup.

"This is Liz," I said, sitting down at the table. I picked up the big yellow mug of coffee that Travis sat in front of me. He motioned he was taking Bailey out the back, and I nodded and smiled.

"Liz, I just wanted to call and see how you're doing."

I didn't want to talk to him, but I needed to know if there was something else going on. He sounded exhausted. I knew how he felt. It had been a long day. "I'm okay. Just tired."

"Yeah, we finally finished at the accident scene and I'm back at the office. I'm going home in a few minutes."

"Where do you want me to start tomorrow?" I kept my voice civil even though I wanted to scream at him. I knew I had to keep things as peaceful as possible for Bella's sake and if I wanted to keep my job.

"We'll have a briefing at nine. I'm thinking about pairing you up with Garcia until Rodriguez gets back. I think he's taking three months paternity leave. I thought I had another month to worry about finding someone to replace him."

"Have you heard any more about Connolly?" I took another drink of coffee. I felt bad that she was hurt, and I wanted to know who had knifed her, but part of me was happy I didn't have to work with her. Garcia and I get along fine.

"No, I called the doctor, and she said Megan should be able to answer questions tomorrow. Do you want to run by the hospital in the morning and see if she'll talk to you? I would, but I've got a meeting with the Chief at eight. Hopefully, it will be over by nine. We want to talk about this accident and how things were handled."

Connolly would talk to Mitch before she'd talk to me, but I said, "I'll give it a try. I can't see her opening up to me, though."

"Just try. If she won't, I'll go talk to her after the briefing. It would be nice to have somewhere to look for whoever did that to her."

"Yes." Connolly needed to come clean and tell us what was going on. Maybe Mitch could get her to talk.

"Okay, I'm going to get off here. Did you call Bella?"

"Not yet, but I will after I eat something." My stomach dipped, and I took a deep breath. I wasn't looking forward to telling our daughter about Renetta. I wasn't sure how she'd take it. Probably not well.

"Okay, tell her I'll call her later. I didn't even ask. Did someone plow you out?"

"Yes. Travis."

I could feel him bristle. Then he gave another tired sigh. "Okay, I'll see you in the morning."

"Okay. 'Night." I could tell there was more he wanted to say that I didn't want to hear. He didn't like it that Travis was now part of my life. He wanted to go back to the way things were before I found out about him and Jenn. But I just couldn't.

Travis and Bailey came back in, and Travis sat a bowl of beef soup in front of me. The smell made my stomach gurgle with hunger. Travis went back to the stove and filled a bowl for himself. "I noticed you didn't tell Mitch about your door being open."

"No, I didn't want him to come over tonight. I must've left it open this morning, but I never do. It's really weird."

Travis nodded. "I don't like it. I'm glad Bailey's here. Would you like me to stay overnight?" His voice was suggestive, and he looked deep into my eyes. Everything inside of me quivered at the promise in his look.

I decided him staying might not be a good idea in my vulnerable state, but I wasn't going to tell him that. "Thank you, but I'll be fine. I have a gun." I smiled at him.

Travis smiled back. "And you know how to use it."

After we ate, Travis took Bailey out one more time while I did the dishes. Then he leaned in and gave me a quick peck on the lips and took off for home.

I put a finger up to my lips. Travis had hugged me, kissed my cheek, but he'd never kissed me on the lips before. I'd felt a surge of electricity race through me at his touch. *Heavenly days. I was in trouble. It's a good thing I was too tired to do anything about the way I felt when he kissed me.*

After he left, I made sure all the doors were locked and the alarm on, then I sat down in the living room to call Bella. For once, Bella answered on the first ring.

"How are you, Mama? How was work?"

"It was a crazy day, baby girl. I have something I need to tell you." I gripped my phone, not wanting to say the words.

"Is it Daddy? Is he all right? Oh, please don't tell me that something happened to him. I couldn't stand it."

As much as I'd wanted to kill him in the past year, I knew Bella loved her dad and would be devastated if anything happened to him. "No honey, your dad is fine." I wasn't sure how to tell her about Renetta. Should I just put it out there or try and ease her into it? Finally, I decided Bella would want me to just tell her. "It's Renetta Larson."

"Renetta?" I could hear the frown in her voice and in my mind, I could see her beautiful blue eyes scrunching up in a worried look while she twirled her blonde hair, so like mine, in one hand. "What happened?"

"She was killed."

"Oh no! Oh, that's horrible. Was it a car wreck?"

Her voice cracked and I knew it was going to get worse once she knew everything. "No honey, she was murdered."

"Murdered? Why? What happened?" Bella's questions came in a rush. "Oh Mom, that's horrible." She sobbed.

"Did you know she was living in a homeless camp?"

"Yeah, she told me. I tried to get her to apply for financial help, but she's so proud." I could hear her crying and it broke my heart. "She called a couple of days ago and wanted you to call her. I forgot all about it. She said there was something going on and she really needed to tell someone."

"She wanted to talk to me? Do you know what about?" I hadn't talked to Renetta for ages, why did she want to talk to me unless it had something to do with what happened to her.

"No, I didn't talk to her. She called and left a message and then when I called her back, she didn't answer. You don't think she was already dead by then do you?" She burst into tears again.

I felt sick inside. "I don't know, honey. Do you have any idea what she needed to talk to me about?"

"No, she didn't say what it was. Oh, mom, I feel horrible. I should've kept trying to call her or had you go see if you could find her. Maybe she'd still be alive," Bella cried. "I'm coming home."

"What? No, Bella, you can't come home. For one thing, the freeway's closed. The weather has been horrible since you went back to school."

"I can't stay here. I won't be able to concentrate." Bella sobbed. "I just want to go home."

I felt sick. I knew Bella would take the news hard, but I didn't have any idea she'd want to leave school. "Let's see what the next couple of days bring. There isn't anything you can do, honey."

"I know, but I feel so bad. I should've been there for her. She tried so hard, Mom. She wanted to bring herself up out of the mess Lilly had them in. She worked hard and studied hard. It's just not fair!"

"No, it's not." I felt myself weakening, listening to Bella's sobs. Then I took a deep breath. The last thing I wanted Bella to do was to miss a bunch of school. "We'll find out who did it, honey. You know your dad and I will work on it until we find Ren's killer."

"I know...but I just can't believe anyone would hurt her. I should've tried harder to get in touch with her. If I hadn't met Ben..."

"Who's Ben?" Had she met someone since we got home from Europe? She'd only been back at school a couple of days.

"He's this really cool guy I met in my Econ class last fall. We've been talking and I think he's going to ask me out."

I smiled. Bella changed guys as fast as most girls changed their nail polish, but maybe this Ben would be different. "Is your roommate home?" Bella lived in an apartment with another girl. They'd become friends while spending their first year of college in the dorms together.

"Yes, she just came in."

Relief flooded my chest. "Good. I don't want you to be alone tonight."

"I'm not. And I can call Ben. Can you tell me how it happened?"

"Not right now." Bella had grown up with law enforcement parents. She knew there were times we couldn't say anything about a case we were on. I didn't want her to know that Renetta had been left out in an ice storm until I had to.

We talked for a few more minutes, then I told Bella that her dad would probably call her later. We said goodnight and I disconnected. I hated it that she was so far away, and I couldn't hug her. Bella was my everything, especially since my dad was killed and Mitch and I split. She was my reason to go on living.

It was getting late, I was tired, so I woke Bailey who'd fallen asleep at my feet, and we headed to bed.

I had claimed one of the extra bedrooms for mine. It was the one I'd used when I was a girl, but I'd painted it and put my furniture in it. I couldn't bring myself to sleep in my dad's room even though it was a lot bigger than the one I used. I hadn't taken anything except his clothes out of his room since he was murdered last spring. I knew I needed to, but I hadn't been able to face it yet. It was weird living there without my dad.

Bailey curled up on her bed in my room and went to sleep. I changed into pajamas and brushed my teeth and washed my face. Then I climbed into the soft bed and instantly went to sleep.

A few hours later a sound woke me up. My heart raced. Bailey stood at the end of my bed, looking towards the hall, growling low in her throat.

I eased up on my elbow and reached for my gun which I'd put on the end table next to the bed. My heart pounding, I picked up the gun and got out of bed as quietly as I could. I remembered setting the alarm. If someone had gotten into my house, they had to know the code.

I eased over to the door, pushing Bailey out of the way. "Go lay down," I whispered.

Bailey whimpered but did as she was told.

I pointed the gun towards the hallway. Then I crept towards the kitchen. It was still dark outside, and I didn't want to turn on a light. The yard light shown into the kitchen giving me enough illumination I could see that no one was in there. The alarm on the wall next to the door blinked red. It hadn't been tripped.

I stood still and listened. Who in their right mind would be out on a cold, snowy night like this? I didn't hear anything except Bailey whimpering from the bedroom.

Trying not to make any noise, I walked through the house. Everything was quiet. Once I'd walked through the downstairs, I headed to the upstairs with my gun held out in front of me. The upstairs had one big room and only took up half of the house. I flipped on the light and looked around. It was empty, too.

I went back downstairs. I knew I'd never sleep again that night. The clock on the oven read 4:30 in the morning. I decided to make coffee. The Keurig I'd bought last fall made a cup fast and I sat down at the table to sip it. I had a pad of paper and a pen sitting on the table and I pulled it over, thinking I'd make a list of things I wanted to do that day.

Suddenly, Bailey came barreling down the hall, barking and growling. She hit the kitchen door with her front paws, her bark ferocious.

I grabbed my gun and a flashlight off the counter. I fumbled with the alarm. Once it was off, I opened the door. Bailey took off like a shot. I shined the flashlight on the ground. There were footsteps on the snow that had piled up on my deck.

Chapter 17

Chapter 17—Mitch

Mitch sighed as he let himself into his office. Almost everyone scheduled to work that night was still at the wreck. They'd found everyone, thank goodness, and no one was dead. Several had cuts and bruises, but it could've been worse.

Mitch knew he was too wired to go home and go to bed. He should work on paperwork, but he needed to get his mind off it for a few minutes. It had been a taxing day. He sat at his desk and powered up his computer. He checked his emails.

His heartbeat quickened when he saw an email from PJ Severance, the investigator he'd hired two weeks earlier. "Finally," Mitch said to the empty room. He grinned, already anticipating telling Liz that he'd found her mother.

Mr. Ellisen, we think we've found Melanie Scott. She left Hood River in the nineties and changed her name to Lisa Margolin. I'm including all the information I found on her. You can get in touch with her at the phone number I've sent.

There was a number for Lisa Margolin at the bottom of the email along with a doc file. Mitch decided to read the file later. He wanted to talk to Liz's mother.

He called the number. It rang and rang, but no one answered. Finally, a tinny voice came on the line asking him to leave a message.

"Ms. Margolin, my name is Mitchel Ellisen. I live in Hood River, and I've been looking for you. I think you might be my wife's mother. Please call me at this number." He left his number and hung up. He grinned thinking how excited Liz and Bella would be when he told them he'd located Liz's mother.

Mitch clicked the doc file included in the email and the page filled. His heart sank when he read the information. Melanie Scott was arrested for selling drugs not long before she left Hood River. Then she was arrested again a couple of years later for the same thing. She over-dosed in 2004 and almost died. After that, she changed her name to Lisa Margolin and seemed to clean up her act for a few years. But the more Mitch read, the more he understood why Liz's dad had kept her away from their girls.

He sat back in his chair and ran his hands over his face. Maybe it would be best to let sleeping dogs lie. If he told Liz he'd found her mother, only to have Lisa Margolin bring more trouble to Liz's life, it wouldn't help his cause any. And did he really want a known druggie in Bella's life? He wished he'd read the file before calling Lisa Margolin. What was he thinking? If she called back, he'd just have to tell her he'd gotten the wrong number.

He shut down his computer thinking he'd go home and try to come up with another plan to get Liz to see how much he loved her. He'd been in hopes that this would work. That he'd find her mother and she'd have a reasonable explanation for why she left her family and never got in touch with them again.

A druggie. Crap. Mitch would have rather found out she'd died in a car wreck or was abducted or anything besides a known drug dealer.

He stood up and grabbed his coat from off the rack. He needed to go home and try and sleep. Just as he got to the door, his office phone rang. Mitch thought about ignoring it and going home. Whoever was after him would leave a message. But he knew as Sheriff, he needed to be responsible in case there was another wreck or someone in danger.

He picked up the phone and said, "Sheriff Ellisen."

A man's voice said, "Sheriff Ellisen, this is Erick Gates in Salem. I'm the sheriff for Marion County and I think we have a perp in common."

"Who?" Did Sheriff Gates have a serial killer in Salem?

"Lisa Margolin. I heard you've been looking for her. I need to know why and if you've found her."

Mitch threw his coat back on the rack and sat down at his desk. "I just got an email from a PI I hired to find her. She said Lisa is in Salem, that she's a drug dealer and has been in jail a few times. How did you know I was looking for her?"

"We're keeping a close eye on her. One of my officers found out that your PI was nosing around and let me know."

"What's going on with her? Why are you keeping an eye on her?" Mitch braced himself for more bad news.

"Before I answer that," Sheriff Gates said, "I need to know why you're looking for her."

Mitch didn't want to tell him that Lisa Margolin was his wife's mother. Instead, he said, "Her name came up here in Hood River. She may be related to someone close to me."

"You'd better hope not for their sake. Lisa Margolin will—and has—done anything for her next hit. We're looking into her for the murder of a local car dealer."

"Murder?" Mitch's insides froze. Time seemed to stand still. What had he done? "What makes you think she was involved in his murder?"

"She was with him the night he went missing. Then she disappeared."

Chapter 18

Chapter 18—Liz

I slammed and locked the door. Then I ran to my bedroom and threw on jeans and a sweatshirt. I jammed my feet into winter boots and went back to the door. I could hear Bailey barking a long way off.

I stepped out the door. "Bailey! Come here, girl."

The yard light gave enough illumination to see the pathway to the garage. There were footprints coming from the garage to the house, and it looked like they went back again. I put my iPhone camera on and took pictures of the footprints.

I called Bailey again and the dog came running back to me. I opened the door and Bailey shot in. She went to her water bowl and slurped up a bunch of water. Then she turned to me.

"What did you see, girl? Was there someone out there?" I knew there must've been, but who? Did Mitch have someone checking up on me, making sure Travis wasn't staying the night? Surely not. Mitch would come himself, not send someone. And Bailey wouldn't act that way around Mitch. So, who was out there? Had they been there earlier and left the kitchen door open?

"Who did Dad give the code to?" I asked Bailey, who looked up at me like she wanted to answer.

"I know he gave it to Travis, Mitch, Bella and I, but he must've given it to someone else." I made myself another mug of coffee. I knew I'd have to change the code on the alarm. I decided to do that before I went to work later that morning. Then I had a thought. Had Mitch given the code to Jenn? Had they used my dad's house for their rendezvous? But no, Jenn's husband was in Salem most of the time. They wouldn't need dad's house. Or would they?

I felt nauseous as I dug around in the drawer next to the counter where my dad had kept the instructions that came with his appliances. Sure enough, there was one for the alarm. I looked it over and realized it wouldn't be hard to change the code. I'd have to remember to give the new code to Travis and Bella. They were the only two I felt should have it besides me.

Later that morning, after Travis came to plow out the driveway, I headed to work. I hadn't said anything about my nocturnal visitor because I didn't want Travis to worry.

The snow had quit falling sometime in the night, and the roads into town were covered, but plowed. My first stop was the hospital. I dreaded seeing Connolly, but I knew someone had to find out what was going on with her. I parked my Jeep and went inside and up to the second floor.

The nurse on duty looked up and smiled when she saw me. "Good morning. Here to check on Deputy Connolly?"

"As a matter of fact, yes, I am." She must've seen my uniform and put two and two together.

"You're in luck. She came to in the night and she seems lucid. Come on back and I'll let her know she has company."

I followed the nurse, whose nametag read, Bridget Martin, RN, back to a room two doors down from the nurse's station. The smell of antiseptic tickled my nostrils. I glanced in rooms as we passed and saw people sitting up in bed watching television or sound asleep, snoring.

"Good morning, Deputy. I've brought you some company." The nurse's cheery voice rang out over the television in the corner that was on a news channel out of Portland talking about the snow storm.

Connolly looked up expectantly, until she saw who it was, then she turned her head away.

Nurse Martin seemed surprised, but her phone went off before she could say anything, and she took off down the hallway. I walked around the bed and looked down at Connolly. "How are you doing this morning?"

"I'm fine. What are you doing here?" Connolly squinted at me, and I realized she didn't have her glasses on.

"Mitch asked me to stop by and check on you. He had a meeting with the police chief this morning." I stood next to her bed, my hands on my hips and my feet spread. My radio squawked, and I reached up and turned it down. Connolly looked like she'd been through a war. Her face and hands bruised. I would've felt bad if she hadn't been such a pain in my butt for so long. Okay, I felt bad. I hate to see anyone beat up.

"Well, as you can see, I'm doing fine." She licked the split on her upper lip and looked up at the television. A reporter stood at the on-ramp to Interstate 84, with snow blowing around her like a blizzard.

I watched it long enough to see more snow in the forecast, then I turned back to Connolly, "What happened, Connolly? Who stabbed you?"

Connolly shook her head. "It was an accident." She lowered her voice. "As if you care."

"Of course, I care. We can't have people beating up our deputies." I stared at her.

"Just leave it, Detective. It's not your business and I'm not telling you anything."

Connolly had called me "Detective" with disgust in her voice since I'd been promoted. She told everyone that I only got the promotion because I was married to the boss. She should be delighted that Mitch and I were divorcing.

Now, she felt around for the bedside table, and I pushed it over near her. Connolly grabbed her glasses and shoved them onto her face. "Are Lilly and her son in jail?"

"No one wanted to press charges, so they're both out on the street." I'd talked to Deputy Garcia on the way into town and she'd told me Lilly had never left Hood River because Brad decided not to press charges.

Connolly nodded. "I'm not surprised."

My mic squawked, and I reached up to turn it down further. "Tell me who hurt you, Connolly. We need to stop them from doing it again." It must've been a guy she'd hooked up with.

Connolly shifted in the bed and grimaced. "It's none of your business, Detective. Now, leave." She pointed to the door. "I have nothing to say."

"Okay. I told Mitch you wouldn't talk to me, but he wanted me to try." I headed for the door. Then I turned back. "If you're in an abusive relationship, you need to tell Mitch. He can help." It must've been a guy. Why else would she be so secretive about it?

"Out!" Connolly screamed.

As I walked down the hall, Nurse Martin came running. "What's going on? Is she okay?"

"She's fine. If she can yell like that, she'll probably make a full recovery." I stopped for a minute to talk to her. I wanted to roll my eyes but didn't think that was professional.

Nurse Martin laughed, then covered her mouth with her hand. "I'm sorry, I shouldn't laugh, but you're right."

"She won't say who stabbed her. If she tells you, please call me." I took one of my cards out of my vest and handed it to her.

The nurse slipped the card into her pocket, nodded and walked back to Connolly's room.

I headed to the maternity section to check on Jolene. To my surprise when I arrived at the door, Enrique sat in a chair holding his newborn son. My heart melted as I squatted down next to them. "Oh, Enrique. He's gorgeous."

Enrique gave me his big smile. "Going to be a lady killer, just like his old man." He turned the baby around so I could see him better.

"Well, he resembles Jolene..." I couldn't help but tease him.

"Ha, ha. He's the spitting image of me and you know it." We stood and he held the baby out to me. "Would you like to hold your godson?"

Tears formed in my eyes. "I'm his godmother? Oh, Enrique, I can't believe you'd pick me."

"Why not? I know if he needed you, you'd be there or die trying. And Jolene loves you, so that's good enough for me."

I laughed and brushed tears away. Then I slipped off my coat and work vest and held my arms out for the baby.

The baby blinked up at me and yawned. He smelled of baby lotion and that new baby smell I loved. I reached out my finger and touched his soft cheek.

"You're boring him already." Enrique grinned.

Just then the bathroom door opened, and Jolene came out. Her long dark hair was pulled back into a low ponytail. She looked exhausted, but beautiful in that way new mothers did. "What do you think of your godson, Lizzy?"

"He's absolutely adorable. Good thing he looks like you." I grinned at Enrique who shook his head.

He went to his wife and helped her to the easy chair in the corner. I sat on the edge of the bed, the baby snuggled in my arms. He had lots of dark hair and big brown eyes. "What's his name?"

"Julio Jonathan Rodriquez." Enrique said.

"Nice strong names." I loved the feel of him in my arms. It made me remember how Bella had felt the first time I held her. So tiny and sweet.

"After my dad," Jolene said. "And Julio after Enrique's dad."

"Great names." I smiled at the baby. "I'm so glad everything went okay and he's here." I never once thought he wouldn't be okay, but with a preemie, you never knew.

"So, what's going on with the case?" Enrique asked.

"Not much. Call me when you get home and settled, and I'll fill you in." I didn't want to talk about death when I was holding new life in my arms. I didn't want to think about Renetta and how she'd been this tiny once. Had Lilly loved her and promised she'd always take care of her back then? Or had she been so self-absorbed she didn't care?

He nodded, and I spent the next few moments holding the baby and visiting his parents. Then I reluctantly gave him back and put my vest and coat on. "I'd better get into the office. Mitch called for a briefing at nine."

They invited me over to see the baby anytime, and I told them I'd be there.

After I left the hospital, I drove to work. I parked outside the sheriff's office and went inside. I could hear people talking around the coffee maker. I walked in and poured myself a cup.

Deputy Garcia stood next to the coffee machine. She smiled. "Nice to have you back, Detective."

"Thanks." I nodded and took a swig of coffee, hoping it would keep me awake the rest of the day.

When you first looked at Garcia, you might think she wasn't cut out to be a deputy. She was pretty, with dark hair and soft brown eyes. She wasn't tall. She looked chunky and you might think she was soft, but you'd be wrong. The woman was made of muscle. She lifted more than most guys on the force. I loved it when a perp misjudged her and the way their eyes grew large when she dropped them where they stood.

Now, she motioned to Deputy Walls who stood next to her. Walls was tall and slim, but she was strong, too. The two women worked out together every morning. I'd been planning on joining them. "We were just talking about the murder. I heard you and Rodriquez caught the case."

"Yes, but Enrique's wife just had the baby. So, he'll be off work for a few months." I really wished Jolene had timed it better. I needed Enrique on this case. But I knew babies tend to come in their timing, not mine.

"Who will be working with you? Connolly?" Walls asked.

"The sheriff called a meeting this morning. I'm sure he'll inform everyone of what their duties are." I smiled at the two women, then headed to my desk. I knew I had to be careful. Before Mitch and I split, I would've told the deputies what Mitch told me, unless he asked me not to. But I didn't feel I had that right anymore. And I didn't want to tell Garcia that she was my new partner in case Mitch changed his mind.

Enrique and I, as the two detectives for Hood River County, shared a small office. The deputies were in a large room with several desks and Mitch had an office in the back. Several deputies were working at their computers when I walked by.

The two desks in our office were clean for a change. Enrique had been keeping his clean, I'm sure he was thinking he'd be taking paternity leave, and I had left mine clean when I took time off. I hung my coat on a rack and sat at my desk and turned on my computer. I was working on my paperwork for the previous day when Garcia stuck her head in.

"Sheriff wants us all in the conference room in two." She held up two fingers.

I looked up. "Got it." I gathered everything I wanted to take with me. Garcia left and I finished my notes and headed to the conference room.

I nodded to several deputies when I walked in. Mitch stood with his arms crossed, talking to Ramon Walker, the undersheriff. Ramon had his arms dangling at his side. He looked like a wrestler with a big neck and big shoulders and arms. He was about 5'9" and had to look up to Mitch's 6'3". He was bald and wore a cap most of the time. I'd always thought he had mean eyes, but Mitch said that made him good at his job. He and Mitch were close. Ramon and I had never seen eye to eye. I wondered if he and Connolly were in cahoots to get rid of me.

It looked as though Mitch had pulled the whole crew in for the morning briefing. His eyes met mine briefly, then flickered away. Ramon didn't bother to look my way.

When our marriage had fractured, I'd immediately taken a six-month leave of absence. That left Mitch with the aftermath of what had happened. I knew that some in the department probably thought it was cowardly of me to leave him to face the music alone. But he made the mess. Why should I have to deal with it?

Now, I was back, and all eyes turned to look at me as I took a seat next to Garcia. I held my head high and looked each deputy in the eye.

Mitch cleared his voice. "We've got a lot to get through this morning. As I'm sure you all know, the body of Renetta Larson was found yesterday on Westcliff Drive. This is what we know so far. Renetta was living in a homeless camp on the opposite side of the freeway from where her body was found. She is the daughter of a famous, or should I say infamous, local woman, Lilly Larson."

Groans went up around the room. I couldn't blame them. There had been many run-ins with Lilly in the last few years and the officer or deputy who was unlucky enough to have to deal with her came away with some injury or another. Usually, it was a bite or a kick in the crotch.

Mitch held up his hand. "I know. But Renetta wasn't like her mother. She was a nice young girl who worked hard and studied hard and was trying to better herself. I need each of you to remember that as we work to solve this case." He looked down at the clipboard in his hands. "Liz, you and Garcia are lead on the case now that Rodriquez is out for paternity leave."

There was clapping and shouts of "Yay, the baby's here." I looked around the room and grinned at how excited everyone was for Enrique and Jolene. "Boy or girl?" someone shouted, and we spent a couple minutes talking about Julio Jonathan Rodriguez.

"Sheriff," Molly Walls held up her hand. She had scraped her blonde hair back into a bun. Everyone who had long hair wore it up when we worked. No need to give perps something to grab onto.

Mitch nodded for her to continue.

"Is it true that Deputy Connolly is in the hospital with a stab wound?"

"I was getting to that." He glanced at me. "Did you have time to see her this morning?"

"Yes, but just as I thought, she wouldn't tell me anything except it wasn't Lilly who stabbed her. Maybe she'll open up to you." I could see the resignation in his eyes and knew he didn't want to deal with Connolly's problems, but he was the boss, and it was his job.

Lots of questions floated around the room and Mitch cut them off by saying to me, "Can you tell everyone about your call to the warming shelter yesterday?"

I nodded and filled them all in on what had gone down at the shelter.

"We need some kind of protection from Lilly," one guy said with a smirk. "I don't want my ear bit off."

"No kidding," Mitch agreed. He gave out assignments and after he'd finished with the briefing, he let everyone except Garcia and me go. "Let's go in my office," he said.

"Want me in on this?" Ramon asked.

Mitch shook his head. "No, you know what's going on. Keep the ship running."

Ramon nodded. It was his job to make sure the office ran right. He oversaw the scheduling, hired receptionists and any other non-law enforcement personnel. Mitch was always telling him to keep the ship running because Mitch hated the day-to-day boring jobs. I thought he was lucky to have Ramon because Ramon always had his back.

We followed Mitch into his office, and Garcia closed the door. "Sit down." He motioned us to the two chairs in front of his desk. He sat in his chair and leaned forward, rubbing his eyes. "There are some things I need to tell you I didn't want to say in front of everyone." He looked down at the papers in front of him. "I had a meeting with Chief Pauley this morning. He was at the crime scene yesterday. The way Renetta was laid out with the snow built up around her like a berm or a frame," he said, and shook his head, "We're thinking this might be worse than we first thought."

"How can it be worse, boss?" Garcia asked. "It's pretty bad already."

"I know, but we're concerned Renetta's murder may have been the work of a serial killer."

Chapter 19

C hapter 19—Connolly

After looking at her phone for what seemed like the hundredth time, Megan Connolly laid it on the hospital bed next to her and stared out the window. Why hadn't he called? He had to know that she was worried. He should've called by now.

Outside the sky was a deep blue and the snow was so white. Megan loved winter. She loved skiing and snowshoeing. She loved the cold. Summer made her sweat, and she didn't like it that much. But winter, especially a winter like this one was turning out to be, was the best.

She moved and grimaced at the pain from the wound in her side. It had been deeper than she'd thought. After he'd left, she'd thought about going into the emergency room and getting it looked at, but the call came for a disturbance at the warming shelter, and she hoped she'd be okay long enough to find out what was going on there. She really didn't want the sheriff or anyone at the department to know she'd been stabbed.

If they didn't know by now, they would soon. She knew Detective Ellisen would enjoy spreading the word around the office. Why couldn't she keep her mouth shut? She was always in someone else's business. If Connolly had gone to see the doctor instead of taking the call to the shelter, the detective wouldn't have found out. She was pretty sure the sheriff would not have ratted her out if she'd asked him not to.

Little did she know that she'd get in a fight with Lilly at the shelter and chase her down the block. Crazy woman. Connolly shook her head. She knew Lilly was volatile, but she hadn't realized she was plain crazy too. To bite Brad's ear and try to bite the Detective. Not smart, Lil.

Her phone rang, and Connolly's heart thumped. She picked up thinking it had to be him, but it was one of the other deputies so she hit the off button. She didn't want to talk to anyone except him. Why didn't he call? She knew he hadn't meant to hurt her. They'd had a few skirmishes before that were kind of exciting. Connolly had to admit, only to herself, that she'd liked it when he'd pretended he was mad, and held her down on the bed, threatening to spank her.

She smiled at the memory. Looking back, she realized she'd been a little too eager for the spanking and it had turned him off. He wanted her to pretend to be frightened. He didn't realize how strong she was. If she wanted to, she knew she could stop him from hurting her. She should've taken the knife away from him the moment she saw it, but she'd known she could take it any time she wanted to. She'd gotten side-tracked by his actions and forgot for a minute that he had a knife in his hand. Her bad. She wouldn't do that again.

The door to her room opened and Connolly looked over, hoping it was him. But she was disappointed when the nurse stuck her head in and said, "Oh, good you're awake. You've got company," and the Sheriff strode in.

Sheriff Ellisen walked over to the bed and pulled a hardback chair closer. He sat down. "Hello Deputy."

"Sheriff." She let her gaze meet his then flitter away. She didn't want him to read anything in her expression.

"So, do you want to tell me what happened?" He leaned forward, his hand against the bedrail.

She shook her head. "It was stupid of me. The knife slipped." She hoped he'd buy her story. How could she tell him she'd been sliced by a knife when she knew better? She really felt dumb. It was bad enough to get hurt, but to have the people she worked with know something was going on, was worse.

Mitch gave her a look of disbelief. "Who was holding the knife?"

She thought for a few seconds. "I was."

"Connolly, tell me the truth. Who did this to you?"

"It's true. I was using it to open a can of soup because my can opener stopped working, and the stupid thing slipped and went into my side." She'd been working on her story since the Detective left earlier.

"Uh-huh. You sticking to that story?" The sheriff leaned back in his chair.

She could hear the unbelief in his voice and grimaced. How could she tell him the truth? She knew it had been an accident, but the sheriff might not believe it. "I'm fine. The doctor said it was a clean cut and will heal okay."

He raised his eyes and looked at her but didn't say anything.

"I probably should've gone to emergency instead of trying to help the Detective, but I thought I'd be fine until I could get here. I had a bandage on the wound."

"Yes, and it bled through. You know better than to let a stab wound go unattended." He gave her a stern look.

She nodded. "I'm sorry." Don't cry, she told herself. You can't let him see how weak you are.

"How long are they keeping you?"

"I should be out tomorrow. I can be back at work in a few days." She hoped.

Mitch stood. He shook his head. "I need you to stay home until that wound heals. You don't want to open it up again."

She watched as he put the chair back where he'd got it. "Yes, sir."

"And Connolly..." He turned, and she looked up at him, seeing the worry in his eyes.

"Yes?"

"If you're in some kind of abusive situation, you need to get out. There are resources...and I'll help all I can."She cut him off. "I'm not being abused, Sir. I promise."

He nodded, but she could tell he wasn't convinced.

After he said goodbye and went out the door, Connolly wiped tears from her eyes. It wasn't like her to cry. She hadn't cried since...she couldn't remember, but it had been a long time. She looked at her phone. Still nothing. She leaned back against the pillow and felt more tears form in her eyes. She hit the pump beside her for more pain meds.

Awhile later, Connolly woke up to the vibration of her phone against her side. Her heart quickened. Maybe this time...but she picked it up, and it was Deputy Williams. She took the call.

After she said hello, Deputy Williams' voice came through. "Hey, how are you doing?"

Williams was the only one in the sheriff's office that Connolly felt like she could call her friend, besides the sheriff. She smiled when she heard his voice. "I'm doing okay."

"Sheriff told us you'd been stabbed. What's going on, Megan?"

No one at work ever called her Megan. She blinked. "I cut myself with a knife. It was deeper than I first thought." There was no way she'd ever tell someone from work the truth. Things had a way of spreading around the office like a bad flu, and she didn't want them talking about her.

"Rumors are flying high around here. Some think Lilly Larson knifed you and you don't want to tell on her because she's your supplier."

"Jeez," Connolly said. "You'd think they'd have better things to think about right now."

"Oh, they do. Sheriff's asking some people to work double shifts since you and Rodriquez are both out."

"Sorry." She wasn't really. When she was there she worked harder than three people.

"Not a problem for me. He hasn't asked me yet and I've learned how to duck."

Connolly laughed. Williams wasn't the greatest deputy. He never went the extra mile. He tried his best to stay off the sheriff's radar, and he hung around the lunchroom when he should have been working. The only thing he was really good for was information. If you wanted to know something, Todd was your man. And he liked Detective Ellisen only marginally better than Connolly did.

"Have you heard anything more about the investigation?"

"Lilly was found with a piece of Brad Thomas's ear stuck in her teeth."

Despite herself, Connolly laughed at his poor joke. It made her side ache, and she put her hand on it and pressed down. "All kidding aside."

She heard him sigh. "Not much. Sheriff pulled Liz and Anna Garcia into his office after the briefing. I'm working on finding out what he said to them. He appointed Garcia to partner with your hero, Liz, until you get back to work. Lucky girl."

Connolly rolled her eyes. "If you hear anything, will you let me know? I hate being side-lined for days. Maybe I can do some computer work if you give me names of suspects."

"Right now, the only suspects we have are Brad Thomas and Lilly. I wouldn't put it past her to kill her own daughter if she thought there was money or drugs in it for her."

"Lilly's a piece of work. What about that friend of hers?" Connolly watched a blackbird land on the windowsill, its inky color a stark contrast to the whiteness of the snow.

"Which one?"

Connolly turned her gaze to the snow-laden parking lot, but she wasn't seeing it. "She's been hanging around this crazy woman who hit town a couple months ago. I think the woman has a daughter with her. They live in the homeless camp near Lilly and Renetta."

"Do you want me to give that information to the Detective?"

"No, they'll figure it out."

"That's on you. I don't want involved. Sheriff will rip you a new one for not saying anything sooner."

"I'll tell him I just remembered." She wasn't worried about the sheriff. If she found out something important, he'd be fine.

Williams chuckled. "You're braver than I am."

Chapter 20

Chapter 20—Liz

I stared at Mitch. Garcia drew in a sharp breath. "A serial killer? What makes you think that?"

Mitch leaned back in his chair and crossed his arms over his chest. "The berm the killer built around her body."

We both nodded. It had seemed strange. Was it the work of a serial killer?

Mitch tucked his hands into his vest pockets. "Why would someone frame her body unless they wanted to showcase their work?"

"A serial killer in Hood River?" Garcia choked on the words.

"They can be anywhere," Mitch said. He had a frown between his eyes, and I noticed his face was grey. This was eating at him. I knew he was good at his job. If Mitch thought there might be a serial killer in our valley, we needed to take all precautions.

I was having trouble getting my head around a serial killer in our small town too. Hood River had always had a low crime rate. I looked at Mitch and he stared back. His face was creased with worry.

"I don't want this getting out yet. If it does, people will go apeshit," he said, rubbing the back of his neck.

"How are we going to keep it quiet?" I asked. I knew how the grapevine worked. It would be all over Hood River in a matter of hours.

Mitch quirked an eyebrow. "We'll try to keep it contained. If we have to tell the rest of the team, we will. But before we do that, let's try to find the SOB and put him away."

"How do we find him?" Garcia asked. I knew this was something she'd never dealt with before. This was something Mitch and I had never dealt with either.

"You're good with online information," Mitch said to Garcia. "I want you to look for any serial killers in Oregon or Washington in the last ten years. These guys can go on a killing spree, then stop for years before they start up again. If you find any known serial killers or anyone at all who fits the profile, report back to me." He looked at his notes, then turned back towards her. "And I want you to stay on that until you find something."

Garcia nodded.

He looked at me. "Keep looking at Renetta's friends and acquaintances. Find out who Lilly hangs out with. Just in case I'm wrong, we can't let anyone slip past our notice."

I nodded. I wished Enrique was working. I missed bouncing ideas off him.

"Go back to the warming shelter and see if anyone there knows anything. There are people who stay there who don't live at the camp. Some of them have their own camping spots around the valley. I'm sorry, but you're going to have to talk to all of them. And Liz, take one of the other deputies with you if Garcia is busy."

I thought fast. Garcia and Rodriquez were the best deputies. "Any suggestions?"

Mitch took off his cap and rubbed the back of his head. "Well, Connolly's out for a while. Williams isn't doing much right now. Take him with you."

Garcia and I both groaned. Mitch raised an eyebrow. "How about Cooper West? I know he's new, but he's a good kid. He's trying to learn the ropes. Have you met him yet?"

"No, he must've come on board while I was on leave." A new kid? Just who I wanted to work a serial murder case with.

"I'll introduce you."

Just my luck, I thought. We get a murder case, and my choices of backup are Williams, who does everything in his power to duck out of work, and a rookie. I glanced at Garcia, and she mouthed, "West."

"Okay. Anything else?" I asked Mitch.

"Just be careful out there. We don't know for sure this guy is a serial killer, but we don't know that he isn't. If you find anything suspicious, report back to me."

We both nodded and stood. Garcia headed for the door, but I hesitated. "I talked to Bella. She's insisting on coming home."

"Absolutely not," Mitch said. He sat back in his chair, and I heard the familiar squeak it always made.

"You'll talk to her?" I hoped our daughter would listen to her dad. I didn't want her in Hood River if we had a serial killer on our hands.

"Yes, I'll talk to her. I don't want her near Hood River until we've found this guy."

When I walked into the common area, Mitch was behind me. "West. You'll team with Detective Ellisen today." He nodded at me.

Cooper West was young. Really young. I would guess him at early twenties. He must've just finished the academy. He had red hair and freckles. His fair skin was bright red when he nodded at me.

I turned to Garcia. She grinned. "I'll hurry with my computer search."

"Thank you," I said, softly. Then I turned to the new kid. "We haven't met, but I'm Detective Ellisen."

He nodded, his face growing more red. I glanced at Mitch. He smiled and went back to his office. Jerk. How was I supposed to find a serial killer with a baby as backup?

"Let's go, West. I'll drive."

"Yes, ma'am."

It was going to be a long day.

West loped behind me out to the SUV like a new puppy. He was all legs and arms. I wondered how long it would be before I could dump him back at the office with a mound of paperwork.

As we drew near to the SUV, I climbed in the driver's side and started the car. West looked lost for a second until I waved him inside.

Once we were both seated with our belts on, I turned to him. "Listen, we all have to start somewhere, and you're getting thrown into this with no lead in. I'm sorry, but with Rodriquez and Connolly both out, we need you to step up."

"Yes, ma'am." He nodded.

"And quit calling me ma'am." He made me feel like I was one hundred years old.

"Yes, ma'am, I mean sir..."

I sighed. "Liz will do. Most of us go by our last names, but since the sheriff and I have the same last name, everyone calls me Liz."

"Okay, Liz." He didn't look happy about using my name, but hopefully by the end of the shift he'd be used to it. Or not.

"I need to go back and talk to Renetta's mother. Last time I saw her she was at the warming shelter, but she may have gone back to the bridge. There were several people down there yesterday."

He nodded and mumbled something.

I shook my head. "You keep your eyes open all the time. I know they told you that in the academy, but it's really important. Crap. I wish you'd had some time on the force before you got thrown into a murder case."

"I've been a deputy for three months."

"That long?" I could barely remember my rookie days. I know I made a lot of mistakes, but I was eager to learn, and I saw that in West too.

I drove back down Oak Street to the shelter, hoping Lilly was there and I wouldn't have to chase her all over town.

When we pulled in the place looked deserted. West said the obvious. "Doesn't look like anyone's here."

I rolled my eyes. "Let's see if anyone's in the office."

We got out of the car and walked over to the office door. The manager, Joe Hinds, motioned us inside.

"Hey Detective, welcome back." Joe was a retired schoolteacher with a big heart. He'd taught me in middle school. I'd always enjoyed talking with him.

"Hey, Joe. Thanks." I walked in and held the door for West. "This is Deputy Cooper West."

Joe nodded at West who stuck his hand out. After they shook, Joe said, "Hear you had some excitement last night." He grinned and shook his head. "I don't know how Lilly gets away with some of the crap she pulls."

"Lilly's the reason we're here. Have you seen her today?" I looked out the window at the deserted parking lot. Usually, if there were people staying there, they were outside smoking and talking.

Joe shook his head. "No, she might be at the Senior Center having breakfast. That's where most folks are right now."

So, that explained why it was so quiet. "But probably not Lilly?"

He shrugged. "More likely not, but you can check. She doesn't usually go for breakfast."

I thanked him, and we left. I glanced at West. "Lilly won't go for breakfast. She doesn't eat enough to keep a bird alive. Let's go back to the bridge. Maybe she's down there." I saw the disappointment cross his face. If he was anything like the boys Bella brought home, he was probably starved. "We can stop by McDonald's for a breakfast sandwich if you're hungry," I said.

He shook his head. "I'll be fine."

We climbed back into the SUV, and I headed towards the bridge. I was eager to talk to Lilly, if she'd talk to me.

The freeway was still closed in both directions, but the snow had stopped coming down, so hopefully they'd get it plowed and traffic moving again. As we turned towards the bridge, we saw several large semi-trucks sitting on the side of the road, waiting for the freeway to open.

It looked like the same people who were there the day before were still huddling around a fire under the bridge. I parked and we went out to talk to them.

"Lil ain't here," one woman called as we walked up. "She didn't show up this morning. I'm a little worried about her."

"Did you stay at the warming shelter last night?" I asked, hoping they all did.

The woman, who wore the same huge purple coat and pajama pants as the day before, nodded. "Yeah, we was there. But Lil didn't show up." She shook her head and her hood fell back revealing greasy blonde hair. "Not like her. She's usually around." She squinted up at me. "You throw her in jail?"

"No, I'm sure you heard what she did to Brad?" I knew news traveled fast among the homeless population and assumed they already knew.

There was a chorus of yesses. "He didn't press charges, so they let her go." I looked around the group. "Anyone know where she might've gone?"

Most people shook their heads. Some didn't acknowledge my question. "If you see her, please ask her to get in touch with me," I told the woman in the purple coat. I had little hope that she'd pass on the message.

She laughed. "Sure. I'll tell her to go up to the sheriff's office. I know she'll run right up there."

I knew I was fighting a losing battle. I smiled. "I'm worried about her. Her daughter was murdered. What if the killer is after Lilly too?"

That stopped the laughter. The woman looked scared.

When we couldn't get anything more out of them, West and I turned to go. We'd almost made it back to our rig when a young woman came hurrying over to us. "You've got to help Lilly. Please, you've got to find her."

"We'll do our best. If there's anything you know that will help us find her, please tell me."

The girl shook her head. "I'm so scared for her. She was shooting off her mouth, telling everyone that she'd come into a lot of money, and then Ren was killed. What if they kill Lilly too?"

"Who did she tell about the money?"

The girl raised her hands and shrugged. "Everyone."

"Do you know how much money she had?" West asked.

I gave him a surprised look. The girl shook her head again. "No but knowing Lil she probably spent most of what she had on drugs and booze."

West handed her his card. "If you hear anything, please let us know. And if we can help you in any way..."

She smiled and it transformed her face, causing West's face to turn red again. "I will. Thank you."

She waved and walked back to the group under the bridge.

"Where are we going next?" West asked.

"It sounds like we need to find Lilly."

Chapter 21

C hapter 21

West agreed, and we drove from the bridge to the homeless camp by the freeway, and then to the Senior Center. No one had seen or heard from Lilly. Where was she? Was she okay? I knew she might be shacked up with some guy and I hoped she'd turn up soon.

Mitch called as we were leaving the Senior Center. "Anything?" he asked.

"No, except Lilly's gone missing."

"She could be anywhere."

I looked at West and rolled my eyes. He grinned. "I know, but I'm worried about her. Apparently, she's been shooting her mouth off, telling everyone that she's got lots of money."

"Does anyone know how much?" Mitch sounded skeptical, and I didn't blame him. Lilly was always making herself out to be better than anyone else. She probably made up the story about coming into money.

"Not anyone we've talked to so far."

"Okay, well, you can head back to the office. I'd like a meeting before you guys go home for the day. I think Garcia has come up with something important. She's waving me into your office."

I glanced at my watch. It was almost four, and we were off at five. Where did the day go? I wondered. "Hungry?" I asked West, feeling bad we hadn't stopped for lunch earlier.

"A little."

"Want to stop at one of the food trucks and get something to take back to the office?"

"Sure."

There were three or four food trucks on Tucker Road. One had Mexican food, one with pizza and one with Chinese food. Out further, there was one with veggie bowls.

I pulled into the parking lot and we both got out, hoping someone was around. The only truck open was the pizza truck. We ordered their largest pepperoni pizza so we could share it. I didn't realize how hungry I was until I got back in the SUV with the pizza and the smell of warm cheese and pepperoni made me want to dive right in. It was the thought of driving in the snow and trying to eat pizza that kept me from it.

Back at the office, West carried the pizza into my tiny space where Garcia was grinning at us from behind my computer. "You guys are great! I was starving."

Mitch came in and helped himself to a piece. "Mmm, this is good." He looked around at the rest of us. "Tell them what you found," he told Garcia between bites.

Anna Garcia wiped her mouth with a napkin. "I found Lilly's family. And she's right, they are big money. BIG!"

"Who are they?" I felt my eyes widen in shock. Lilly came from money? Who would've ever thought that? I grabbed a piece of pizza and ate half of it in one bite.

Garcia smiled and took another bite of pizza. As soon as she swallowed, she said, "Ever hear of the Abbott family?"

"Sounds familiar," I said, trying to remember what I knew about them.

"They have furniture stores all over the Northwest."

"And Lilly is related to them?" Talk about being amazed. I assumed her family was dirt poor like she was.

Garcia nodded. "It looks like Lilly is the sole remaining heir to the fortune."

West choked, and I sat up abruptly in my chair. "Say that again."

"Lilly Larson aka Lillian Abbott is the only child of furniture mogul, Kenneth Abbott. The family lawyer, one Gilbert Caruthers, has been trying to track Lilly down since her father died last fall."

I finished my second piece and threw my napkin in the trash. "How did you find that out?"

Garcia shrugged. "I started searching for missing heiresses in California. When that didn't work, I broadened it to include the Pacific Northwest and bingo, up popped the Abbott family who was missing an heiress. At first, I didn't think it was our Lilly, but look at this." She scooted the computer towards me and there on the screen was a picture of a younger Lilly. This woman looked more like the one I'd known when the girls were young. She was gorgeous, with long black hair, big blue eyes and a figure that would make most women green with envy.

"Wow," I said, staring at the picture.

"Wow," West repeated. A deep red flush covered his face.

Mitch grinned. "Hard to believe that's our Lilly, huh?"

"But why would she end up being homeless in Hood River? She could've bought most of the hotels in the valley. Could Lilly have a double?" That made more sense to me. Why would Lilly leave the comfort of a wealthy family to be homeless?

"We'll find out. I've got a call in to the attorney. Maybe he can shed some light on it. It's kind of a coincidence if Lilly has a doppelganger that has the same name."

I chewed on my thumbnail, trying to come up with scenarios where Lilly would be an heiress. "If it is her, she must've had a falling out with her family and moved here before Renetta was born."

I looked at Mitch. "So maybe instead of a local killer, there's someone in Lilly's past that doesn't want her to inherit her family money."

"It's possible," Mitch said.

"This just gets stranger and stranger." I glanced at West. "Go home, West. You look beat. We'll go back out tomorrow."

West grabbed the last slice of pizza and headed for the door. "Goodnight."

We all mumbled goodnight back at him. Then Mitch motioned me to his office. "I need to talk to you a minute, Liz."

Garcia ducked her head. Some friend, I thought as I headed to Mitch's office.

He followed me in and closed the door. This was the first time we'd been alone since I'd gotten back from my trip. I didn't know what he wanted to talk about. My heart sank. I was tired and hoped he wasn't going to get into something personal.

He motioned to the chair on the other side of his desk. I sat down with a sigh.

"I talked to Bella." He sat in his office chair and leaned back.

"What did she say?" Relief flowed through me. I was happy he wanted to talk about Bella, not anything between us.

"She said she wants to come home, but she understands why we don't want her to. She's pretty broken up about Renetta."

I nodded. "Did she tell you that Renetta called her wanting to get in touch with me?"

"Yeah. I wish we knew why." Mitch ran a hand over his head and down his neck. "But there's something else. I'm worried about Connolly. Her story about stabbing herself doesn't add up."

"I don't think so either. What do you think's going on?" Connolly was the least of my worries, but he was right, something was going on with the deputy.

He shrugged. "Have you heard any rumors around the department?"

"No one has said anything, but I've been busy since I got back. Do you want me to talk to Williams? They seem to be pals."

"Connolly and Williams?" Mitch looked shocked, and I wondered how he missed that.

"Yeah, I've seen them whispering together in the break room. You hadn't noticed?"

"No, but I don't pay attention to that kind of thing."

I knew that was true. Mitch did his best to keep himself above the conflicts or friendships in the department. "Well, they were hanging out before I left for Europe. They'd go to lunch together, and she spent a lot of time sitting by his desk when he was pretending to be working on something."

Mitch shook his head. "Do you think it's more than friendship?"

"No, but how would I know? Did you talk to Garcia? She might have some idea what's going on." The thought of the lazy Deputy Williams having enough energy to hurt Connolly was funny, but I didn't laugh. It would be horrible for the morale of the office if we had an abusive deputy.

He sat forward in his chair, and I heard it squeak again when he moved. "I haven't yet. I wanted to talk to you about it first."

I realized that Mitch was missing our working relationship. We'd always bounced things back and forth. I wondered who he talked to now. Maybe Ramon? I knew they were close, but Ramon kept his head more in the business side of things. I sighed. It wasn't any of my business, but I still wondered.

There was a tap on the door and Garcia stuck her head in. "I'm sorry to interrupt, but Connolly has disappeared."

Chapter 22

C hapter 22

"What do you mean she disappeared?" Mitch asked, his eyes boring into Garcia's.

Garcia shrugged. "The hospital just called. When the nurse went in to check her vitals, she was gone. They've searched the hospital, but she's not there."

"Did you call her phone?" Mitch closed his eyes for a second.

"Yup, no answer. Want me to drive over to her house?"

Mitch rubbed the back of his neck. "I'll go." He looked at me, acted like he wanted to say something, then shook his head and grabbed his jacket.

After he left, I asked Garcia if she knew what was going on with Connolly.

"No, but Williams might. They're thick as thieves lately." She stepped to the door, and I heard her ask someone if Williams was around.

"No, he left twenty minutes ago."

"Of course, he did," I said. I stood up and made my way to my office with Garcia right behind me. "Why don't you call him? See if he knows anything."

She nodded and took her phone out. I grabbed my coat and backpack out of my office. I was beat and thought I'd head home. If Travis hadn't plowed my driveway, I'd have to. I wasn't looking forward to that. One more thing that Mitch always took care of that I had to worry about now.

Garcia met me in the front office. "Williams said he doesn't know where she is. He talked to her earlier, but she didn't say anything about leaving the hospital."

"She's probably with a friend and has her phone off." I pulled on my coat. "Although I can't imagine Connolly having friends."

Garcia snorted.

I grinned. "I'm heading home. Let me know if you hear anything about Connolly or Lilly."

She shrugged into her jacket. "You'll probably hear before I will."

I wasn't so sure of that.

The main roads to the small town of Odell where I lived were plowed, but Davis Drive wasn't, and it took me a while to get home. I breathed a sigh of relief when I saw Travis had beat me to plowing the drive.

Bailey was waiting for me when I walked in the house. "Hey girl, how are you? Do you need to go outside?" I held the door open, and she ran out into the snow.

I wondered how long she'd been in the house. Travis must've finished plowing and let her inside. I sat on a kitchen chair and took my boots off. When I got up to make coffee, I noticed a note on the coffee pot.

I hope you had a good day. I put Bailey in the house about 4 p.m. Call me if you want to talk.

Travis

I smiled as I poured a cup of coffee. Travis and I had a crazy relationship. I knew he wanted more than friendship; I just didn't know what I wanted. Until I could get my head together, I knew it was better to keep a distance between us.

Mitch called as I was heating soup for dinner. I put the bowl in the microwave, hit the buttons and grabbed my phone from off the counter where I'd laid it when I walked in the door.

"Hey, did you find her?" I had visions of Connolly sitting in her easy chair, drinking hot chocolate, and not caring that people were worried about her.

"No. She's not home. I talked to her neighbor, and he said he hasn't seen her. I'm getting a little tired of people disappearing in this town."

"First Lilly and now Connolly. That is weird." I wasn't worried about Connolly. I knew she could take care of herself.

"I wouldn't be so worried if I wasn't afraid there's a serial killer running around town."

"And if it wasn't so cold out. Connolly, I'm sure, is with someone. A friend or boyfriend." I shook my head even though he couldn't see me. "She has resources. I'm sure she'll turn up tomorrow."

"Sounds like Lilly has resources too."

"Yeah, it's hard to believe she comes from so much money. I've known her forever. She never acted like she had money when the girls were young. I think she was happy with Renetta's dad. But she fell apart when he died."

"And why didn't she go back to her family? They had enough money to care for her and Renetta."

"There must've been a big falling out. Maybe we should be looking into the Abbott family? Maybe they had Renetta killed because she stands to inherit so much money?"

My microwave dinged, and I opened the door and took the bowl out. The soup smelled heavenly, and I mentally thanked Travis for making it for me.

"And now they have Lilly? I guess it's possible."

"Somewhere to look anyway." I put a piece of bread in the toaster and carried my bowl to the table.

"Okay, we'll hit it again tomorrow. Get some rest."

"I will."

I was about to push the off button when I heard him say, "I miss you, Liz. I wish you'd come home."

My heart sank. I could hear the regret in his voice. What could I say? I'd told him I needed time. This was not what I wanted, but how could I ever trust him again? "I can't," I whispered, and touched the off button on the phone.

My appetite had vanished. I heard the toaster pop and ignored it. Instead, I sat down and stared at my soup, thinking about Mitch and what I was going to do about my job and working with him. "It might not work out," I said into the empty room. "I may have to find another job."

I knew that in a way, Mitch and I wanted the same thing. We both wanted our lives to go back to the way they were before the affair. But I couldn't get past the hurt.

I forced myself to put those thoughts away and concentrate on Renetta's murder. Did Lilly's family have Renetta killed? That made more sense to me than that there was a serial killer in town. I forced myself to take a bite of the soup. It was so good; I gobbled it down.

I'd just gotten up to put my bowl in the dishwasher and throw away the now cold toast when I heard Bailey barking outside. I went to the door and flipped on the outside light. She was standing with her nose against the garage, barking her head off. I whistled, and she came to me.

"What's going on, girl?" I bent down and patted her head. She was wet with snow, and I felt the cold as she pushed against me. I led her into the house and flipped off the yard light. Was someone in my garage? I turned off the kitchen light so I could see outside. Did I see a gleam of light moving around the garage? What were they after? Were they trying to steal my Jeep?

Anger burned bright within me. How dare someone try to steal from me. I stuck my feet into my boots and grabbed my gun and flashlight. Then I told Bailey to wait while I went out to check out the garage. I crept to the door and put my ear against it. Did I hear someone moving around inside? I wasn't about to let them take anything, especially my jeep.

I threw open the door and yelled, "Sheriff's Department! Put your hands up."

Nothing moved.

I yelled again. Still nothing. I glanced at my car. The interior light was on as if someone had just touched the door handle. It faded off. I put my flashlight and gun in front of me and walked into the garage. I reached over to the wall and flipped on the overhead light.

My heart pounded. The garage is a large room. It's big enough to house two cars plus store a lot of stuff. My dad's pickup still sat where he'd left it when he died almost a year ago. I hadn't had the heart to sell it. I walked around my Jeep, shining my flashlight inside. Then I did the same with Dad's pickup. Nothing. I looked around. There wasn't anywhere to hide. Where had the intruder gone?

Then I noticed an open window at the back of the garage. I whirled around to the door and hurried through it to the back of the building. There weren't any footprints in the snow until I reached the window. Footsteps led away from the garage.

I ran through the orchard, my gun out in front of me. Whoever had been in my garage was fast. I couldn't see anyone through the snow that was falling in my eyes. I kept running. I'd gone past my ranch foreman's home when the yard light came on and blinded me for a few seconds.

José came outside. "What's going on?" he yelled from his front porch.

"Intruder," I yelled as I started running again.

The intruder was heading for the road. I followed, trying to run in the snow-packed driveway. I could hear José behind me. Just as I crested a rise in the driveway, I saw car lights pop on and a car fishtail it down to the road. I ran faster, trying to see what make of car it was, but my boot got stuck in the snow and my foot came out of it.

I stopped and put my hands on my knees trying to catch my breath. As soon as I could move, I grabbed my boot, stuck my foot back in and kicked the snow. "Dang it! I'm so sick and tired of this snow."

José ran up next to me. "Did you get a look at them, Leez?"

"No, I couldn't get close enough." I stood up and shook my head. "I couldn't run fast enough in the snow. Have you noticed anyone hanging around the farm lately?"

"No, the guys in the cabins come and go, but I haven't seen anyone I didn't know." He was panting.

"Let's go back." I started walking down the drive. "Bailey barked, and I went to see what was going on and someone was in the garage."

José looked worried. "You think they were trying to steal your car?"

"Maybe. Or looking for something they could sell." A shiver ran over me. That didn't explain the other times I'd noticed someone hanging around my house.

He nodded. "I'll keep a closer eye on things."

I thanked him. We'd made it back to his house, and I said goodnight and headed back to mine. Who had been in my garage? What did they want and was it the same person who'd tried to get in my house the day before?

Chapter 23

Chapter 23—Mitch

Mitch felt beat up as he pulled into his driveway. It had been one of the longest days of his career as a sheriff. His eyes stung, his shoulders and arms ached, and depression clung to him like the smell of a skunk.

He climbed out of his vehicle and walked towards the house. How he missed coming home to Bella singing at the top of her lungs, or Liz fixing dinner. He missed his girls. Even though he hadn't lost his daughter, things were different since Liz left.

He let himself into the house. It was cold and silent. He wished he'd read the full report on Liz's mother, Lisa Margolin, before calling her. What if she demanded to meet Liz? How was he going to tell Liz that he'd found her mother, and she was wanted for murder? Maybe Lisa wouldn't call. Probably she wouldn't. Most people who were wanted by the police would do just about anything to stay out of the law's way.

His phone rang, and he glanced down, hoping it was Liz. It was Connolly, and he clicked on the button to answer. He'd been trying to get hold of her all day. "Hey Connolly, are you okay?"

"Yes, I'm fine. Sorry to worry everyone. I needed to get out of that hospital. They were driving me crazy, waking me up every twenty minutes, poking me with needles, and asking the same stupid questions over and over."

Mitch could imagine the questions. "Well, you need to tell me what's going on, Megan. I don't buy it that you stabbed yourself." Mitch wandered over to the refrigerator and opened the door, hoping a good fairy had left supper for him.

"I know it sounds crazy, Sheriff, but that's what happened. I wasn't paying attention to how I was holding the knife and it slipped."

Mitch sighed. He'd have to give her the benefit of the doubt, but he still didn't buy it. "So, how are you feeling? Where are you? I've been by your house several times and you aren't there."

"I'm staying with a friend. And I'm feeling much better. What's going on with the investigation?"

Mitch closed the refrigerator and opened the freezer compartment. He wished he'd picked up something to eat on his way home, but he wasn't going back out now unless he had to. He grabbed a frozen pizza. He'd only had two pieces at the office. He could handle a couple more.

"Liz and Garcia have been working hard. I'm worried something else is going on." He turned on the oven and set the temperature.

"What do you mean?"

"Just that this doesn't feel like a regular murder, if there even is such a thing. I'm afraid we may have a serial murderer on our hands."

Connolly gasped. "What makes you think that?"

"The way he displayed her body. And now Lilly is missing." Mitch felt sick. It was his job to find out who had killed Renetta and where Lilly had gone, and he didn't have any better idea now than he had when they'd first discovered Renetta's body. This was such a shit-show.

"Lilly is missing?"

"Yes, we've been looking for her all day. And apparently, she's some sort of heiress." He grabbed a can of sardines and a package of crackers from the pantry. He'd munch on them while he waited for the pizza.

"Lilly's an heiress? You've got to be kidding me." Connolly snickered. "She must've been disinherited. Can't say I blame her family."

Mitch chuckled. "Who would have thought." He filled Connolly in on what Garcia had discovered about Lilly.

"So, you're thinking Lilly's family had her killed? Or a serial killer did it?"

"I don't know what I'm thinking. It could be either way. We need to find out who the killer is and stop this madness." Mitch could hear the worry in his voice. His re-election campaign was coming up in a few months and he knew he'd never be elected Sheriff again if he didn't find out who killed Renetta Larson. He had to find the killer.

"I'll be back in the office as soon as I can. You need my skills. In the meantime, I can do computer work from home," Connolly said.

"Are you sure you're up to it?" Mitch could use her computer skills. Garcia was good, but Connolly was better.

"Of course. If you only have the Detective and Garcia working this case with you, you need me big time. I'll start doing research into Lilly's family tonight. I'm sure there's something Garcia missed."

Mitch did an eye roll. Connolly always thought herself the best at everything, which really got on his other deputies' nerves. But he needed her dogged attention to this, so he didn't say anything. "Okay, do what you can. And Connolly, don't say anything about the serial killer angle. I don't want that getting out."

"Got it."

They said goodbye and Mitch tossed his phone on the counter. He took the frozen pizza from the box and put it in the oven and set the timer, but he wasn't hungry anymore. He put the sardines and crackers back in the pantry.

Chapter 24

Chapter 24—Liz

I didn't sleep well that night. I kept getting up and checking outside to make sure no one was around. When I did get to sleep, I dreamt about car thefts and someone stalking Renetta.

When I finally gave in and got out of bed, I let Bailey out and looked around the snow-covered lawn and driveway. I didn't see any new prints in the snow. Was someone trying to scare me or steal from me?

My first thought was Connolly. Would she come here trying to scare me? What good would that do her? Did she honestly think I'd be scared enough to quit the Department? Ha! In her dreams. But who was creeping around my place?

I got ready and went to work. When I walked in the door, Garcia came out of my office. "Do you ever go home?" I asked her.

She laughed. "Yeah, I just got here. I have some things to tell you."

I followed her into my office and took off my coat, hanging it on the coat rack. "What's up?"

"You were right. Connolly finally called the Sheriff. She's staying with a friend for a few days."

"I'm amazed she has any." I wasn't trying to be facetious. Connolly wasn't the type to make friends easily. She thought she was better than everyone and I'd never known her to have a close friend in the department, unless you counted Williams.

Garcia laughed. "Me, too." Then she sobered. "One of the night deputies found Brad Thomas wandering around in the snow last night. He was incoherent, so they took him to the hospital to be evaluated."

"Overdose?" The guy looked like a junkie, so I wouldn't have been surprised.

"Probably, but I haven't heard. It got down to sixteen degrees. He could've died out there."

"I need to see if he knows where Lilly is. I take it no one's seen her yet?"

Garcia shook her head. "Still missing." She looked down at the pad she carried. "Some guy called for you. Said his name is Jolly. Know anyone by that name?"

"Jolly? I think he's one of the guys Enrique and I talked to at the homeless camp. What did he want?" My pulse kicked up a few beats. Had Jolly found out something about the murder? I sure hoped so.

"He said he had something to tell you. Reception said he wouldn't talk to anyone but you." She shrugged.

"Okay, I'll go see him. Anything else going on?" As if that wasn't enough, I needed to know what I was facing. And I wanted to find out fast and get out to the homeless camp to see what Jolly had to tell me.

"The Sheriff hasn't come in. He called and said he's following a lead and will be in later."

I nodded, wondering what lead he was following. Or was he avoiding me because of our conversation the night before? "Want to go with me to talk to Jolly?" I asked Garcia, hoping she'd say yes, so I didn't have to take the rookie.

"Sure. Let me get my coat. Can we get coffee on the way?"

"You bet." I nodded to West as we walked through the main room. He nodded once, then went back to whatever he was looking at on his computer.

We drove through Dutch Bros. While we waited in line, Garcia said, "Do you think this snow will ever end?"

"I hope so." It had stopped snowing during the night, but it was starting again. I told Garcia about my intruder.

"Have you told the sheriff?"

"No, not yet." I wasn't sure I would tell Mitch. What could he do? And it would give him an excuse to stop by my house.

She must've heard something in my voice. "You don't think it's him, do you?"

"No, he'd come to the door and demand to be let in."

She laughed. "True. But Liz, that worries me. Especially since the Sheriff thinks we're dealing with a serial killer."

I drove up to the window and paid for our drinks. "Be safe out there," the young girl at the window said.

I thanked her and drove off. "I don't think a serial killer would try to get into my garage." I really didn't, but the hair on the back of my neck stood up. Was I being watched by a killer?

Garcia took a sip of her hot coffee. "Really? They like to stalk their prey. It's part of the game. You know that. You need to tell the Sheriff."

"And have him insist on moving in?" I shook my head. "Please don't say anything, Anna. I'm sure it's someone looking for something to steal."

"I don't like the thought of you being way out there by yourself. At least come stay with me until this is over."

I smiled. "Thank you, but I'm fine. I have my dog, Bailey, to warn me and my gun close by. And my orchard foreman, José, isn't that far away. Let's just find out who is doing this and arrest them. Then we all can sleep better."

I drove down Hospital Hill and turned left towards the homeless camp. "Jolly wouldn't go to the shelter before. I hope he's not frozen solid in his tent."

I pulled up and parked next to the camp. There was no sign of life. We got out and headed towards the tent I'd seen Jolly go into the day of Renetta's murder. It was too cold for him to sleep outside. I'd have to convince him to go to the shelter. If he was still alive. "Jolly! It's Detective Ellisen."

Nothing stirred inside.

I tried again. "Jolly, Mr. Weathers!"

Garcia walked around looking at the other tents. We heard a fire crackling behind a motorhome and headed that way.

Jolly Weathers stood next to the fire with a coffeepot in his hand. "Good morning, Detectives. Would you like a cup of coffee?"

"No, thank you. We just had one." There was no way I was drinking out of the mug he held out to us. "Are you staying warm?"

"Sure. Sure." He nodded several times. "I brought my sleeping bag out and slept by the fire."

I shivered. "I heard you want to talk to me."

He nodded. His nose was running, and he swiped it with his gloved hand. "I remembered something." He took a sip of coffee and stared at the fire. "Thought you might want to know."

"What's that?" I moved my feet, trying to keep them from freezing.

"Some dude came by the camp asking about Lilly. It was a few days before Ren died." He stopped and shook his head. "I sort of forgot because of all that happened."

I nodded. "Did he say why he wanted to talk to Lilly?"

"Just that he needed to find her. He was well-dressed. Clean. Drove a nice car. I thought, well, old Lil has come up in the world if one of her Johns is rich like that."

Garcia took out a notebook and pen.

"Can you tell us anything else about him?" I asked. The smoke came our way, and I waved it away with my hand. My eyes stung, and I coughed. We moved over a couple of feet to get out of its way.

"Yeah, he came back yesterday. Said he really needed to find Lil. I told him to try the shelter up the street some." He pointed East of us in the general direction of the street.

"And what did he do?"

Jolly shrugged. "He left."

"What did he look like?" Garcia asked. "Was he tall, short, heavyset or thin? Did you see his hair color?"

"He was tall, with light brown hair. Dressed nice, like I told ya. He was average size, I guess. Not fat, but not skinny."

"Is there anything you can think of that will help us look for him?" I asked.

Jolly thought about it. He rubbed at his whiskers. "He drove one of them fancy cars. Starts with an L. Can't remember what they're called. But it was black and shiny."

"A Lexus?" I asked.

Jolly shrugged. "I just remember it was a big car, and it started with an L. Can't remember the rest." He shook his head. "Oh, it had a sticker on the back window. I noticed that when he drove away."

"A sticker? Did you see what it said?"

"No, I don't see too good these days. It looked official. Like a government sticker of some kind."

Garcia and I stared at each other. Then we turned back to Jolly. "Have you seen Lilly in the last couple of days?" I asked.

He shook his head. "Not many staying here in this cold weather. Just me and Brad. But he didn't come home last night."

Garcia and I looked at each other. "You need to stay at the shelter until the weather improves," I told him.

"Nah, I don't want to stay there. Too many people." He stirred the fire with a long stick.

"Are you sure you wouldn't be more comfortable somewhere warm?" Garcia asked Jolly.

Jolly shook his head. "Nah, I can't stand to be closed in."

We thanked him and headed back to the SUV. Once we were inside, I turned to Garcia. "A government car? What is going on with Lilly?"

Chapter 25

Garcia shrugged. "A lot more than we ever thought, that's for sure."

I nodded. "Let's go see if we can get anything out of Brad Thomas." I started the SUV and headed back to town and the hospital. There were few vehicles on the road because of the snow. Most people were holding up at home. I was thankful for that.

While I drove, Garcia called Mitch and told him what Jolly had said. He asked her to track down the driver of the Lexus.

As I started up Hospital Hill, a car slid down the hill sideways. It was headed straight for us. I tried to maneuver away from it, heading for the sidewalk, but the SUV didn't want to cooperate.

"Watch out!" Garcia put her hand on the dash.

I watched as the car slid toward us in slow motion. I pulled the SUV over, and the other car slid down the hill, finally stopping before it hit the motel at the bottom.

"I'll bet that was a fun ride," Garcia said.

The vehicle straightened out and headed West on Cascade. My hands were shaking, which never happens. It was a close call. "And that's why people should stay home on days like today."

Garcia nodded, and I eased the county SUV back on the road and drove slowly to the hospital.

Once inside, we made our way to the nurse's station.

A young woman in blue scrubs looked up from her computer and smiled. "What can I do for you officers?"

Her nametag read Heather Parks, RN. She was slender with blonde hair pulled back into a ponytail.

"We're here to check on Brad Thomas," I said, and she nodded and checked her computer monitor.

"He's in ICU. We're monitoring him because of his mental state."

"Can you tell us what's going on?" I asked. "We heard he was wandering around outside in the snow last night."

"That's right. One of your officers picked him up and brought him in. You'll need to talk to his doctor, but I can tell you he isn't responsive."

"Can we see him?" Garcia asked.

The nurse nodded. "Sure, but I doubt it will do any good."

We followed her down the hall to the critical care unit. She buzzed us in, wished us luck, and went back the way we'd come.

Garcia and I met with the nurse in the ICU. "Has there been any change since they brought him in?" I asked. What had caused Brad's mental breakdown? He must've overdosed. Had he, like I first suspected, killed Renetta?

The nurse answered my question. "Not really. He started to come to a little while ago and whispered something. It sounded like a name. But his voice was so faint, it was hard to hear him."

She showed us to the door of Brad's room, and we went in. She looked at the whiteboard attached to the wall. "Looks like he has Dr. Hanson. Let me get him for you."

We thanked her and she hurried out.

Brad was lying in bed, his face as white as the sheets covering him. I walked over to the bed. "Brad? It's Detective Ellisen. Can you hear me?"

He stirred but didn't open his eyes.

"Brad?" I reached out and touched his shoulder and he jerked awake. He stared at me; panic written all over his face.

"Renetta," he whispered.

"What about Renetta?" I asked. I glanced up at Garcia. Was he going to confess that he'd killed her?

Garcia's eyes grew enormous. We both turned back to Brad.

He blinked twice, then it was as though the lights went out. He closed his eyes and no amount of trying on my or Garcia's part would wake him.

We stared at him. "Come on, Brad," I said. "Wake up and tell us what's going on. Did you kill your sister?"

He didn't move.

"Brad, what happened to Renetta?" I reached out and shook his shoulder. He didn't move.

"I don't think he's going to wake up again," Garcia said.

I leaned over Brad, close to his ear, and said, "Lilly's family is looking for her."

Nothing but the beep of the heart monitor.

I tried again. "Do you know where Lilly is? Come on, Brad. Give us something."

Nothing.

"Brad, do you know who killed Renetta?"

He stirred and whispered, "Renetta. Sorry." His eyes opened, then rolled back in his head.

Garcia and I looked at each other. We both tried to get him awake, but he didn't open his eyes again or say anything else. We looked up as a man dressed in a white coat walked in. His name tag read Dr. Mark Hanson.

"Hello officers. What can I do for you?" He held a clipboard in his hands and wore a stethoscope around his neck. His white lab coat was open, and he had on a brown and black checked shirt and black cargo pants. He was young, probably late twenties to early thirties, and I felt old. Here was a good-looking guy, and he was twenty years younger than me. Sigh.

We explained to him why we were checking on Brad. He shook his head. "He was in a bad way when he came in. He had lots of oxycodone in his system. We gave him Naloxone as soon as he was brought in."

"How soon do you think he'll start waking up?" I asked.

"He'll probably start stirring soon. He may stay in a state of late time withdrawal syndrome and have insomnia, restlessness, raised REM sleep, epileptic phenomena and even delirium which can last for up to two months."

Great. Hopefully, Brad will wake up sooner rather than later. "Will you let us know if he wakes up?" I asked.

"Yes, I'll tell the nurse on duty to call you." Dr. Hanson wrote something on Brad's chart and hung it up by the head of the bed. Then he touched the screen on the laptop that sat next to the bed. It came on and he started typing.

Garcia and I thanked him and walked out of the room. "Nice looking doctor," she said. "Is it me, or do they get younger every year?"

I sighed. "It's not you. I'm going to check on Enrique and Jolene before we leave." I turned towards the elevator, wanting to see my little godson again.

Garcia nodded, and we headed to the maternity unit, only to find they'd gone home the night before.

"Shoot. I wanted some baby snuggles. I'll call and make sure they're okay." I pulled my phone from my pocket.

We walked down the corridor, our boots making thumping sounds on the tile floor. "I've heard several people are taking food to them. You know how well-liked Enrique and Jolene are," Garcia said.

"Yup, they have a lot of great friends and family." I flipped through my contacts. I wanted to check and make sure they had what they needed. I knew Enrique would understand that I was busy, but I needed to do something. After all, I was the baby's godmother.

I made the call as we headed out to the car. Enrique picked up. After we greeted each other, he said, "We're doing fine, Liz. Sounds like you've got a big case on your hands. Wish I was there to help."

"Don't worry about it. Your job is to take care of Jolene and my godson."

Enrique chuckled. "Jolene's mom is coming to stay for a couple of days. I can leave them for a few hours and help if you need me."

Did I hear hope in his voice? He'd probably love to get out of the house if all of his in-laws were descending on them. "Do you have enough food?"

"Oh yes. The family has brought tons of food, so don't worry about that. Just come visit when you can."

I promised him I would and said goodbye. Garcia and I walked out into the frosty morning.

I glanced up at the sky. It wasn't snowing at that moment, but it looked like it would start again any time. "I'm worried about Lilly. Shall we check the warming shelter again? Maybe she came in during the night."

"Sure." Garcia blew on her gloved hands to warm them. "I hate to say it, but I'm getting sick of this weather."

"Yeah, me, too." We headed to the SUV. But when we checked the shelter, they still hadn't seen her.

"Do you think her family found her?" Garcia asked when we got back to the SUV. "I can't help but wonder if she's a threat to them. Maybe they told her they'd kill Renetta if she didn't sign the papers to give up her inheritance."

"That's possible." I chewed on my lower lip. My lips were dry from the cold, and I pulled lip moisturizer out of my pack and covered them. "Let's check the hotels in town. See if we can find the black Lexus." I slipped my moisturizer back into my pack and started the vehicle heading towards town.

We pulled up in front of the Hood River Hotel on Oak Street and parked. The clerk on duty wasn't much help. He was a young guy, with short dark hair and black glasses. His name tag identified him as Rick. I had a feeling he hadn't been working there long.

"We haven't had anyone check in for a couple of days. With the roads closed, most people have already gotten rooms. We've had some extend their stay, but I don't know what vehicle they're driving."

I motioned to his computer screen. "Could you check your files? Don't they have to list the make of their car when they check in?"

He frowned. "Oh, yeah."

He checked the guest registration. After a few minutes of him looking at the screen and muttering to himself, he said, "No Lexus drivers that I can see."

We thanked him and started for the door when it opened, and a man walked in. He was dressed in jeans and a dark sweater. He carried a black down jacket over his arm. Garcia and I watched him stride across the room and get on the elevator.

I turned back to the desk clerk. "Who is he?"

He shrugged. "He said he's stuck here because of the weather."

I wondered if he was our guy. We went outside and looked at the cars parked on the side of the road next to the hotel. Sure enough, a large black Lexus sedan sat two spaces down from the door. I walked around the back of it to see if it was a government issued car. I found the sticker Jolly had mentioned, but it was a parking sticker. I shook my head. Garcia and I looked at each other and headed back into the hotel.

Chapter 26

Chapter 26

Mitch called just as we opened the door. "Hey, ODOT opened the freeway. Thought you should know. I'm sure people will head out of town as fast as they can."

ODOT did their best to keep the freeway open if they could. "Okay, thanks. We found the Lexus that Jolly Weathers told us about. We're at the Hood River Hotel. We'll see if the owner is in a hurry to leave town."

"Sounds good. What are your plans for the afternoon?"

I glanced at my watch. It was close to lunchtime. My stomach was feeling empty. "I don't know. Is there anything you need us to do, or should we head back to the office after lunch?"

"Why don't you head back? We need a meeting to regroup and see what everyone has so far. I'll call it for one o'clock."

"Got it. See you then."

He hung up and Garcia opened the door to the hotel. Word must've gotten out because the lobby was full of people waiting in line to check out. "Let's go get a coffee and stand by the Lexus. I have a feeling he'll be wanting to leave town."

"Okay." Garcia turned and stepped back onto the sidewalk. She headed towards Ground Espresso, the coffee shop on the next block.

While she went in and placed our orders, I stood out on the sidewalk and kept an eye on the Lexus. I didn't want the owner to leave while we were inside.

Soon, Garcia came out carrying two cups. She handed me one and sipped out of the other. "Mmm, pure heaven."

"Thanks." I took the lid off and blew on my coffee before taking a drink. She was right. The coffee warmed me from the inside out.

We stood by the Lexus for ten minutes before the driver appeared. But it wasn't a man like Jolly had told us, it was a woman. Garcia and I exchanged confused looks before approaching her.

"Good afternoon, ma'am. I'm Detective Liz Ellisen and this is Deputy Anna Garcia of the Hood River Sheriff's office. We need to see your identification, please."

She stopped in the middle of the sidewalk and looked at us. She was dressed in black pants, a black sweater and a white down coat. On her feet were black dress boots that I doubted would do her much good in the snow. She had pulled her long blonde hair back into a sleek ponytail, and she wore small silver hoops in her ears.

"Whatever for?" She let go of the handle of her suitcase and pulled a large white leather wallet out of her bag.

"Are you the driver of that car?" I pointed to the Lexus.

"Yes, why?" She gave me a confused look.

"Were you at the homeless camp on the West end of town this morning?" Garcia asked. She took a notebook and pen out of her pocket, handed her coffee to me, and prepared to take notes.

The woman shook her head. "No, I've been in the hotel hoping that 84 would open. I've got a meeting in Pendleton tomorrow morning."

"May I ask what you're doing in Hood River?" I asked, glancing down at her license. Her name was Kara Jefferson. I handed the license to Garcia.

"Sure. The highway going East closed, and I had to find somewhere to spend the night. I'm heading to Pendleton to take a deposition in a criminal trial my office is involved with. What's this about, officers?" Her perfectly arched eyebrows rose to the top of her face.

"Do you know Lillian Abbott?" I watched her carefully, hoping her expression would give her away.

Something passed over her face, but she covered it quickly with a blank look. "No, should I?"

I would swear she was lying to me. "And you're just passing through?"

She nodded. "I'm sorry I can't help you."

Garcia jotted her information in her notebook and handed the license back to her. "Okay, drive safe," she said.

The woman smiled, grabbed her suitcase, and walked to her car.

I looked at Garcia. "Okay, what's going on? There are a lot of nice cars in Hood River, but two black Lexus sedans in one day?"

Garcia shook her head. "Very weird. But I got her license number in case she wasn't telling the truth."

We headed back to our SUV. Before we could get in, a man came out of the hotel and slid into the Lexus on the passenger side. Garcia and I both headed towards the Lexus, wanting to catch him before they drove away.

"Sir!" I called, holding up my hand. "Sir!"

He noticed me, and a look of resignation crossed his face. He stepped back out of the car. "What can I do for you, officer?"

"I need to see your identification, please." I hurried over to him with Garcia trailing me.

He was wearing a charcoal grey suit and white shirt. It was unusual to see a man dressed like that in Hood River. We were lucky to see them wearing jeans and a flannel shirt instead of pajamas. I noticed Garcia looked star-struck and smiled inwardly. Then I introduced us to him and asked the same question I'd asked the woman with him.

He sighed and took his wallet out of his back pants pocket. After removing his driver's license he handed it to me. "Yes, I was at the homeless camp and talked to Mr. Weathers. I was looking for Lillian Abbott. She's the daughter of my client, Kenneth Abbott."

"Lillian Abbott?" I read his name, Jason Morris, and handed his license to Garcia.

He nodded. "I'm an investigator for the firm that handles the Abbott's estate. Mr. Abbott recently died, and we've been looking for his heir. We finally figured out she moved to Hood River many years ago and has been living in a homeless camp, so I went to see if she was there." He shook his head and put his hands on his hips. "Mr. Abbott would be horrified if he knew how his daughter has been living."

"Did he know he had a granddaughter?" I couldn't help the aggressive tone of my voice. If Mr. Abbott was so dang rich, why hadn't he helped Renetta?

The man shrugged. "I don't know. He never mentioned her."

Why would Lilly not tell her family about Renetta? Or had she told them, and they refused to acknowledge her because Lilly had her with someone they didn't like? Was that it? I knew it happened a lot in wealthy families.

"We're investigating Lillian's daughter's murder. Do you know anything about that?" I kept a close watch on his face.

He shook his head. "Her daughter was murdered. That's too bad. I couldn't find Lillian. Kara and I are headed to Pendleton for a deposition and to gather some information on another case. We thought we'd come back here after we've finished there." He nodded to the woman in the car.

"Okay, we'll let you go. Do you have a card? Just in case we find Lilly, I can let you know."

Garcia handed his license back and he took it and put it back in his wallet. Then he fished a business card out of his pocket and handed it to me, said goodbye, got in the car and we watched as they drove away.

"There's something I'm missing with those two," I told Garcia. I didn't like the cavalier way he acted about Renetta. It was as though she didn't matter.

"I agree. They were in a big hurry to get out of town." She shook her head and gave me a grin. "Good-looking guy, though. Think they're a couple?"

I shrugged. "I wouldn't be surprised, but they may just be colleagues."

"I wouldn't mind working with him. The guy can wear a suit."

I rolled my eyes. We walked back to the SUV. My phone rang as I opened the door. It was Mitch. What was he calling for again so soon? "What's up?"

"Hope you aren't hungry. We've got another body."

Chapter 27

Chapter 27—Connolly

Connolly awoke to silence. Her heart was beating fast. She looked around. The room was dim, with afternoon shadows lurking in the corners. Where was she? Then she remembered and settled back on the pillows. She was lying on the sofa in her boyfriend's living room. He had picked her up from the hospital and brought her to his place, then insisted she spend the night. He'd been so sweet, begging her to forgive him for the accident.

Of course, she forgave him. He hadn't let the knife slip on purpose. She knew that. She looked around his living room. The TV had been on when she fell asleep, but it was off now. The house was so quiet. Had he gone out?

She called his name. When he didn't answer, she threw the blanket back and sat up, clutching her side, which ached from her wound.

Maybe he'd gone into the bathroom. His house was a single level ranch that had been added onto. He had a master suite and three guest rooms. It was beautiful, and Megan could see herself living there one day if things worked out. She hoped they did. They had been so careful to keep their affair a secret. It was more his idea than hers. She wanted to shout it out to the world, but he'd asked for a little longer before they told anyone.

She struggled to her feet, feeling the urge to pee. "I hope you aren't going to be in there all day," she called as she headed for the bathroom. She hoped he was in the shower. Maybe she could catch a glimpse of his gorgeous body. But when she got there, the door was open, but he wasn't there. She peed first, then looked in his bedroom. He wasn't there either. Megan frowned.

She looked through the rest of the house, but there was no sign of him. She headed back into the kitchen to see if he'd left a note but didn't find one. Her cell phone sat on the table. She picked it up and called him, but he didn't answer. Strange. She went back to the sofa and grabbing the remote; she turned on a movie. Surely, he'd show up soon.

But the movie ended with no word from him. Megan called his cell several times, but he didn't pick up. It was getting late in the day, and she wanted a shower. She knew she could take one in his bathroom, but she didn't have clean clothes with her.

Finally, after trying his cell again for what felt like the hundredth time, she called an Uber driver. If he wasn't home by the time the driver arrived, she'd leave him a note.

It didn't take long for the driver to arrive. Megan grabbed her coat and bag and let herself out, locking the door behind her. She was worried about her boyfriend but thought he must've run into some friends at one of the bars in town and got to talking. It was easy to lose track of time when you were visiting with friends. He'd get home, find her note and call her, she was sure.

The Uber driver helped her to his car. He was an older man and didn't seem worried about driving on the snowy roads. When she asked him, he said, "Nah, I've lived here all my life. Snow doesn't bother me none."

Megan was glad she'd gotten him. He let her off in front of her house on May Street. "Stay warm," he told her, giving her a smile.

"I will. You, too." Megan let herself into the house. She shivered and went straight to the thermostat to turn up the heat. She took her coat off and started to hang it in the hall closet when she realized something was wrong.

The closet door was open, and her coats and jackets were on the floor. Her heart pounded. She knew she hadn't left her closet this way. She put her coat on the back of the sofa in her living room and looked around.

The living room seemed untouched, but an uneasy shiver skittered over her skin. She went back to the closet and the safe where she kept her service revolver. It wasn't there. She remembered having it with her at the shelter, but she didn't remember what happened to it when the ambulance took her to the hospital.

She walked to the hall and listened. Not hearing anything, she made her way to the last bedroom down the hall. It was the largest, and she'd made it into an ensuite with a connecting bathroom. She also had one guest room and a home office that she used mostly for paying bills and computer work.

She gasped when she opened the door to her room. Someone had tossed it. Her comforter was on the floor. The closet door was open, and her clothes were on the floor or hanging crooked on their hangers. Someone took the totes she had stored extra clothes in off the shelf and left them lying open on the floor.

Megan frowned. She hurried to her home office. She had put her other gun, a .45, in the safe in there. Megan hoped it was still there and the house was as empty as it felt. She kept a gun there plus the few pieces of jewelry she had. Most she'd inherited from her mom and grandmother. Someone had ransacked the office as well. She hurried to the desk and looked under it where she'd had the safe installed. It was still intact, thank you God.

With shaking fingers, Megan opened the safe and took out the revolver. She loaded it and shut the safe. Then she went back into her kitchen and called her boyfriend. He still didn't answer, so she called the sheriff.

Sheriff Ellisen answered, sounding rushed. "Hey Connolly. Are you okay?"

"Not really." She told him about her house being tossed. She wasn't the nervous sort, but she felt weird being in her house alone.

"Was the door unlocked?"

Megan silently berated herself for not checking the door into the garage. She headed there while she talked. "The front door was locked. I had to use my key to get in, but I didn't try the door into the garage. I'll do that now."

She walked through the kitchen to the garage door. It was partially open. She always left it closed. "Uh, Sheriff, this door is open." She backed away. "I always leave it locked." She frowned. Had her boyfriend been there? Why would he toss her house? It didn't make sense, but nothing about this made sense.

She still had her .45 in her hand. She pushed the garage door open and looked inside. It was gloomy in there, and she stopped and listened. Nothing moved. She eased into the garage. Her head felt fuzzy, and she had to grab onto the doorframe to stay upright.

"Sheriff's Department," she called in a loud voice. "Come out with your hands up."

Still, nothing moved. She said it again. "Sheriff's Department. I have a gun. Come out with your hands up."

A noise at the back of the room startled her, and she swung in that direction, keeping her gun in front of her. Then a shot rang out and Megan dropped to the floor.

She could hear the sheriff's voice from far away. "Megan, are you okay? Get out of there."

She had enough presence of mind to get up, hurry into the kitchen and close the door into the garage. She'd just locked it when the blast from a gun hit the door, shattering the wood.

"Megan! What's going on?" the sheriff yelled from her phone which she still clutched in her hand.

"Shots fired." Megan yelled into the phone.

"Get out of there. I'm on my way."

She nodded, then realized he couldn't see her. She headed for the front door. Should she let herself out or stay inside? Where was the shooter now?

In the distance, she heard a siren and knew Mitch was on his way. "Hurry, please hurry," she whispered as she let herself out the front door. She ran to the road, holding her side, which ached with a ferocity she had never felt before. Gritting her teeth, she ran toward the siren.

Chapter 28

Chapter 28—Liz

Garcia and I ran to the SUV and climbed in. While I drove, Garcia talked to Mitch. "Connolly just called," I heard him say. "She's being shot at. I'm going there first. As soon as I can, I'll be at the crime scene."

"What is going on?" I shouted. "Why's Connolly being shot at?" Even though I'd wanted to shoot her myself a few times, I didn't know of her making anyone else that mad.

Garcia put Mitch on speaker. "I don't know. Connolly called and said she was at home, and someone had been there going through her stuff. Then she found the door into the garage open. When she went in, someone shot at her."

"Good heavens. This town has gone nuts," Garcia exclaimed.

"You two head to the crime scene. I'll be there as soon as I can. I'm calling the city for back-up. I'll call you once I have things secured at Connolly's."

"Okay," Garcia said, then clicked off her phone. "Victim is just off Whiskey Creek Road," she said. "By the creek on the south side."

I turned the SUV towards the East side of town. Whiskey Creek was off Highway 35 just before the train trestle over the highway. It was a small, picturesque road that connected the highway to Eastside Road. There were large old oak and pine trees on both sides that shaded the drive. The drive was most beautiful in autumn when brilliant hues of orange and red from the leaves washed over it. It was also gorgeous in the winter, with snow covering the ground and weighing down the tree limbs. I'd always loved to turn onto Whiskey Creek and take in the beauty of the short drive. Now, it would forever be fixed in my mind as a crime scene.

Lights flashed as we turned onto the road. We could see the emergency vehicles parked along the right side of the road. A firefighter from the local fire department was out directing traffic. Enrique parked his pickup on the opposite side, facing us. I parked behind one of the first responders, and we got out.

Whiskey Creek was over an embankment. It wasn't far down to the creek, but it looked like the body was about twenty feet from where we stood. Several people congregated there. "Let's do this."

"What's Rodriquez doing here?" Garcia asked as we made our way through the snow and slush down the hill to the creek. "Shouldn't he be home with the new baby?"

I shrugged. "He lives near here." We continued down the slope, our boots slipping in the snow. The hill rose on the other side of the creek into an orchard. Snow rose halfway up the trees. Once we were back on level ground, Enrique came to meet us.

"Another young woman," he said, shaking his head. He had dressed in a black winter jacket and snow pants. On his head was a green stocking cap that was covered in snow.

"Who found her?" I asked, looking around the area. Deputies stood close to the body. Dr. King was down on her knees next to her.

"Couple of teenage boys down here playing around. Found her lying next to that rock over there." Enrique pointed to a rock a few feet from us. He shook his head. "Poor kids."

I looked around. "Where are they?" Worry gnawed at me. I wanted to make sure the boys were all right.

"After they stopped puking their guts up, Winkler put them in the back of her car." He pointed to a county SUV parked next to the road. Deputy Winkler stood next to it talking to the young men through the window.

"Okay, we'll go check on them as soon as we talk to Doc. Has someone called their parents?" I hated to think of how traumatized the boys were. I hoped their parents would get help for them.

"They're on the way."

I nodded. "Do you recognize the victim?" I asked, heading towards the body. My footsteps were steady, but inside I wanted to stop and not go down there. I didn't want to see who was lying at the bottom. I shook my head. What was the matter with me? I'd never shied away from a crime scene before.

Enrique and Garcia fell into step beside me. "Yeah," Enrique said, his voice sad. "It's Willow Evans."

"Why is that name familiar?" I asked, knowing I should know her. Was she an old friend of Bella's, too? I hope not.

"She's a friend of Renetta's."

"You're kidding me." I stopped and stared at him. He and Garcia stopped, too.

Enrique shook his head. "No, we saw her at lunch the other day. Remember, she was with Kari Young."

I remembered. The bigger girl with the long blonde braids. "Has anyone talked to Amy?" I knew this would be another blow for the young woman.

He shook his head. "I thought you might want to."

We started walking towards the crime scene again. I nodded. "Yeah, I would. Garcia and I will go after we talk to the boys who found her. I don't suppose there's any way we can keep this quiet for a while?"

He nodded. "You know this is Hood River, right? Too many people with scanners and word spreads so fast everyone knows before it happens."

"That's for sure," Garcia agreed. "You can't keep anything quiet in this valley."

"Do you know if Mitch called in the Major Crimes Team?" I asked. The Gorge Major Crimes Team comprised of officers from The Dalles Police, Hood River Police, Wasco County Sheriff's Department, Hood River County Sheriff's Department, Sherman County Sheriff's Department, and the State Police. They were typically called in when something of this caliber occurred.

"Second murder in a week? I'm sure he did. But they just opened the freeway a while ago, so they aren't here yet."

We were getting closer to the body and Dr. King looked up when she heard us. "Liz, come here." She motioned me over and I went, feeling the questioning looks Enrique and Garcia were giving me.

She raised up on her knees and pulled back the victim's coat and sweater. The white skin of her torso had several ugly red punctures. "Looks like she was stabbed," I said, squatting next to her so I could get a better look.

Dr. King nodded. "But look closely at the wounds. What do you see?"

At first, all I saw were multiple stab wounds. The icy water caused Willow's skin to shrivel and turn blue from the cold. The red wounds stood out and the longer I looked, the more they formed a pattern. "Is that a heart?" I asked, pointing at the wounds.

"Looks like it to me," Dr. King said, gazing down at the victim.

"Oh, shit." I jumped up and grabbed Enrique by the arm. "Is he leaving us a clue?"

"Looks that way to me." Enrique walked around the body, looking at every inch of snow and then back at the victim.

Dr. King stood and shook her head. "We need to get her to the morgue so I can look her over. There may be more clues."

I took my phone out and took a picture of the wounds. "At least it's a lead of sorts. Maybe it will help us."

Dr. King nodded to her assistant to help her put Willow in a body bag. I thought a lot of the doctor. She had a lot of heart and made sure victims were treated with respect.

"Do you think she was in the water for long?" I looked around at the swirling, freezing water flowing past us. It wasn't a big creek and not deep, but it was so cold out I was surprised it wasn't frozen solid.

"Hard to say. We'll know more after I get her back to the morgue and have time to look at her." She watched while her assistant spread out the body bag.

I nodded, knowing the doc would say that. I felt sick, thinking about another autopsy that I'd have to attend. Autopsies were one of the worst parts of my job.

Garcia walked around taking pictures of everything and making notes in her notebook. I saw her stop and talk to the other deputies, but I couldn't hear what they were saying.

Enrique watched the doctor and her assistant. "What's going on with this guy?"

"Maybe Mitch is right and we're looking at a serial killer." Would he kill again? Willow's murder was so soon after Renetta's that I worried he was ramping up, enjoying the kill. "We have to stop him before he kills again."

"So, you think this is a serial killer? How are Lilly and her family involved? None of this makes sense." Enrique took a piece of gum out of his pocket, unwrapped it, and stuck it in his mouth.

"No, it doesn't. We need to keep digging until we can fit all the pieces together." I stomped my feet, trying to warm them. "Why can't killers do their thing in the summer? Why do it now when we have to be out here freezing our butts off?"

He snapped his gum. "I'm going to tell Jolene that I need to come back to work at least part time." He held up his hands. "Not that I don't think you can handle this without me, but with Connolly out, I know you're short-handed."

I nodded. I couldn't help but feel relieved. We needed Enrique on this case. "I'm sorry. I know you want time with your new little one, but we could use you, that's for sure." I brushed at the spit up on his jacket. "Baby get you?"

He looked down and smiled. "Yeah, he spits up a lot. I hope that stops soon." He brushed his fingers over his coat.

I smiled, then gave him a worried look. "Are you sure you can leave them and work this case? It may consume us for a while." I watched as different expressions crossed his face, a little worry, and a lot of determination.

"I'm sure Jo will understand." His jaws worked as he chewed his gum.

"You think so?" I glanced at him, aware of his struggle dividing his time between his wife and new baby and his commitment to the team. I hoped Jo would understand that we needed Enrique, and he wanted to help. Our job was hard on spouses, and some handled it better than others. Jo was supportive, but since she'd just had a baby, she might want her husband around.

"Probably not." He grinned. "But her mom will be there to tell her how lucky she is to have such a great husband and she'll agree. Everything will be fine."

I chuckled, hoping he was right.

We looked at the area around the body, taking pictures and making notes, until Dr. King was ready to transport Willow's body to the morgue. I didn't see any obvious signs that someone had dumped her there, but there were so many tracks in the snow from the boys who found her and the first responders. It was hard to tell.

While Garcia and the other deputies canvassed a wide swath around where the body was found, Enrique and I walked to where the boys who'd found her were running towards a couple who'd just pulled up.

Deputy Winkler headed our way when she saw us. "Detectives." She nodded. Her nose was red from the cold, and she swiped at it with a gloved hand. "The parents just arrived."

Two tall people each held a boy in their arms. They looked up at us as we approached. A closer look and I realized the boys were younger than we'd been told. They were tall like their parents.

I introduced myself and Enrique. "I'm so sorry you had to find her," I said softly to the oldest boy. He nodded, but didn't move out of his dad's arms. The younger boy had his head buried in his mom's shoulder.

"They're pretty traumatized, Detective," the father said. "We need to get them home."

"I understand, but I need to talk to them before they forget what they saw." I moved a little closer. "Is there anything you can tell me?" I asked the boys.

"She was just lying there. We thought it was a blanket or something," the older boy said. His brother shook his head and burrowed closer to his mom.

"Did you see anyone else around? Maybe before you found her?"

He shook his head.

"Okay, your folks are going to take you home. We'll come by and see you later, okay?" I kept my voice gentle, and they both nodded. We wrote down the parents' names, address and the boys' names and let them go.

"I don't think we'll get much out of them," Enrique said, popping his gum. We watched as they got into their Chevy Tahoe and drove away.

"Probably not, but we need to talk to them again, anyway. They may have seen something that their brains are not wanting to face right now."

He shook his head. "Poor kids."

"Yeah." I was afraid they'd have nightmares for years after today.

We walked back to the crime scene. Dr. King was heading for her van. "I'll let you know as soon as I'm ready to do the autopsy," she said, waving at us as she left.

Garcia walked towards us as the first responders started packing up to leave. "Did you find out anything?" I asked as she walked over next to us.

She shook her head. "Not really. One boy had a phone and called his parents and they called it in. They told the boys to walk out to the road and wait for them or a police officer to get there." She looked down at her notes. "Jeff Gannon was the first one on the scene. He said the boys were hysterical, talking and crying and pointing down to the creek. He put them in his pickup and walked over to look. He said one thing that was interesting."

"What's that?"

Garcia held out an evidence bag with an object in it. "He found a child's hair clip lying next to the body."

Chapter 29

Chapter 29

Enrique and I stared at the object and then at each other. I felt the hair on the back of my neck stand up. This was looking more and more like the work of a serial killer who, for some twisted reason, was using a child's possession to leave clues for us. I squeezed my hands into fists.

"Mitch told me he was concerned about a serial killer, but I thought serial killers take souvenirs, not leave them," Enrique said.

"This is bizarre," Garcia agreed. She looked at me. "I wonder what the boss will think?"

Just then, Mitch pulled up. We watched him get out of his truck and head for us. "I guess we'll find out. Is Connolly okay?" I asked when he walked up.

Mitch nodded. "Yeah, for now. I took her back to the hospital. Her stitches broke open." He frowned. "I've got Williams looking for the shooter. Wasco County and The Dalles Police will be here soon to help us. What have we got here?"

I really looked at him for the first time in months. He'd aged since our break-up. His hair, which was once a sandy blond, was now more grey than blond, and he had deep wrinkles around his eyes.

We told him what had happened, and Garcia showed him the hair clip.

Mitch looked at me. "Someone needs to go talk to the boys while this is still fresh on their minds. Then we need to find out who the victim was close to."

"We know she was friends with Amy Bryne, who was also friends with Renetta," I said.

He nodded. "Good place to start." He looked at Enrique. "Are you back?"

Enrique nodded. "Yeah, I think you guys need me. I'll take the rest of my paternity leave after we find this SOB."

Mitch nodded. "Good. Liz, you and Garcia go talk to the friends of the victim. Rodriquez and I will talk to the boys as soon as we finish here."

"Okay." I wanted to speak to the boys again to see if I could get them to tell me something...anything. But I'd have to let Mitch and Enrique do it. I knew I couldn't be everywhere.

Garcia and I headed for the SUV. After we got in and I'd started the engine, I turned to her. "Let's go talk to Britney Fraizer again. She has a beautiful little girl. I'd like to show her the hair clip."

Garcia agreed, and I headed towards Highline Drive. The snowplows were out, but they hadn't been able to do the secondary roads because they were so busy with the main roads. I was concerned about Britney and the children and wanted to check on them, anyway. I doubted her husband had made it home yet.

We pulled into the driveway and the SUV bucked through the soft powdery snow. Garcia had one hand on the door and the other on the dashboard. I gritted my teeth and held onto the steering wheel with both hands. We both sighed with relief when I pulled up in front of the house and stopped.

Britney met us at the door with her little boy in her arms and her little girl hanging on her pants leg. "Oh, it's so good to see you. We've felt so stranded. Ethan still hasn't been able to get home."

Gone was the well-put-together woman I'd seen two days before. In front of us was a woman in sweats, her hair piled in an untidy bun on her head and no makeup.

She backed up and we stepped inside, closing the door leaving the freezing temperatures outside. "I wanted to make sure you're all right."

"That is so nice of you. We're okay. But we're running out of firewood. If the electricity goes off again, we'll be in trouble." She gnawed on the tip of her thumb. "I wish the freeway would open."

"It has," Garcia told her, and Britney's eyes filled with relief.

"Oh, that's wonderful. Ethan is probably on his way. Last time we talked, he was going to head out as soon as he heard it was open."

"We have something we'd like you to look at, if you don't mind?" I asked her.

A tiny frown marred her forehead. "Of course not. What is it?"

Garcia pulled the evidence bag out of her pocket with the hair clip inside. She held it up and Britney frowned. Then Kennedy said, "That's mine!"

Chapter 30

C hapter 30

I bent down next to the little girl. "Are you sure, honey?"

She nodded. "That's my favorite." She reached for it, but Garcia held it out of her reach.

Britney nodded, biting her lip. "Her grandma gave it to her. We thought we lost it at the grocery store."

"Huh-uh, Mommy. I losted it from my dresser. It was there and then it was gone." She shrugged her tiny shoulders. "'Member?"

Britney smiled. "I guess you're right." She looked at us. "Now I remember. We looked everywhere. She was so upset. She and Grandma Fraizer are close. And Grandma sent that one all the way from Hawaii."

The little girl nodded, her eyes big. "Can I have it now?"

"I'm sorry, sweetie. We have to keep it for a little longer. Then we'll give it to you, I promise." I nodded at Garcia, and she put the evidence bag with the hair clip in it back in her pocket. I could tell from the look on her face that she hated keeping it from the little girl.

"But I want it." Kennedy's lips trembled.

"It's okay, honey," her mom said, putting her arm around her daughter. "Grandma said she'll send you another one."

"Is there anything else that you've noticed has gone missing lately?" I asked, thinking of the child's bracelet we found next to Renetta's body.

"I don't think so." Britney bounced her little boy on her hip.

"Yes, there is, Mommy." Kennedy tugged on her mom's shirt. "My bracelet and my bear." She shrugged. "All my stuff keeps disappearing."

Britney frowned. "Oh, that's right. We first missed the bracelet, but thought it fell off your wrist at the grocery store. Then you said your bear was missing."

Kennedy nodded, her blonde ponytail bouncing against her back. "My pink bear, daddy gave me."

"When did you notice it was gone?" I asked Britney. I didn't like this. It sounded more and more like a serial killer. Did Britney and her family know the killer? Was it the missing Ethan? I sure hoped not for their sake.

Garcia got her notepad out and jotted down notes.

"About a week ago." Her eyes widened, and she backed up a step. "Oh heavens, you don't think..." Her eyes grew huge, and panic swept across her face. "You don't think someone was here?"

"Why don't you call your husband and see if he's on his way?" I asked, reaching out for the baby.

Britney put him into my arms, and he started playing with my jacket zipper.

Then she called her husband who answered and told her he was on the way. Tears formed in her eyes as she took her baby back and thanked me.

"Be sure and lock all the doors. In fact, why don't you go around and make sure everything is locked before we leave?"

She nodded, handed the baby back and took off down the hall. After returning and confirming that everything was securely locked, she took the baby and we left.

"This case is getting stranger by the second," Garcia said, as we walked out to the car. "Do you think the husband is the killer?"

"He would be my number one suspect if he hadn't been in Portland for a few days. We'll need to confirm that he actually was in Portland."

She nodded. "Why would a killer take a little girl's things and leave them at the murder scene? This is just bizarre."

"I think if we can figure that out, we'll have a better chance of finding out who he is." It was sounding more and more like Mitch was right and we had a serial killer on our hands. Except, there were so many suspects. Was one of our local people a serial killer?

We trudged through the snow back to our county SUV and got in. "Brrr! It's so cold." I started the vehicle and turned the heat on high. I sent a silent thank you to whoever invented heated seats and turned mine up to the highest setting.

"I'm thinking this weather will never improve," Garcia said. She buckled her seatbelt and turned to me. "What do you think is going on with Connolly?"

I shrugged, put the SUV in reverse and turned it back towards the main road. "I don't know. Her story doesn't add up." I didn't really care what was going on with Connolly. Whatever she was doing was way down my list of worries.

"No, it doesn't. Sheriff said Connolly told him she was using a knife, and it slipped and went into her stomach. How many times have you ever heard of that happening?" Garcia raised her eyebrows.

"None. Usually, if someone has an injury while using a knife, they cut their fingers or hand. Her story is weird. And why didn't she head to the hospital instead of meeting me at the warming shelter? No one would've blamed her for that?" I shook my head. "I really don't have time to worry about her. Finding out who killed Renetta and Willow are more important."

"Yes, but it's still strange. Makes me wonder if she's into something she shouldn't be."

"Possible. Who knows with Connolly?"

"Liz, there's something I should tell you."

I frowned and gave her a quick glance. "About Connolly?"

She nodded. "I hate saying anything because I don't enjoy stirring things up at the office."

"She's trying to get me fired?" Nothing new there. Connolly had been trying to get rid of me for years.

Garcia turned to look at me. She brushed snow off her pants leg. "You know. Good. I hated to bring it up, but I felt like I should warn you.

"Thanks. She's tried to get rid of me since she took this job. Not sure what she has against me, but now she has a better chance because Mitch and I are no longer together."

"I don't think the sheriff wants to lose you. You're too good of a detective, but Connolly will try to make things harder for you."

Why was Garcia warning me now? Was she genuinely worried that Mitch might let me go, or was there something else eating at her? Did she want to be a detective? The competition in the office was fierce. If I left, Mitch would have to either bring in an outsider or insist one of the other deputies try to make detective level.

"I appreciate you telling me." I didn't like Connolly going behind my back and trying to get me fired, but it wasn't surprising. I knew I'd have to address the issue, but not now. Now I needed to solve this case and get this killer locked up tight.

I didn't want to drive down the steep part of Highline Drive, so I turned south, and we made our way back to Eastside Road and to town that way.

"I hope Mitch calls a meeting some time tonight. We need to see what everyone else has found out." I wanted to know if he and Enrique had found out anything from the boys who'd discovered Willow's body.

"Me, too," Garcia agreed.

I drove back through town to Amy Bryne's house. When we pulled in behind her minivan, we saw another car in the driveway. "Why don't you run the plates on that car? I'd like to know who's visiting Amy."

Garcia nodded and did as I asked. When she got the information, she looked over at me with raised eyebrows. "You'll never guess."

"Who?"

"Willow Evans."

I opened my door. "Let's go see if Amy's home, and if she knows anything about Willow's murder."

We headed to the front door. Amy must've been looking out. She opened the door before I knocked. "What's going on?"

"Is it okay if we come in?" I asked. The house smelled of vanilla scented candles. I glanced around and saw Amy had them lit and sitting on the coffee table.

She nodded and backed into the room. Her eyes were wide with concern. "Is it Willow? Is she okay?"

Garcia stepped in behind me and closed the door.

"I'm sorry to inform you..." I didn't get far when a wail erupted out of Amy's mouth.

She held her hands up in front of her face and backed away. "No, no, no! Please don't tell me something has happened to her."

We eased her into the living room and helped her sit on the sofa. I sat next to her. "Why would you say that? Was someone threatening her?"

"No, but she didn't go home last night. And when I woke up this morning, her car was parked in my driveway. I've been trying to call her all day."

I put my hand on her arm. "I'm sorry. Willow's body was found in Whiskey Creek this morning."

She shook her head and cried, big fat tears running down her cheeks. "I can't..." She shook her head again. "I just can't do this without her."

"Do what, Amy?" I kept my voice soft.

She threw her right hand out. "Any of this. Life. Willow was my anchor. She knew how to take care of things. She's the one person in the world that I could count on." Amy swiped at her eyes. "My ex is trying to take my kids from me. Willow has money. We were going to fight him." She burst into tears again.

"Where are the kids now?" I asked.

She looked up and I saw tears forming in her eyes. "I think they're with their grandma in Portland. My ex took them to her while I move." Her words trailed off and she wouldn't look me in the eyes. "What will I do now?"

"Is there someone we can call to come stay with you?" Garcia asked.

Amy nodded. "My sister, Jill, lives in town." She took her phone out of her back pocket and hit a button to call her sister, but the call didn't go through. "That's odd. I paid my bill, but my phone's dead."

"Let me try." I took my phone out. "What's her number?" She gave it to me, and I dialed Jill's number.

"I'll be right there," she said when she'd answered, and I'd told her what was going on. She didn't hesitate and I was happy that Amy had family support.

"Your sister is on the way," I told her.

She nodded and wiped her nose on her sweater sleeve.

"We need to ask you a few questions. When was the last time you saw Willow?" I kept my voice gentle, hoping she would open up to me.

"Yesterday morning before she went to work. She came by to help me pack." She wiped tears from her eyes.

"Do you know of anyone who had a grudge against her? Anyone who had threatened her?" I watched her closely, trying to figure out if she was telling the truth.

"Just my ex." She fidgeted with her sweater sleeve, pulling it down over her hands and pushing it back up.

"Your ex threatened her?" I asked.

"Well, he was mad because she helped me leave him. He said she'd get hers someday." Amy's eyes flicked around the room. What was she searching for? She seemed tense, but of course she just heard her friend was dead. Was there something else that I needed to be aware of?

"How long ago was that?" Did Amy's ex have something to do with Willow's death?

She shrugged. "I moved out about a year ago. He was mad that I took the kids. He took me to court, and we ended up with joint custody."

"He never made any other threats against you or Willow?"

Amy tugged on her hair, winding it around her fingers. "Well, he wasn't happy about Willow and me. He made some nasty remarks about us moving in together."

"You and Willow were a couple?" I hadn't seen that coming. Would Amy's ex be upset by her falling for a woman?

"Yes." A fresh batch of tears poured down her face. "I never thought I'd want another woman that way. You know? But Willow is such an amazing person." She grabbed a Kleenex and swiped her eyes. "I think it was bad enough that I left him, but when I replaced him with a woman..." She stopped and shook her head. "He really had a hard time with that."

The door opened and a young woman hurried in. She was smaller than Amy, but she looked enough like her that I immediately knew she was her sister. She went to Amy and wrapped her in her arms. "I'm so sorry," she cried.

Amy clung to her sister. After a while, she calmed down a little, and I said, "I'm sorry to keep bothering you, but I have a couple more questions. Is that okay?"

She nodded, but I could tell by the look on her face that she wanted Garcia and me to leave. We get that a lot when we interview people.

"Can you give us your ex's phone number? I'd like to talk to him." I kept a close look on her expression and watched as her eyes widened.

"Colin would never..."

"No, probably not, but we need to eliminate him." I held up my pen and notepad letting her know I needed his number.

"Okay." She told me the number and where he lived.

I thanked her. "Is there anyone you can think of that Willow might have confided in if she was having trouble with someone? Like maybe a sister, or another close friend?"

Amy shook her head. "No, not really. I mean, we were best friends, then things changed between us. But we're still besties. We tell each other everything." She looked at Jill. "Did she have anyone at the hospital that she seemed close to? I can't think of anyone."

"Not really. There were people she was friendly with, but no one super close." She rubbed Amy's shoulders.

"You worked with Willow?" I asked. Jill's hands kneaded Amy's shoulders. Amy winced. Was Jill giving her some kind of warning?

Jill nodded. "We both worked in admitting. Willow was well-liked by the staff and the doctors, but she didn't really hang out with anyone except Amy and me."

But Rodriguez and I had seen her at lunch with Kari Young. "What about Kari Young?"

"No," Amy said. "They had a falling out and hadn't spoken in months."

"Do you know what the falling out was about?" I asked. Interestingly, they didn't act like they were mad at each other when I saw them at lunch.

Amy shrugged. "Willow said she couldn't trust Kari. She'd told her some things and Kari spread it around." She shrugged again. "I don't think it was a big deal, but it upset Willow."

"Okay." I wrote Kari's name down with a question mark next to it, put my notebook and pen back in my pocket and stood up. "Thank you for your time." I handed Amy my card. "If you think of anything, please call me."

Amy nodded.

Garcia and I let ourselves out and trudged through the snow to the SUV. "What do you think?" I asked once we were sitting inside with the motor running and the heat on full blast.

"I think we should try to find out what the falling out was all about."

"Yeah." I put the SUV in reverse and backed out of the drive. "Something isn't adding up."

Garcia said, "I'll see if I can find out anything about Willow. Maybe there's information out there about her that will give us insight."

"Okay. I don't know what to think about this case. How is Willow tied in with Renetta and Lilly? I thought maybe Lilly's family wanted to get rid of her and Renetta so they could have the money she's supposed to inherit. But why would they kill Willow?"

"Do you think we have two killers running around Hood River? Or maybe Willow's murder is to throw us off the investigation or send us in the wrong direction."

"That's possible."

"I was sure at first that Brad Thomas was the killer. He fits the profile. Jealous half-brother. Wants the money for himself."

"Yeah, my money was on him, too. Now, I just don't know what to think."

"And then we have the serial killer angle. Could this all be a coincidence and we've got a crazed killer on our hands?"

Garcia sighed. "I guess we have to figure that out."

Chapter 31

C hapter 31

I drove to the address Amy had given us for her ex. He lived in a small duplex on West Eugene Street. It was painted grey and set back off the road. There was one car in the drive which was covered in snow so we couldn't tell what kind of car it was. It hadn't been moved in days. The driveway wasn't plowed, so I parked in the street and Garcia and I made our way to the door. The walk hadn't been shoveled for days and I wondered if we'd find him home.

I rang the bell and listened for movement inside. Nothing. I rang it again. We waited a couple minutes, and I banged on the door. "Sheriff's department. Open up."

Still nothing. I turned to Garcia. "Doesn't look like he's home."

She took her phone out. "What's his number?" I gave it to her, and she called, but we couldn't hear it ring inside. "I'll call Amy and see if she knows where else he might be."

Amy answered right away. Garcia talked to her for a couple of minutes, then ended the call. "She doesn't think he has a girlfriend. She said we could check in with his job. They might know where he is."

"Where does he work?"

Garcia glanced down at her notebook. "He works for Steadman Construction."

"Let's go back to the car and see if we can get a number for them." We hurried as fast as the deep snow would let us. "Have I mentioned I'm getting a little tired of all of this snow?"

Garcia laughed. "You and everyone else in town."

We climbed into the SUV, and I turned it on so we could warm up. Garcia looked up the construction company's number and called while we waited.

A deep voice answered, and she put the phone on speaker. "Yeah, this is Mike."

Garcia introduced herself and told him we were looking for Colin Symons. "We understand he works for you?"

We heard a sigh on the other end of the line. "Yeah, what's he done now?"

"We just need to talk to him. Do you know where he is?"

"No, I wish I did. He hasn't shown up for work or called in the last week. Not that there's been much going on with this snow. If you find him, tell him to call me."

"Is it like him to take off and not call you?" Garcia asked.

"No. He's probably thinking we aren't working in this weather. But I've got an inside job I need him to help with." He was quiet a second, then said, "He just needs to communicate with me."

He sounded frustrated, and I wondered how long he'd been trying to get hold of Colin. "Has he been missing for a while?"

"Not missing exactly," the man said, "But he hasn't been returning my calls and that's not like him. He's usually an excellent employee."

I looked at Garcia and raised my eyebrows. She nodded.

"If you hear from him, please have him get in touch with us." Garcia gave him her number.

Mike said he would, and she ended the call. She looked at me. "Wonder where Mr. Symons could be."

I looked up and down the street at the houses. No one moved around. No vehicles drove by. It was so quiet. A few houses down smoke curled from the chimney of a small green house, but other than that nothing stirred. "Everything is so quiet."

Garcia followed my gaze. "It's the snow, it insulates the sounds. Do you think we should check out his house?

I glanced up at the house. "There were no lights on. The TV wasn't on. We didn't hear his cell phone ring when we called him. I don't think we have cause to break in. He might be shacked up with some girl. Just because Amy doesn't know of any girlfriends doesn't mean there isn't one."

Garcia nodded. "So, we keep looking for him."

"Yup."

We drove back to the office. Garcia was going to try to find out what she could about Willow Evans and Renetta to see if she could find a common denominator. I wanted to find Lilly. I thought I'd take West with me, and we'd go back to the warming shelter, homeless camp, and down to the bridge and talk to everyone again.

Mitch called as we walked through the door. "What's up?" I asked.

"We got nothing more from the two boys who found Willow Evans. They both said they were out playing in the snow and decided to walk along the creek before turning back. The older boy said they saw what looked like a bundle of rags. They thought they saw it move, so they went to investigate thinking someone may have dumped puppies or kittens. Apparently, the whole family is animal crazy. When they saw Willow, the younger boy screamed, and they ran."

Not surprising. Poor kids. "Did they go back?"

"No, they called their parents who told them to go up to the road and wait for them to get there. Poor kids are going to have nightmares for a while."

"Yeah, no doubt." I felt disappointed that he didn't get more from the boys, but not surprised. I told him about our talk with Britney Fraizer and Kennedy. "It sounds like someone has been taking Kennedy's things and placing them at the murder scenes. If what they said is true, the killer has one more item to get rid of."

"The bear?"

I heard the same despair in his voice that I felt in my heart. If we didn't find the killer, he was planning to kill at least one more person. Maybe more. "It hasn't turned up yet."

Mitch sighed. "It's getting late. Why don't you both go home and we'll hit it hard again in the morning."

We agreed, knowing there wasn't much we could do in the dark.

After an uneventful night, I drove to work the next morning. Garcia was already there. We talked about our next step in the investigation. I asked West if he wanted to ride with me that morning and he agreed.

Mitch came in soon after me. I had poured myself a cup of coffee and said to him, "Garcia is staying here to work on the computer, and West and I are going to try to find Lilly, if that's okay with you?"

"Yes, that's fine. Why don't you head down to the bridge first? See if Lilly has shown up and if not, talk to the people there. I'm sure one of them knows something."

"Okay." I hit the end button and motioned to West. "Ready?"

He nodded and followed me out to the SUV.

I drove down to the bridge. When we pulled up and stopped, it looked like the same people standing around the fire as the day before. I put the SUV in Park, and we stepped out. We got curious and nervous glances as we walked up to the fire.

I started with a hello that no one acknowledged. Then I said, "We really need to find Lilly. If you know where she is, please let us know."

No one looked up or spoke. I sweetened the deal. "If you tell me where she is, I'll spring for coffee from Starbucks for everyone here."

A few heads bobbed. The woman I'd noticed last time we were there wearing the purple coat finally spoke up. "If we knew anything, we'd tell you. But Lils is always off somewhere. She don't answer to nobody."

"I think she's out looking for her kid's killer," a man I didn't remember seeing before said. He stirred the fire with a long stick and sparks flew.

"What makes you think that?" I asked, stepping closer to the fire and holding my gloved hands over it trying to find some warmth.

He shrugged. "'Cause she said she was going to find the SOB and shoot him herself."

I walked closer, a feeling of dread deep in my gut. "Does Lilly have a gun?"

He shook his head and shrugged. "Must if she's going to shoot someone, but I never seen one."

"Anybody? This is important. I don't want Lilly getting herself killed." The thought of Lilly having a gun terrified me.

A young girl sidled up to West. She gave him a gapped-tooth smile. To his credit he smiled back. "Do you know where Lilly went?" he asked.

"Maybe." She fluttered her lashes at him. I did my best not to smile at the pained look on his face.

"Maybe you should tell us. You don't want anything to happen to her, do you?"

She shook her head and gave him another smile. "Maybe you should take me out for coffee, and I'll tell you everything I know."

West turned his head towards me with a terrified look in his eyes.

I came to his aid. "Sorry, we're on duty and West has a girlfriend." I didn't know if he did or not, but I smiled inside at the look of relief on his face.

"Yeah, but we will go get you a coffee if you tell us what you know."

She moved closer to him. The smell of smoke and body odor clung to her clothes and West stepped back. "And a breakfast sandwich?"

He nodded. "Sure."

Everyone had gone quiet. The fire crackled and popped while we all waited to see what she'd say. Then she surprised me.

"Go talk to that Senator's wife."

Jenn. My nerve endings burned. What did Jenn have to do with this? "The senator's wife? What makes you think she knows anything?"

The girl gave West another come-hither smile. Then she looked at me. "Because me and Lils went over to McDonald's this morning and she picked Lils up in that fancy car of hers. That's why."

Chapter 32

C hapter 32

I thanked the girl and West and I ran to the coffee shop to buy coffee for everyone. Then we hit McDonald's for breakfast sandwiches. We delivered them and took off. I called Jenn on the way to her house. I hadn't talked to her since the fiasco in Germany when she'd tried to ruin my trip with Bella and led us a song and dance across Cologne looking for her.

She didn't answer. I left a message. "Jenn, what's going on? Why do you have Lilly Larson with you? Call me."

West had been quiet the whole time we'd been in the vehicle. After we left the gathering under the bridge he said, "Who is the senator's wife?"

"Jennifer Lockwood. I can't imagine why she'd be with Lilly. It's not like her to be charitable."

"Maybe Lilly knows something that Jennifer doesn't want known."

Out of the mouth of babes, I thought. If Ray had been screwing around with Lilly, Jenn would want to keep it quiet. She'd do anything to protect his reputation. I couldn't imagine the fastidious Ray Lockwood wanting Lilly Larson. But Lilly must have skills that drew men to her like flies to an outhouse, because it sounded like she'd been with a lot of men. Had she been with Mitch? The thought of the two of them made me gag. I held my hand up to my mouth and pretended to cough.

"Possibly. I can't imagine any other reason she'd pick Lilly up." I drummed my gloved fingers on the steering wheel. "Where would she take her?"

"Do you have a number for the Senator? Maybe he knows."

Why hadn't I thought of that? I went through my contacts until I found Ray's number. He, of course, didn't answer, so I left him a message to call me. I hadn't really expected him to answer. Jenn told me the man never answered his phone. Just let it go to voicemail in case he didn't want to talk to the caller. "We'll head over to their house."

West nodded, and I turned the car towards the West side of the valley. Jenn and Ray lived at the top of Riordan Hill Drive, with a view that was to die for. Jenn had almost lost her view, plus her senator husband and most of his money, when she'd had an affair with Mitch. But she finally talked Ray around, and they were still together.

Mitch and I weren't that lucky. If you wanted to call it luck. Since I couldn't decide if I wanted a divorce or wanted to try again. That wasn't fair to Mitch, but how fair had he been to me? I needed to decide. I thought I'd made up my mind, but I was having trouble with the finality of the divorce. Maybe I just needed to bite the bullet and file.

Luckily, Riordan Hill had been plowed, and we made it up in the county SUV with no problems. I heard West take a sharp breath when he saw the house. It was dark grey with rock half-way up the walls. The front was all glass and looked out over the valley. I had serious house-envy every time I came up here.

"Gorgeous, huh?" I said, looking up at the enormous structure. Six-thousand square feet of architectural beauty.

"You might say that. Are these people rich, or what?"

I nodded. "Yeah, old money. Ray's family owned a lot of land in the valley among other things." I parked, and we got out and went to the front door. I rang the bell and we waited.

"Doesn't look like anyone's home," West said, stepping back and looking up at the tall windows.

"It would be hard to tell in this house. They could go weeks without going into every room." I rang the bell again. Nothing. "Let's go around back and see if their cars are in the garage."

We walked around the outside of the house to the back and the five-car garage. I went up to the side door and peeked in the window. I knew they had a motorhome they never used, a Mercedes sports car they didn't use in the winter, Ray had a pickup and each of them had a Mercedes Sedan. There were two open spots.

"Dang. Looks like they're not here." I tried Jenn's number again, but it went to voicemail. I hated to do it. I'd promised myself I wouldn't talk to Mitch about Jenn again, but maybe he knew something. I called his cell.

Mitch picked up. "Liz?"

I filled him in on what we'd learned from the girl under the bridge. "West and I are at Jenn's house. No one's home. Do you have any idea where she'd take Lilly?"

"No. I can't imagine Jenn taking Lilly anywhere. Did you try Ray's cell?"

"Yes. He doesn't answer either." Why couldn't one of them answer? They were annoying me.

Mitch swore. "I don't have any idea what Jenn's up to. Ray may be in Salem. Hopefully, one of them will call you back."

"Okay, we'll go back to the office." I didn't know what else to do and maybe Garcia had found information on Willow Evans.

"Good. I'm calling a meeting at eleven this morning. We need to regroup and see where everyone is on the investigation."

Back at the office, we all met in the conference room. Mitch asked for updates. Most of us had nothing except more questions. Garcia told everyone about the jewelry that was found at both murder sites.

"So, this guy is a serial murderer?" asked West.

Mitch frowned. "More than one murder, West."

West blushed and I felt sorry for him. He was so young.

"I need you to be diligent in your inquiries. I don't like this jewelry thing. And if the FBI gets wind of it, we'll lose our investigation. They'll be in here like bees on a hive."

He looked at Garcia, then at me. "Are you sure the child's mother knew nothing?"

"She didn't seem to. Her little girl knew more than she did," I answered, and Garcia nodded her agreement.

Mitch shook his head and rubbed the back of his neck. "I really don't like this."

"And there's also the missing teddy bear," I said. The room buzzed with electricity, as people leaned forward and took more notice.

He looked up at me. "Yes, the teddy bear. Tell everyone." He made a sweeping gesture with his arm.

"The little girl said someone also stole her teddy bear."

The room grew silent, and everyone looked at Mitch. I knew what they were thinking. It was the same thing as I thought. He was planning at least one more murder.

Someone in the back of the room spoke up, "That could mean he's planning another killing."

Mitch nodded. "That's what we're afraid of. We've got to find this SOB." He turned to Garcia. "Did you find anything in your search?"

Garcia shook her head. "Not really. I looked at both of their Facebook accounts, Instagram, and Snap Chat. There were a couple of pictures on Renetta's social media with Willow in them. Amy was there, too, so it looked like maybe they all hung out together a few times. Willow didn't post often, and there wasn't any mention of Renetta that I could find. No pictures of her or Amy."

Mitch looked up. "No one found Renetta's laptop?"

Most everyone shook their heads.

"Maybe the killer got rid of it," I said. "Since Garcia was able to bring up her social media through her phone, I doubt there's much else on there."

"Okay, keep digging. You may find something yet." He turned to Enrique. "Do you want to tell everyone what we found out today?"

"Sure." Enrique grinned. "Mitch and I found Willow Evans' sister. She gave us an earful about Amy Bryne and her sister's relationship with her. It turns out that Amy and Willow have been dating for some time. Amy wanted to move in with Willow, but according to the sister, Becka Phillips, Willow didn't like children. She told Amy that she didn't want to raise her kids, so she'd have to make other arrangements for them if she wanted a long-term relationship with Willow."

"What arrangements did she make?" I asked. "She told Garcia and me that they were with her ex's stepmom. Was the stepmom going to raise them?"

Enrique shook his head. "Becka didn't know what they'd finally agreed on. She thought Amy's ex had them. She was really upset about her sister's death, but we could tell she wasn't happy with the way her sister felt about the children."

Mitch nodded. "Probably because she had about ten of her own."

"Maybe that's why Willow didn't want any," Williams said, and everyone chuckled. Ten children could be a little overwhelming.

"What about Connolly? Have you heard anything from her lately?" Garcia asked Mitch, changing the subject.

He took a deep breath. "Still in the hospital. Still won't come clean about the boyfriend." He rubbed the back of his neck. "Does anyone here know who she was dating?"

No one admitted they knew, and I couldn't help but wonder if someone knew and didn't want to say. I looked at Williams. He was the only one Connolly had a friendship with within the department. He sat with his head down, doodling on a piece of paper.

"Do you think it was her boyfriend who was shooting at her?" Garcia asked.

Mitch shrugged. "I don't know. Williams didn't find the shooter."

Williams sat up. "I asked the neighbors, and no one will admit they saw or heard anything except the sirens when Mitch arrived."

"They didn't hear the gun shots?" Mitch asked.

Williams tugged on his earlobe. I'd noticed he did that when asked a question he didn't want to answer. "They said they did not. There were only two neighbors at home when it happened. Both are elderly. One was taking a nap and the other had the TV up so high, he couldn't hear me ringing the doorbell."

"Have you talked to Connolly?" Mitch asked him.

Williams shrugged. "A couple of times."

Mitch crossed his arms over his chest and narrowed his eyes. "Did she give you any idea what's going on with her?"

"I don't think she knows who shot at her. She went home and someone was there. She was looking in the garage when he or she fired at her. That's when she ran out of the house and called you." Williams shrugged as if to say that's all he knew.

"Okay, stay on it. I want to find that shooter ASAP. Everyone else stay on the murder investigation. We'll meet back here tomorrow at the same time." Mitch pushed people out of his way to get to me. I don't remember a time in our marriage when he was that anxious to talk to me. Maybe in the early years, but I doubted it.

"Liz, I need to talk to you. Alone."

My heart sank. Not now, I thought. Please just let us get this murder solved. Then we can deal with our personal lives. But of course, I didn't say that. I followed him to his office and shut the door.

Chapter 33

Chapter 33—Connolly

They'd given Connolly oxycodone for the pain, and she'd been asleep for a while when she startled and sat up in bed. The pain grabbed her, and she took a deep breath. She reached for the button to push for more pain meds, but it wasn't on the bed beside her.

She felt around. It was dark in the room, and she wondered if the PCA pump had fallen off the bed. The call button for the nurse was gone too. How was she going to get a nurse to give her more meds? She eased back into a horizontal position and closed her eyes, willing the pain away.

That's when she felt something. A presence in the room. She opened her eyes and struggled to get up. A hard hand on her shoulder kept her in place. She looked up. Without her glasses, she couldn't make out his features, but it looked like her boyfriend.

A warmth spread through her chest that he was there. She said his name and he leaned over. "You're here."

"What's going on, Megan? I went by your house and the sheriff was there. I followed the ambulance here."

She tried raising up again, but he held her in place. "Why didn't you say something? You could've come with me."

He shook his head. "I'd had too much to drink. Didn't want to get a DUI."

"Where were you all day?" She frowned. "You didn't come back to your house, so I went home. Then someone shot at me." She tried to sit up again, but the pain was too intense. She laid back down.

"I don't know who was shooting at you," he whispered. "I'm trying to find out."

"No, you might get hurt."

"You've got to keep our relationship quiet, Megan. Promise me you won't tell anyone that we're involved. My wife will take my kids from me if she thinks I've already found someone else."

Megan frowned. "She can't expect you not to date. You've been single for a while."

"Just promise me that you won't say anything. Promise?" His voice got deeper and the hand on her shoulder squeezed until Megan winced.

"Of course, if that's what you want. It's nobody's business anyway." She struggled to see his face.

He bent down and picked something up off the floor. "Here's the nurse's button. I can tell you're in pain." He hit the button. "Someone will be right in. Take care of yourself, Megan."

"But...when will I see you again?"

"Soon."

Megan watched him leave and then laid back and closed her eyes. They'd only been dating for a couple months, but he was adamant that she didn't tell anyone. It was starting to get on her nerves. Why have a boyfriend if she couldn't tell people or be seen with him? She knew he'd been in a brutal custody battle with his ex, but this was getting ridiculous.

The nurse came in and gave her more oxycodone. While she waited for it to take effect, she thought about her boyfriend and their relationship. What wasn't he telling her? Why did he want to keep them a secret? It was driving her nuts. She knew it was important that she find out what it was. She needed to make a note for herself, but she was having trouble staying awake. She reached for her cell phone to call Mitch, but it needed to be charged. It wasn't long after that she was asleep.

Chapter 34

Mitch sat at his desk and rubbed the back of his neck. "Have you heard from Bella today?"

My heart sank. What was our daughter up to? I stood near the door, my arms crossed in front of me. "No, why?"

"She's in Portland. She wants me to drive down and pick her up." He narrowed his eyes. "I wish she'd stayed at school."

"Crap." I pulled out the chair in front of his desk and sank into it. "Why won't that girl listen? This is the last place she needs to be."

He nodded. "I'm tempted to tell her to turn around and go back to school, but I wouldn't put it past her to come home anyway."

"No, I wouldn't either." I bit a hangnail on my thumb. "She's so stubborn." Just like her father.

"I wonder where she gets that?" Mitch grinned at me.

"You." I couldn't hold a candle to him when it came to being stubborn.

Apparently, Mitch didn't agree. "Ha. And you aren't stubborn?"

"Nope." It was like the old days, sparring with him. But we had a serious issue and I sobered up. "What are we going to do?"

"I guess one of us will have to go get her. She said she could get an Uber, but I don't want her riding through that gorge with just anybody."

I nodded. "Now we have to figure out how to keep her safe and solve this crime. There are so many suspects, it's making my head swim."

Mitch stood. "I'll go. I don't want both of you girls stuck in the gorge. It will only take me a couple hours to drive to Portland and back. Why don't you go home and get some rest? Who knows what tomorrow might bring?" He walked around the desk and held out his hand to help me up.

I jumped out of the chair without his help and headed to the door. "Is Bella staying with you?"

Mitch frowned. "Do you want her to? I assumed she'd spend part of the time with me and part with you. We're both so busy with these murders, but I'm sure she has friends who are still in town."

"How long does she plan to be home?" I felt a little miffed that she'd called her dad and not me, but Bella knew I'd tell her to stay in school and she had Mitch wrapped around her little finger.

Mitch opened the door and stood back for me to walk out. "Probably a couple of weeks. She said she can finish her classes online, so she won't miss out on this semester."

"Well, that's good. But I wish she'd stayed in Corvallis until we find the killer."

"Me, too."

We walked out to the main room. The night receptionist was clocking in, and she raised her hand in greeting.

"I'm going to head out. I'll call you when we get back to town." Mitch grabbed his coat off the coat rack and walked out.

I grabbed mine and walked out to my Jeep. My mind was busy with thoughts of Renetta and Willow's murder and Bella coming home. I hoped I could talk her into staying with her dad. I didn't want her at my house. What if the person I'd run off came back? I'd have to make sure she stayed with Mitch. Was it the same person that shot at Connolly?

It had gotten dark while I was at the office and I made my way to the parking lot where I'd left my Jeep, carefully trying to avoid the ice. The drive home was easier than it had been for the last few days. We hadn't had a lot of new snow, and the roads were all plowed. I drove through the heights, out Tucker Road to Odell Highway and home.

The outside lights weren't on when I drove in and hit the garage door opener. I pulled the Jeep into the garage, turned it off and headed for the house. The motion lights didn't come on as I approached the front door and I frowned, wondering why they weren't turning on. I touched the flashlight on my phone and moved the light around the yard. Everything looked okay, but I felt the small hairs on my neck stand up. Where was Bailey?

I didn't hear her welcoming barks from inside the house. I called Travis. His phone rang several times and went to voicemail. "This is Travis. Leave me a message."

"It's Liz. Call me when you get this."

What's going on? I wondered as I took my gun out and held it in front of me. This didn't feel right. Travis had been there because there was a path shoveled to the front door, but it had been a while because the path had some snow covering it. The house was dark. Everything in me told me to stay outside. Call for reinforcements. Wouldn't my colleagues laugh if I called in that I was frightened to go into my own house? I could just imagine what Connolly would say.

I walked to the front door. My arms and legs felt jittery. I took a deep breath and reached for the doorknob. It turned easily in my hand. My heart thundered. Someone had been here. Had Mitch come by before he went to get Bella? But no, we'd left at the same time. Had

Travis been here and forgot to lock the door? But wouldn't he have left Bailey?

I reached into the kitchen and flipped on the light. Everything looked normal. "Who's in there?" I called out. "Come out with your hands up."

Nothing. I stepped further into the house. I felt someone there. I felt their presence. "Come out now, or I'll shoot the second I see you."

Nothing stirred inside the house. I made my way in with my gun held out in front of me. I was out here on this farm alone. José lived close, but not close enough. I went through the house room by room not finding anyone. I took a deep breath and let it out, thankful no one was in my house, but I knew someone had been there. Why? Were they just trying to scare me?

I had turned every light on in the house and I went back through turning them off. As I got to the bedroom that Bella used when she was here, something caught my eye that I hadn't noticed when I checked out the room the first time. I walked in and over to the bed. It was exactly like it was the last time I'd seen it except for a pink teddy bear propped up against the pillows. My heart skipped a beat. I didn't remember Bella leaving a pink teddy bear last time she was home. I looked closer and saw a piece of paper tucked underneath the bear's arm.

I pulled it out and cried out when I read the message. **Drop the investigation or your little girl is dead.**

Chapter 35

C hapter 35

Bella!

I hit Mitch's number on my phone. It rang once and he answered. "Hey Liz, I'm about halfway to Portland. I'll grab Bella and be back in Hood River in a couple of hours."

"Mitch, you've got to convince Bella to go back to school. She can't come here. Someone is threatening her." My words came out in a rush. My heart pounded like thunder.

"Slow down. What's going on?" His voice was sharp, and I know he heard the fear in mine.

"She can't come back here. Someone's been in my house." I felt eyes on me and turned to the large kitchen window. Was there someone out there watching me? I made sure the door was locked, the alarm on and went into the living room where the blinds were pulled, and no one could see in.

"Get out now," Mitch said. "Go to Enrique's and stay there until I can get back to town."

"You don't understand," I cried. "He's been here. He knows about Bella!" I knew I was losing it. I glanced around wildly.

"How do you know he's been there?"

"I found a note and a teddy bear on the bed in Bella's room."

"A teddy bear? What color?"

My heart skipped a beat. "Pink."

"Shit. Please, Lizzy. Go back to town. Stay with Enrique and Jolene. I'll call and tell them you're coming. I'm sure the killer is long gone, but I want you out of there."

From somewhere deep within me, I pulled myself back from the edge of insanity. "No. I'm okay. I need to find him. Just protect our daughter."

"You know I will. But be reasonable. Get out of there now."

"I'll be fine. Mitch, you need to drive Bella back to Corvallis." I gritted my teeth and made fists out of both hands. I was not going to let anyone hurt my daughter.

There was silence for a couple moments. "If he knows who she is, he knows where she goes to school."

"Oh, no." My heart sank. I hadn't thought of that. "What are we going to do?"

"We're going to find this SOB and keep a close eye on Bella. Now, please Liz, get out of there. Call me when you're at Enrique's."

I told Mitch I'd call Enrique and clicked off my phone. Then I went through my house, room by room, with my gun held out in front of me and my heart beating a staccato in my chest. I eased into the bedrooms and bathrooms. Checked out the upstairs. Nothing else seemed to be touched. But how was he getting in without setting off the alarm?

I checked the back door, and it was locked. Then I went back to the front door and checked the lock on it. It had been tampered with. I called Enrique and filled him in.

"I'll grab an evidence kit and be right there," he said. "We'll see if he left any prints."

I had no more than hung up when lights flashed against the kitchen window. I went to look and saw Travis stopping in front of my house.

He got out and let Bailey out. I turned off the alarm and opened the door. "Hey, good, you're home," he said, leading Bailey up the walk. "I'm sorry I'm late bringing Bailey home, but I had unexpected company and she stayed for dinner."

She? Travis had a date? My heart skittered. I didn't have any right to be upset by him dating. *But who was this chick? And why was she inviting herself to dinner?*

"That's okay. I'm kind of glad you were late. I've had a break-in."

Travis stopped in front of me and looked towards the house then back at me. "A break-in? Were you robbed? What's going on?"

Bailey bounded over and barked. I reached down to pet her. "No. I haven't said anything, but someone has been here before. I've seen footprints in the snow the last couple of nights. I chased them away last night and tonight when I got home, the motion lights were turned off and the front door unlocked."

"And you didn't tell anyone? This is insane, Liz." He strode towards the house with Bailey and I following him.

Travis walked to the door and examined it. He shook his head. "Do you have any idea what they were after? Do you think someone was trying to scare you?"

"Yeah, I know they were."

His eyes blazed. "Mitch. He thinks if he scares you, you'll go back to him."

"No." I put my hand up to stop him from saying more. "It wasn't Mitch. I'm pretty sure it's the killer. He left a note." I shivered and handed him the baggy with the note.

Travis took the note, looked at it, said a few choice words, then pulled me towards him and wrapped his arms around me. "You're freezing. Let's go in and have coffee and you can tell me everything. I feel like I've really been out of the loop lately."

"It's not your fault." I stepped past him into my kitchen and shut the door after he came in. Bailey went to her water dish and lapped up the water, then looked at me expectantly. "I think she's hungry." I went to the cupboard where I keep her food and got the bag out, filling her bowl.   "It's my fault. I've been trying to stay away and give you some space."

I put the coffee on and then put my arms around him. "I'm sorry. I know you've been more than patient. I just...I'm not..."

He held me close and kissed the top of my head. "You're not ready. I know that. I just wonder if you'll ever be."

I heard the sadness in his voice and wished I could convince him or myself that he's the one I want. I loved the feel of his arms around me. Travis is the most gorgeous man. Tall, dark, handsome with dark brown eyes I could drown in. And he'd made it clear that he wanted me. Why couldn't I embrace that? Why was I so conflicted about him and about Mitch? It was hard to throw away twenty-five years of marriage. Even when you had every reason to. "So, who was your company?"

Travis chuckled. "Feeling a little jealous?"

"Maybe." I leaned back into his arms and looked at him. "You might as well say. Bailey will tell me after you go home."

He laughed. "Just an old school friend. She grew up here. She's visiting her parents, and her husband is coming next week."

"She's married?" I squeaked and he nodded.

Relief coursed through me. I didn't want Travis to have a girl-friend. That should tell me something. It must've been obvious to him because he grinned, and his eyes sparkled. He pulled me closer and touched his lips to mine. He was hesitant, giving me room to back away if I wanted, but I didn't want that. I wanted to feel his closeness. I leaned into the kiss, and he moved his lips from mine and looked at me for a second, then his lips took mine in a kiss so intense I thought I might faint.

Lights flashed and I thought it was from the electricity we generated, but Travis raised his head and said, "Looks like the calvary has arrived."

I turned out of his arms and saw Enrique stepping out of his pickup.

Enrique's grin covered his face. "Looks like I interrupted something." He held up the evidence kit. "Just carry on. I'll dust for fingerprints."

My mouth curved into a smile. I had wondered how my friend would feel if I divorced Mitch, now I knew. "It's the front door," I said, matching his strides.

Travis took Bailey inside while Enrique dusted for prints, and I watched him. "Tell me everything," he said.

"About Travis?"

"No, about the break-in. You can tell Jo about Travis. I'm sure she'll want to hear the mushy stuff." He chuckled and shook his head. "Kind of telling that your first thought was Travis, not the perp."

He was right and I gave him a goofy smile. Then I told him what had been going on.

"Why didn't you say something?" He put the black powder on the doorknob.

I shrugged. "I just thought it was someone trying to scare me. I didn't think about it being the killer." My insides quaked. How could I have been so dumb?

He finished what he was doing and put the kit away. "Hmm, no prints. Looks like he wore gloves. Do you want me to try and get prints somewhere else?"

I took gloves out of my pocket and put them on. "The paper he wrote the message on."

Enrique followed me back into the kitchen and I picked up the evidence bags with the bear and note in them and handed them to him.

"I'll send it to the lab and see if we get any matches. Hopefully, it won't take them two months to get back to us." He put the two baggies in his coat pocket.

Travis and Bailey came back into the kitchen and Travis made coffee. "Want a cup?" he asked Enrique.

"No, I'll take these back to the office. I take it you're going to stay around for a while?" He gave Travis a sharp look.

Travis put the coffee beans away. "Yes."

Enrique nodded. "Good. Come see Jonathan, Liz. He's so amazing."

"I will." I followed him to the door. He stepped out, then turned back to me. "You know that Jo and I only want what's best for you, don't you?"

I smiled. "Of course I do."

He reached over and gave my arm a squeeze. "Stay safe." Then he took off for his pickup.

Travis handed me a mug of coffee when I went back into the kitchen. "Here you go. Are you hungry? You don't have much in your fridge, but I could make you an omelet and toast."

My stomach rumbled. "That sounds great. But I can make it."

"Sit." He motioned to the table with a spatula he'd just pulled from the utensil drawer.

I sat and watched him cook. Mitch had never been good in the kitchen. Travis was a great cook and I loved watching him. Bailey gobbled down her food, then came to lay down next to my chair.

"I don't like you staying here alone," Travis said. He slid the omelet onto a plate, added a piece of buttered toast and placed it in front of me. "I know what you're going to say."

"What am I going to say?" I took a bite of the warm eggs and swallowed.

He poured himself a cup of coffee and sat at the table next to me. "That you're a detective and you can handle any bad guy that comes around and tries to kill you."

I reached over and took his hand. "I know you're worried. I am, too. But I can't let this jerk win. I have to take him down. I have too much at stake. And maybe the only way to do that is to make him think he can get to me."

Chapter 36

Chapter 36

Travis grabbed my hand. "Liz, please, listen to me. You have to be careful. I need you. Bella needs you."

I gripped his hand. "I'm not going to do anything stupid, Travis. But I am going to do my job. If this monster thinks he can hurt my little girl, he has another think coming." I finished my dinner, got up and put my dishes in the dishwasher.

Travis watched me, a worried frown between his eyes. It was an awkward moment between us. I knew we needed to talk about what had happened earlier, but I couldn't concentrate on my love life when my daughter was in danger. I think Travis knew that. He didn't say anything, just looked at me.

My phone rang. I took it out of my pocket and looked at it. Jenn. I raised my eyebrows and showed Travis the phone. "I need to take this."

He nodded.

I hit the on button. Jenn's excited voice broke in on my greeting. "I'm on my way to your house. I've got Lilly Larson with me. You've got to do something with her, Liz. She's driving me insane."

"What are you talking about? Why is Lilly with you?"

"It's a long story. I'll be there in fifteen minutes." She hung up.

"What's that all about?" Travis asked.

I filled him in as best I could. "We've been trying to find Lilly all day. I have no idea why she's with Jenn, but I guess we'll find out." I poured us each another cup of coffee. "I'm going to change out of my work clothes. Will you stay?"

Travis looked surprised. "Of course, I'm staying. You aren't getting rid of me."

I smiled, touched his lips with my finger, heard his intake of breath and moved away just before he grabbed my waist. "I'll be right back."

Travis's eyes were dark with desire, and it took everything in me to walk away. My heart was beating fast. My breath was lodged in my throat, and I realized during all that was going on how much this man was starting to mean to me.

Not now, Liz, I told myself as I went into my bedroom and closed the door.

By the time I changed into jeans and a coral sweatshirt, Jenn was pulling into my drive. Travis stood looking out the kitchen window. His broad back and big shoulders caught my attention, then I blinked and walked over next to him. "Well, this should be interesting."

Travis was aware of my history with Jenn. He chuckled.

Jenn came towards the house with her hand on Lilly's arm, pulling her along. Lilly looked around like she was memorizing the place which sent a skitter of uneasiness through me. Was she casing the joint? But no, apparently, she had more money than she knew what to do with.

I went to the door and opened it, letting them in along with a burst of cold air. Jenn shivered. "It's freaking cold out there." She glanced at Travis and frowned. "Hey Travis. What are you doing here?"

It was none of her business and neither of us answered. She smirked. Then in true Jenn fashion she said, "Ray wanted me to pick up Lilly this morning and keep her with me." She rolled her eyes. "The man doesn't understand what he's asking of me. I'm not a cop. Why would he think I could protect her?"

"Protect her from what?" I asked.

Lilly shook off Jenn's hand, looked around, went to the coffee pot and helped herself to a cup of coffee. "Ya got creamer?"

Jenn rolled her eyes. "I don't know. I thought maybe you would. I can't seem to find Mitch. Do you know where he is?"

I nodded. "He went to Portland to get Bella." I watched as Lilly rooted around in my refrigerator. She found what she wanted and poured it into her mug. I cringed at how dirty her hands were.

"Bella's coming home?" Jenn frowned.

"Yes. Where's Ray and what did he say when he asked you to pick up Lilly?" This was crazy. I couldn't think of a reason why Ray would want his wife to pick up Lilly Larson. Unless he knew about Lilly's family. If he thought there was money in it, he would do anything and so would Jenn.

Jenn took her coat off and put it over the back of a chair. She looked at Lilly who was drinking her coffee. "He said, go to the bridge, pick up Lilly Larson and keep her with you until I call you." She shook her head. "So, I did. But Ray hasn't called all day. I've called and texted him numerous times and he hasn't answered, and I can't keep her there overnight. She'd steal me blind."

Lilly looked up and gave Jenn a gapped-tooth smile. "Ya got any cookies?" she asked me.

I opened a drawer that I kept candy bars in and tossed her a Snickers bar. "No, but this might help." The last thing I wanted was her dirty fingers in my cookie jar. Luckily, I didn't have cookies, so it wasn't a problem.

She caught it and opened it, tossing the wrapper on the counter.

Jenn grabbed it and put it in the trash. "This has been going on all day. She has no manners." Jenn was a clean freak. She never had a piece of dust in her house, let alone trash lying around.

Lilly laughed. "Sure, I do."

I pulled out a chair and motioned for Lilly to sit down. She did and I sat next to her. Jenn acted like she was leaving, and I pointed to a chair. "Oh no, you aren't leaving her with me. We need to find Ray and see what this is all about." I turned to Lilly. "Do you know why Ray wanted Jenn to pick you up?"

Lilly shrugged. "Probably wanted sex. Wants it all the time. That thing there is probably cold as a fish." She pointed a dirty finger at Jenn.

Jenn narrowed her eyes. "You need to shut up about that or I'm going to let you walk back to town."

"Just tellin' you what you hubby's been up to." Lilly cackled.

Jenn lunged for Lilly, but Travis caught her and kept her from swinging at the other woman. "She's just trying to upset you."

Jenn's eyes blazed. She grabbed her phone out of her huge Coach bag and hit the on button. "I'm calling Ray again and if he doesn't answer I'm calling Salem. I'm sick of this whore." She glared at Lilly who stuck her tongue out at her.

I wanted to laugh. I glanced at Travis and realized his eyes were full of laughter.

"Ray, dammit, answer your phone or you're going to be sorry." Jenn jabbed a finger on the phone. "Where could he be? This is driving me crazy." She looked up at me. "You call him. Maybe he'll answer for you."

Lilly dug into her coat and came out with a phone. "I'll call. He'll answer for me." She hit a number on her screen and Jenn's breath came out in a hiss. I worried what would happen to Ray if he answered, but he didn't. "Hmm," Lilly said, looking at her phone. "He usually answers." She looked up at Travis, giving him a knowing smile. "I've got some time if you're interested. Big, handsome guy like you, I'll give you a good price."

"No thanks." Travis raised his hands. "I'm good."

"I'll just bet you are, honey." She winked at him.

"Lilly. Stop it," I said. "You aren't soliciting men in my home." Not that I thought she had a chance with Travis, but I had to stop her from driving us all crazy.

Travis looked at me and I smiled. He shook his head.

"See what I've had to put up with all day? This is ridiculous." Jenn hauled her phone out again, hit the button to call Ray and held the phone up to her ear.

This time Ray answered.

"Where are you? I did what you asked, and I've put up with this nasty woman and her comments long enough," Jenn yelled into the phone. Ray said something I couldn't hear, and she said, "You'd better get here soon or I'm leaving her with Liz."

"Oh, no you aren't," I said, loud enough for Ray to hear.

Lilly got up and went to my candy drawer and pulled out another candy bar.

Jenn sank into one of my kitchen chairs, her phone still up to her ear. "You've got to be kidding me," she said, staring at Lilly who grinned at her, showing chocolate covered teeth. "Well, that's just great, but I'm not keeping this flea bag overnight. You need to get your ass home and..." She blinked several times. "He hung up on me. That rat b..."

"What's going on?" I interrupted her tirade.

Jenn pointed at Lilly. "She's an heiress. Did you know that?"

I nodded. "But why is Ray involved?"

"His family and the Abbott family are related somehow. Her attorney," she pointed her phone at Lilly, "Wants her kept safe until they can get bodyguards, or the freakin' FBI, or someone here to protect her."

"Why are they so worried? She's been here for years."

"Because I plan to give my inheritance away. All five-hundred million of it," Lilly said, grinning at Jenn. Jenn gasped.

Chapter 37

Chapter 37—Mitch

Mitch drove through the gorge feeling like he needed to hurry, and he couldn't. The roads were plowed, but they were slick, and he wanted to take his time even though a part of him was urging him to drive faster. Bella sat beside him, talking about school, her new boyfriend, and Renetta. Mitch had a tough time concentrating on her words.

His gut told him that something was going to happen to Liz. He had to get home. His phone beeped and he glanced at it, saw it was Jenn and switched it off.

"Don't want to talk to her?" Bella asked.

"Not now."

"So, do you plan to marry Jenn after you and Mom divorce?"

Mitch heard the strain in her voice and cringed. Bella didn't hate him for what he'd done, but she was mad at him. He didn't blame her. If she and Liz would just give him another chance. It really wasn't his fault. Jenn had come on to him, not the other way around. "No, I'm not going to marry Jenn. She was a huge mistake, Bella, and I hate it that I hurt you and your mom. I'll do anything to make things right with your mom. I love her."

"Even if it means letting her go?" she asked softly.

Mitch felt a pain hit his chest. He tightened his grip on the steering wheel. Could he do it? Could he let Liz go? What if he didn't have a choice? He felt tears running down his face and he knew he was really losing her. He nodded and Bella reached over and rubbed his shoulder. She had tears in her eyes too.

When his phone rang again, Mitch saw it was Liz and answered. "Hey Liz, we're on 184. The freeway has been plowed. We should be back in town in under an hour."

"You need to come to my house, Mitch. We have a situation."

He could hear the strain in her voice and his stomach dropped. "What's going on?"

Liz filled him in. "I don't know what to do with Lilly for the night. She's not safe with Jenn and she's not safe here with me."

"How about putting her in a holding cell until her bodyguards show up?" Lilly would throw a fit, but Mitch didn't really care. He had to keep her safe and if putting her into a holding cell with a guard on duty was the only way to do that, he'd do it.

"That's actually a great idea. She would be safe there."

He heard the relief in Liz's voice and a smile tugged at his lips. Finally, he'd said something that she liked. "Do you want me to meet you at the office?" Mitch asked.

"I'll let you know."

"We'll be there as soon as possible." Mitch's spirits rose. He loved working with Liz, bouncing ideas off her, helping her in any way he could. And it was good for Bella to see that he was trying.

"Okay."

"Hi Mama." Bella said. "I can't wait to see you."

"Hey, babe. I can't wait to see you either." Liz's voice softened. "Are there many people on the roads?"

"Not really," Mitch said. "We're taking it slow. So are most of the other drivers."

"Why don't you head to my house? We're having a party. We can decide what to do with Lilly after you get here."

Mitch liked that idea. "We'll be there soon."

Chapter 38

Chapter 38—Liz

Jenn stirred and Travis helped her into a chair and got her some water. Her face was white and her breathing fast. I knew she couldn't, in her deepest imagination, understand Lilly giving all that money away. I couldn't either.

I looked at Lilly. "Why would you give your inheritance away? Wouldn't it be nice to have a house and money in the bank?"

Lilly shrugged. "Too much trouble and I don't want nothin' to do with that money. I know where it came from." She sat back in the chair and crossed her arms, a mutinous look on her face.

I knew there had to be a story there, but Lilly shut her mouth and wouldn't say anything more about it even though Jenn and I both tried to get her to tell us.

What had gone wrong in her family? Why had she ended up being homeless? She obviously had enough money to buy any house she wanted. It didn't make sense.

"What does Ray want you to do with her?" I asked Jenn.

Jenn ran a hand through her long hair. "He says he'll be here in about fifteen minutes, and he wants me to wait until he gets here. For my money, I'd say put her in jail and let her spend her time there until she decides to go back to Portland and face the music."

"What music?"

Jenn shrugged. "Her family. Whatever went wrong there must be her fault."

"Not hardly," Lilly said. Then she cackled. "You should've seen your face when you passed out. Youse funnier than..."

"Lilly, stop it," I said, pointing my finger at her. "You're making this harder for everyone."

She shrugged. "I don't give a shit." She sank back against her chair and slurped her coffee.

I knew that was true. But even though a small, mean part of me was happy to see Jenn squirm, I didn't want a cat fight to erupt in my kitchen.

I put my phone down. "I guess we wait for reinforcements."

"What ya got to eat in this place besides candy bars?" Lilly asked. "I'm starving. All that skinny ass eats is salad." She pointed to Jenn and scrunched up her face at the thought of salad.

"I'll make you a grilled cheese sandwich," Travis offered. He looked at me. "Would you like one?"

I shook my head. "No thanks. I'm good."

While Travis made Lilly a sandwich, the rest of us sat waiting for Mitch or Ray to appear. I thought about what had been going on. The murders, someone stalking me, Lilly's inheritance. Was it all connected? I didn't see how, but it was strange that it had all happened at the same time. A coincidence, or some strange plot thought out by an expert manipulator. I didn't know and it was driving me crazy.

A car drove down the driveway towards the house and I got up to see who it was. Travis glanced over from his spot by the stove. He walked over. "Who is it?"

"It looks like Ray's white Ford pickup."

Jenn jumped up from the table and stood beside me, looking out. "Yes, thank God! He can take care of her now. I'm going home." She grabbed her coat and purse and headed out to meet Ray.

Travis raised his eyebrows. "She's a real piece of work."

"Tell me about it." I wasn't sure why Jenn and I had remained friends after high school. I didn't think she'd ever progressed emotionally past the twelfth grade.

We watched as Jenn greeted Ray at his truck. He shook his head at whatever she was saying, and she yelled at him. Then she got in her Mercedes SUV and headed down the drive. Ray watched her go, then came into the house.

When he got to the door, he muttered something under his breath, stamped his feet on the mat, and came in.

Lilly looked up and gave him a gapped-tooth smile. I wondered if she'd get her teeth fixed now that she'd inherited her dad's money. What had made her leave that life and become a prostitute? Maybe Ray had the answers. Lilly sure wasn't saying.

Ray looked around the kitchen. "Thanks for helping Jenn with Lilly," he said to me.

Lilly munched on her hot sandwich. For all her talk about Ray, she didn't pay any attention to him. He leaned on the counter, crossed his arms, and looked at her. "Well Lillian, are you ready to go home?"

She shrugged. "Sure."

"Back to Portland?"

She finally looked at him. "Is that old man gone?"

"Your father?"

She didn't say anything.

Ray sighed. "If you don't want the money, you can give it to charity, but you have to sign papers first. It would be easier if you'd go to Portland to the attorney's office to do that."

I heard another vehicle pull into my driveway and looked out. Mitch had pulled up. He and Bella got out and started for the house. I went to greet them.

"Bella!" I pulled her into my arms, just holding her. She hugged me and leaned back.

"What's going on? It looks like you're having a party in there." She motioned towards my kitchen.

"You won't believe it." I felt sick inside thinking of the killer threatening my daughter. I'd make Mitch stay at my house. Or Bella and I would go to his. We wouldn't leave Bella alone for a second until this creep was found.

I backed up and led the way inside. Ray's eyes iced over when he saw Mitch, but he didn't say anything. He was probably glad Jenn had left.

"We've got a situation," I told Mitch.

He stood just inside my kitchen door and nodded. "Sounds like we've got more than one."

Lilly had finished her grilled cheese sandwich and asked Travis for more coffee. She acted like there was nothing going on.

Mitch sat next to her at the table. He looked at her. "It's time we talked, Lilly."

Lilly had a pained look on her face. "What about?"

"I've got two young women dead. One is your daughter. Now I find out that you're worth millions. Is someone after you? Did they kill Renetta to get your money? Have you been threatened?"

"Just by him and that crazy witch he lives with." She pointed at Ray.

Mitch looked at Ray who rolled his eyes, then back at Lilly. "How did they threaten you?"

"We didn't threaten her. My family has been friends with her family forever. Her father made me executor of his Will. When he died, his attorney got in touch with me. He knew I was coming back to Hood River today and he asked me to pick Lilly up and keep her with me until his co-workers could get back from Pendleton to get her."

"Pendleton? The two people I talked to who spent the night at the Hood River Hotel, then headed to Pendleton for a deposition?" I asked.

Ray nodded. "Yeah, they were trying to find Lilly. When they couldn't, they went on to Pendleton. But the weather is worse up there than it is here, and they're stuck."

Mitch looked out the window. "It's snowing again."

"Great." I had a bad feeling I was going to be stuck with not only Lilly and Ray, but my ex-husband for the night. "What are you going to do with her?" I pointed to Lilly who had wandered into my living room and turned on the television.

Ray grimaced. "I know it's a lot to ask, but can she stay here tonight? I'll stay and keep an eye on her, but I can't take her home with me and I have to make sure she gets to Portland to sign those papers."

He was sure anxious for Lilly to sign away her money. I couldn't help but wonder why. I glanced up at Mitch. He nodded once and I knew he felt the same.

"Why don't we all stay? That way I can keep an eye on Lilly and Bella," Mitch said.

I started to protest, but Travis beat me to it. "Oh, I don't think that's necessary, do you?"

"You can leave," Mitch said, "But it's late and I want to make sure that everyone is safe for the night."

Travis looked at me. I smiled and he smiled back. "Well, I don't want to miss the party, so I guess I'll stay too."

Mitch didn't look happy, but that was too bad.

I pulled a pan of lasagna out of the freezer and put it in the oven to cook. Travis made a salad. Mitch and Ray went into the living room and joined Lilly. Bella stayed in the kitchen, telling us about school.

After we ate, Mitch said he'd take the first watch. I'd take the second. Ray decided to stay in the living room where Lilly had fallen asleep after dinner. Bella went to her room, and Travis and I sat in the kitchen.

"You should get some rest," he said. "You have to be up in a couple hours."

I nodded. "There's a bed upstairs. You can lay down and get a few hours of sleep."

"Okay. I will if you will."

I wondered if he meant together, and a delicious thrill raced through me. If only we didn't have a bunch of people here. I led the way up the stairs. Once we were alone, he put his arms around me. "I wish there wasn't a houseful of people here," he whispered.

I snuggled closer to his warmth. "Me, too."

He kissed me, then let me go. "Go get some sleep."

I started for the stairs, then I turned back. "Does this seem like the weirdest thing in the world, all of us being here together?"

He chuckled. "Yeah, all we need is Jenn."

"Oh, we definitely don't need her."

I went downstairs and checked on the men and Lilly. Mitch and Ray were talking quietly, and Lilly was snoring on my sofa. I went to Bella's room and knocked on her door.

She came to the door, wearing a grey sweatshirt with OSU across the top, and matching pajama pants. "This is a weird setup, Mom."

"Oh, I know. But what else were we going to do?"

She shrugged. "Don't you feel strange having Dad and Travis in the same house?" She turned back into the room and motioned me to join her.

I shut the door behind me and sat on her bed. "Yes, but I feel safer with them both here."

She frowned. "So, are you and Travis dating?"

"Would that be a bad thing?" I held my breath, waiting for her answer. Would I not date Travis if she was against it? I didn't know. I love my daughter, but she was growing up and would soon have her own life. Didn't I deserve some happiness?

She shrugged. "I mean, it would be hard on Dad, but he kind of deserves it, I guess."

I reached over and took her hand. "I'm not dating Travis to get even with your dad. In fact, Travis and I haven't dated at all."

"But you like him." She watched me carefully.

Suddenly, I knew what I'd been fighting for so long. I really did like Travis. I wanted to explore a relationship with him. I just hadn't wanted to upset Bella, so I'd kept him at arm's length. "I really do."

She smiled and hugged me. "I don't blame you. He's seriously hot."

I pulled back and looked at the sparkle in her eyes. "He is, isn't he?"

We laughed and she hugged me again. "I know you were really hurt by what Daddy did. I wanted to kill him for hurting you. But I just want you to be happy, Mom. If you like Travis, go for him."

"We'll see what happens." I stood up and ruffled her blonde hair. "First I have to find this killer and put him behind bars."

She nodded and I left her and went to my room. I set the alarm for four hours and after changing into sweats and a tee shirt, I went to bed.

When the alarm rang at four a.m., I got up and went to relieve Mitch. I figured he could sleep in my bed the rest of the night. As I walked down the hall, I heard snoring coming from the living room. I smiled, wondering if it was Ray, Mitch or Lilly.

I stepped into the room and my heart dove to my toes. Ray and Mitch were conked out, and Lilly was gone.

Chapter 39

Chapter 39

I hurried to the bathroom to see if she was there. It was empty. I climbed the stairs, thinking maybe she crawled into bed with Travis—I wouldn't be surprised at anything Lilly did—but she wasn't there.

Back downstairs I hurried into my living room and shook Mitch's shoulder. "Mitch! Lilly's gone."

He blinked and sat up in the recliner. "What? What do you mean she's gone? Did you look through the house?" He got up and stretched.

"I checked the bathrooms and upstairs. I'll go check Dad's office and Bella's room, but I don't think she's here." Some sixth sense that I only got once in a blue moon told me that she had taken off.

Mitch and I went through the house, but she wasn't there. Ray heard us and got up, meeting us in the kitchen. "What's going on?"

"Lilly's missing." The crazy woman had probably called someone to come get her after we were all asleep. She had a serious screw loose somewhere.

"Crap. Where would she go in this weather?" He looked out the window at the snow and shook his head. "I'm sorry I offered to keep an eye on her. She's a mess."

Travis came down the stairs, rubbing his eyes, his shirt unbuttoned. "What's going on?"

"Lilly took off." I watched him button his shirt and my fingers tingled to unbutton it.

He frowned. "How did she get away without someone hearing her?"

Mitch and Ray looked at each other. "I thought she was sound asleep. I drifted off and the next thing I knew, Liz was waking me up to say she was gone," Mitch said.

Ray nodded.

I dragged my thoughts back from Travis' naked chest and did an eye roll. "Well, I guess you guys need to find her."

"Where would she go?" Ray asked. "She doesn't have a car."

Mitch and I stared at each other, then ran for the door. Had Lilly taken one of our cars? But they were all there. We both got our shoes on and grabbed our coats.

"We'd better have a look around in case she's out there in a snowbank," Mitch said.

Ray nodded and went to the counter to make coffee. Travis followed us outside.

The snow had quit again sometime in the night. We followed Lilly's footprints to the driveway. "It looks like she walked down the drive," I said, my breath coming out in frosty clouds of vapor.

Mitch shook his head. "Why would she take off like that?"

"I guess she doesn't want Ray dragging her back to Portland." I looked around for tire tracks on the driveway, but I didn't see any. So, whoever picked her up hadn't driven into the house.

"Did she have a phone?" Travis asked. "You could call her."

"That's probably how she found a ride. We should've taken it away from her last night." I thought about the phone bills I'd seen in the motorhome she'd shared with Renetta. "I can try and call her, but I doubt she'll answer."

To my surprise, Mitch took his phone out of his pocket. "I can see if Garcia can get me her number, but she won't be in the office for a few more hours."

He called the office and left a message for Deputy Garcia to try and find a number for Lilly. After he hung up, he said, "I feel stupid for falling asleep like that."

"Don't feel too bad," I said, "Ray was supposed to be watching her, not you. Wait a minute. Ray has her number."

I hurried back to the house and found Ray drinking coffee and staring at his phone. "Do you have a number for Lilly?"

He nodded. "I just tried to call her. She isn't picking up. Surprise, surprise."

I went back outside. Mitch and Travis stood by Mitch's pickup. "Ray tried to call her, but she didn't answer."

"She must've called someone to pick her up." Travis blew on his hands.

Mitch took his keys out of his pocket. "Probably. I'll drive down to the road and see if I see tire tracks or Lilly frozen in a snowdrift."

"Okay. Do you want me to come with you?" I asked.

He shook his head. "No, go back in and stay warm. If I don't find her, I'll call for help. She could be anywhere."

He took off and we went back inside the house. Travis poured us each a cup of coffee and I sat at the table next to Ray. "Why is she so determined not to go back to Portland to sign papers if she wants to give all her money away?"

"I have no idea. Lilly's always been a law unto herself." Ray took a sip of coffee.

"Did you know all these years that she was an heiress?" I asked.

"Yes. I was afraid if word got out, someone would try and take advantage of her for her money." He shook his head. "I've tried to keep an eye on her and Renetta for the family. But I felt like I had to keep my distance."

I stirred cream into my coffee. "Do you think Renetta's murder has something to do with Lilly's inheritance?"

Ray shrugged. "I wouldn't be surprised. Renetta was a sweet girl. I can't imagine why anyone would want her dead unless..." He stopped and stared out the window looking thoughtful.

"Unless?" I prodded.

Ray blinked and looked at me. "Unless they were trying to control Lilly by threatening Renetta."

"Then it comes back to the family, or whoever benefits from the Will if Lilly doesn't want her inheritance."

Ray nodded.

"Tell me everything you know about Lilly's family."

"I know they were big money in Portland. Big on the social scene until they started dying out. Kenneth Abbott, Lilly's father was a big man with a big personality. I don't know what drove Lilly to leave and pretend she didn't know them. Kenneth never talked about her. I didn't give it much thought that he had a daughter unless I happened to see Lilly on the street. When he got ill and realized he might not make it, he started trying to find Lilly. I think he wanted to make up with her. He asked for my help, and I found her and tried to talk to her." He shrugged.

"Did her dad know that she was living on the streets?"

"Yes. According to his attorney, he tried giving her money, but she wouldn't take it. When he found out about Renetta, he tried paying for her schooling. To my knowledge, Lilly never told Renetta that she had wealthy grandparents."

"Someone knew." Maybe if we could figure out who inherited the Abbott money if Lilly signed off on it, we'd figure out who killed Renetta. But what about Willow? Why kill her? "I need to talk to Lilly's attorney. Can you give me his number?" I grabbed a notepad and pen and looked at him expectantly.

He stood and took his phone out of his pocket, scrolling through his contacts. He gave me the attorney's name and number and I wrote it down.

"I need to go home and get a shower. Who knows what this day will bring?" He grabbed his winter coat off the kitchen chair where he'd put it the night before. "Call me if you find Lilly."

"I will."

Travis grabbed his coat, too. "I'm going out to shovel the sidewalk."

I thanked him and watched as he opened the door and went outside. Ray followed him out and I went to check on Bella who was still sound asleep. Oh, to be young and not have to wake up so early, I thought, smiling at her disheveled hair on the pillow. Love for my daughter struck me in the chest almost taking me to my knees. I knew I'd do anything to protect her.

I eased out of her room and closed the door behind me. Then I went into my office and powered up my laptop. It was too early in the morning to call the Abbott family attorney. I wanted to Google the Abbott family and see where Lilly had come from. I knew there must be quite a story there and I wanted to know what it was.

My phone rang and I took it out of my sweatshirt pocket and saw it was Mitch. "Yeah?"

"I followed Lilly's footprints to the road, but the snowplow has been through and obliterated all the tracks. She must've called someone to pick her up."

"But who? The people she hangs out with don't have cars."

He laughed. "Where have you been? Lilly has friends all over the valley. One of her Johns probably picked her up. She's probably sitting in a diner having breakfast while we're out in the freezing cold looking for her."

"Maybe. I'm trying to find out all I can about her family. Maybe it will lead us to the killer."

"Yeah, if she's the reason both girls were killed. It makes sense that her family might have Renetta killed, but how does Willow fit into it?"

"We'll have to figure that out." I scrolled through pictures of the Abbott family. There were some early pictures of Lilly when she was Lillian Abbott, the young, beautiful daughter of a very wealthy man. She was gorgeous. What had happened to make her give up her lifestyle and become who she was now? It didn't make sense.

Mitch was about to hang up when I said, "Wait a minute. You aren't going to believe what I'm looking at."

"What?"

I touched my screen enlarging the faded photo from many years earlier. It was Lilly at a charity ball, dancing with a man who looked like he was besotted with her. "There's a picture here of Lilly years ago with some guy at a charity function."

"How many years ago?"

"This newspaper is from the nineties."

"Who's the man?"

I looked closer, zooming in on the caption under the picture. "I don't know, it just says Lillian Abbott of Abbott's Furniture, dancing with an unknown male."

"Could it be Brad's father?"

"Maybe. I'll send you the link so you can see him." I drummed my fingers on the keyboard. "You know, Brad told me Lilly had him when she was young and neither she nor his father wanted him. I'd like to know what happened to the father."

"I'll get Garcia working on it. Maybe she can find out who this guy is."

A thought crossed my mind. "Okay, and we need to find Lilly and see if she knows." I stood up and walked around my desk, chewing on my thumbnail and thinking.

"You're being quiet. What are you thinking?"

"If this guy was in love with Lilly, what would have happened to him? Is he the reason she left home?"

"We'll find him. We also need to find out who gets the money if Lilly dies before she gets the chance to give it away."

I agreed and we ended the call. I chewed my thumbnail and looked around the room, deep in thought about the case. Then something grabbed my attention. I'd left my dad's checkbook sitting on top of files on his desk. I'd closed most of his accounts, but I still needed to finish paying some of his bills and I'd left money in this account. There were several thousand dollars in the bank. But it wasn't sitting where I'd left it. I looked around the desk, on the floor, and even opened the desk drawers and looked inside. It was gone.

Chapter 40

C hapter 40—Connolly

Connolly woke up and reached for her phone. She'd forgotten to plug it in before she went under again. She pushed the call button and when the nurse came in, asked her to plug her phone in.

The nurse fiddled with the cord and finally got the phone plugged in. "Is there anything else you need?" she asked.

Megan shook her head. "No, thanks." The nurse smiled and left the room and a couple minutes later Megan's phone lit up with texts.

Sheriff: Megan, hope you're feeling better. Call me when you can talk.

She hit the button to call him, and he answered on the first ring. "This is Mitch."

"Sheriff, this is Connolly. What's going on?" She eased up in the bed, trying not to start the pain exploding again.

"I need to come by and talk to you. We've been looking for the shooter, but not having any luck."

Megan felt dread curdling her stomach. "I don't know how much longer I'll be here."

"I'll be right over. I need to know everyone you've been around lately, so be thinking about that, okay?"

"Okay," she said in a small voice. She had been thinking about it and wondering if it was her boyfriend. He'd been acting squirrelly since their skirmish when he'd knifed her. Accidentally? She'd thought so at the time, but now she was beginning to wonder. She'd thought of him as a law-abiding citizen, but was he? Connolly's heartbeat tripled. Had he killed Renetta? He liked to play rough, did he also like to kill women? Was she next?

She knew of one way to get him to show his cards. She called his cell. He didn't pick up, so she left a voicemail. "The sheriff wants to know everyone I've been hanging around with lately. I have to tell him about us."

She hit end and laid the phone next to her. Five minutes later her phone lit up with an incoming call. It was him.

"You can't tell him about me, Megan. It has to remain our secret."

"Why? I don't understand. He's just trying to find out who was shooting at me. I can tell him you were at Jack's, and you have an alibi." Her voice shook and she hoped he'd think it was because she was on drugs.

"No. Don't say anything. Promise me, Megan. If you do, it will be very bad."

"For you?"

"And you."

He hung up on her without saying more. She didn't understand what was going on with him, but she had a bad feeling. Was he the shooter? Why would he try and hurt her? She thought about the knife slipping. Had it really slipped, or had he knifed her on purpose? She tried to remember exactly what they were doing when it happened.

They'd had words, then he'd tried to make up with her. He'd kissed her and rubbed her shoulders and the next thing she remembered was the knife sliding into her stomach.

Oh heavens, maybe he had done it on purpose?

She knew she needed to tell Mitch everything, but he'd sounded so sure that something bad would happen if she did. She didn't know what to do. Her police training told her to tell Mitch.

Her heart pounded. An ache sliced through her chest. She couldn't breathe. She called for a nurse. When the woman came in, she said, "I'm having a heart attack."

Chapter 41

Chapter 41—Liz

Travis and I fixed breakfast for the three of us—Bella wasn't up yet—and then I went to take a shower. Travis went home to shower and change. Then he planned to bring paperwork back to my house to work on and stay with Bella until Mitch or I could get back to her. I didn't want her alone.

I called Mitch on my way into the office to see if he'd had any luck finding Lilly.

"Not yet." He sounded tired and frustrated. "We checked all the usual places. Who knows where the crazy woman went?"

"I've been thinking about Willow. How does she tie into all of this? I just can't believe it's a coincidence."

"Yeah, me either." He was quiet for a couple minutes. "Why don't you look into Willow's comings and goings the last few days before she was killed while I search for Lilly. Maybe one of us will find out something."

"Okay."

"Oh, I talked to Connolly. I'm heading to the hospital next. I need lots more information before I can find her shooter."

"I didn't mention this before because I didn't think it was important, but someone has been stalking me. They've broken into my house, and last night I noticed that my dad's checkbook is gone."

"And why did you feel it wasn't important to tell me? You could've been killed." I didn't say anything, and he said, "Oh, you thought it was me, didn't you?"

"I'm sorry. I know that was stupid of me, but..."

"No, it wasn't stupid. If I thought it would do any good, I probably would stalk you. But I haven't been, and we need to find out who is and why. Besides, I wouldn't take your dad's money."

I knew that and felt bad thinking it was him. He was a lot of things, but he wasn't a thief.

"Where's Bella?"

"She's home still asleep. Travis is there."

"Well, that makes me feel a whole lot better," he said, sarcastically.

"It's better than her being there alone." I shot back.

"You're right. I'm sorry." He cleared his throat. "Do you want me to send one of the deputies to relieve him?"

"No, we don't have the manpower. Travis has his laptop and is doing some computer work. He also has a gun and a carry permit. He's a good shot and he'll keep an eye on Bella."

"Okay, I'll call you after I leave Connolly."

We hung up and I drove down Hwy 35 towards town. Enrique called as I was nearing the turn into Hood River. I hit the button to talk. "Hey."

"Hey, good morning. I heard you lost Lilly last night."

"Yeah, she's slippery. Have you heard anything this morning?" Did I dare hope they'd found her?

"Nope. No one has seen her. We've been out talking to the folks at the warming shelter, homeless camp and under the bridge."

I sighed. "She could be anywhere."

"Yeah, I have a feeling Ms. Lilly is keeping things from us. Like what her relationship with Brad Thomas really is."

"And why she tried to bite his ear off?"

"Yes. She's crazy as a loon, but I'm not sure that she's not calculating, too."

"What do you mean?" I turned my blinkers on and left the highway to drive over the bridge into town.

"I just don't think she's as dumb as she'd like us to think."

"No, she's not dumb. Just crazy. Has anyone checked on Brad lately?"

"Isn't he still in the hospital?"

I eased around a car doing fifteen miles an hour. It was slick and I felt my tires slide a little before I found traction. "I think so, but who knows. Lilly slipped past us; we should probably check on him."

"Do you want me to head over to the hospital?"

"No, Mitch is going to check on Connolly. I'll have him ask."

My phone beeped with an incoming call. "Oh, that's Mitch. I'd better take it. Do you want to meet me at the office in about fifteen minutes? Maybe we can come up with a game plan for the day."

"Sounds good. I'll be there."

He hung up and I clicked on Mitch's name.

"You'll never believe this," he said. "I just walked into the hospital, and they think Connolly may have had a heart attack and Brad Thomas came to for a little while late last night."

"Came to? Did he say anything?" Maybe we'd get something from him.

"Not that I heard."

"This just keeps getting crazier and crazier. Have you talked to a doctor about Connolly? Is she okay?" I bit my lip. My lips were dry and sore from the cold weather.

"Not yet. They're running tests to check her heart enzymes. I told the nurse to call me as soon as possible. Why don't we meet back at the office? It's almost time for the shift change and I need to talk to everyone and see if anyone has found out anything."

"Sounds good. Enrique and I were heading in anyway."

We hung up and I concentrated on driving through town. There were people out shoveling sidewalks in front of their businesses. A couple side streets had been cordoned off and kids were sledding down them.

The office was busy when I walked in. I waved at the receptionist and kept walking to my office. Enrique was there and greeted me with a cup of coffee.

"Thanks." I took it and smiled at him. "How's Jonathan and Jolene?"

He grinned. "Jonny kept us up most of the night, but you know, I don't care. I let Jolene go back to bed and I just sat in the living room rocking him. Being a dad is great."

"Except for the missed sleep?" I took a sip of coffee.

"Well, yeah, but I don't mind yet. Maybe when he's three or four and is still keeping me up." He grinned.

I nodded. "I talked to Mitch. He's on the way in and wants to have a meeting with everyone."

"Did he say how Connolly's doing?"

I filled him in on Connolly's possible heart problem.

He shook his head. "There's something strange going on with her. She's acted different the last couple of months. You know how she was always at Mitch's side, trying to tell him what to do and how to do it?""Yup. She thinks she's the only deputy the department has."

Enrique nodded. "Well lately, she's been taking time off work, on her phone when she is here, and leaving Mitch and the rest of us alone. It's nice, but weird for her."

I shrugged. "Maybe she hasn't been feeling good. Or maybe there's a guy involved, and she doesn't want to tell anyone in case it doesn't work out."

"Maybe." He didn't sound convinced.

Garcia poked her head in the door to tell us Mitch had arrived and wanted everyone in the conference room ASAP.

Enrique raised his eyebrows and I laughed and followed him out of our office and down the hall to the conference room.

Mitch looked up when we walked in. "Okay, I think everyone's here. Let's talk about what's going on with these two murders. We need to get them solved. People are starting to get nervous. The mayor has called me several times."

There were some grumblings in the room, but mostly everyone agreed. I wondered if Mitch knew the mayor and Jenn were playing around. I'd seen his car at her house soon after I found out about her and Mitch. And talk around town was they were having a hot and heavy affair. I wondered how long Ray would put up with it. He was spending more and more time in Salem.

"What do we know about the victims that we didn't at the last meeting?" Mitch walked over to a Dry Erase board and picked up a marker. He drew a line down the middle of the board and wrote Renetta on one side and Willow on the other.

"We know that Renetta's mother, Lilly Larson, is Lillian Abbott of Abbott's Furniture in Portland, and she stands to inherit a ton of money which she has said she's giving to charity," I said.

"You've got to be kidding me," Deputy Williams said from his chair at the back of the room. "How much is she giving away? I know a great charity."

"Who? The Todd Williams Fund?" Someone asked and everyone laughed.

"You've got it," Williams said. "I can take any extra millions she has laying around." He chuckled and sat forward in his chair. He was more engaged in this conversation than any we'd ever had in this room. I wanted to roll my eyes, but I didn't want to give him the satisfaction.

"I can't believe Lilly is an heiress," Garcia said, scrunching up her nose. "I thought she was a homeless person."

"Do you know why she turned her back on her family?" Mitch asked, looking right at me.

"Nope. She just said she doesn't want any of that man's dirty money. I'm assuming she had a falling out with her father at some point. I tried calling his attorney, but I haven't reached him." And she's certifiably crazy, I thought.

"Why don't you look closer at that, Garcia? See what you can dig up on Kenneth Abbott."

Garcia nodded and wrote something in her notebook.

"And what about Willow? Has anyone found out anything about her?" He looked around the room.

Wells raised her hand. She looked at her phone, swiped her finger over it a couple of times and said, "Willow was in a relationship with Kari Young, but she didn't want children and Kari has a couple, so Willow broke up with her."

"Are you sure? Rodriguez and I interviewed Kari. She didn't mention that she and Willow dated."

"They were at lunch together the day we found Renetta," Enrique reminded me.

I nodded. "That's true. Sounds like we need to have another talk with Kari."

"The only things I know that Renetta and Willow have in common are they were both friends with Amy and Kari." Mitch wrote their names on the Dry Erase Board. "Anybody else have anything to add?"

No one spoke up. I stared at what he'd written. "If we assume that Renetta was killed because she's Lilly's daughter and stands to inherit Lilly's money, why kill Willow, too? It just doesn't make sense."

"Maybe there are two killers," West said, raising his hand.

He was so polite, I thought. His parents raised him well. "No, because the killer left children's jewelry next to both victims, so that suggests the same killer."

West's face turned beet red, and I felt bad, but he had to learn to take criticism.

"There has to be another common denominator between the two murders. Think, people." Mitch looked around the room.

We tossed several ideas around, but no one could come up with a reason for Willow's murder. Mitch finally let us go with a warning, "Keep digging into the victims' lives. We've got to find the killer before he strikes again."

I thought about the teddy bear taken from little Kennedy and placed on Bella's bed. I hurried down the hall to my office and called Bella, just wanting to hear her voice. "Is everything okay there?" I asked when she answered the phone.

"Yeah, Travis is fixing supper. He plans to drag me with him to the store."

"Good. What are we having?" Thank you, Travis, I thought.

"Chicken Fettuccini Alfredo. Travis assures me that he is a good cook. You don't want to be late tonight."

I laughed, told her I'd be home for dinner and hung up. Enrique stepped into our office just as I slipped my phone into my pocket.

"Everything okay?" he asked.

"Yeah, just checking on Bella." I stared at him as another thought hit me. "You know, I almost forgot this, but Bella said Renetta called her a day or two before she was killed and asked for my phone number.

She said that something was terribly wrong, and she wanted to tell me."

"I wonder what it could be. We got the report back on her cell phone and there were calls to Bella, but none to you."

"No, because Bella didn't get back to her. But the fact that she told Bella something was going on, and she needed to call me, tells me that she was worried. I wonder if we've been looking at this case wrong the whole time."

"What do you mean?"

"I'm not sure, but I need to talk to Bella again. Maybe Renetta told her more than she remembered to tell me."

Chapter 42

Chapter 42

The smell of garlic and Italian spices hit me the minute I opened the door at home. Okay, I was going to marry Travis and have his babies. No one cooked like this man. Oh, wait a minute, I was too old to have his babies. Well, a girl could dream, couldn't she?

"Dinner smells heavenly," I said, smiling at him as I slipped out of my coat and hung it in the closet. Bailey whined and nudged me with her nose. I bent down to give her some belly rubs.

"I've been a bachelor long enough that I've learned to cook and clean. Keep that in mind when I annoy you and you want me to leave." He smiled.

"I would be swooning right now, but I'm a homicide detective and it's in the rule books that we can't swoon. It's against the law."

He laughed and pulled me into his arms for a quick hug. "The fettuccini will be ready in ten minutes, Ms. Detective."

My stomach growled and he grinned. "I need to talk to Bella. Is she in her room?"

He put a hand up to his ear. "Can you not hear the music coming from down the hall?"

I smiled. "As a matter of fact, I can. We'll be in for dinner in ten minutes."

He glanced at his watch. "Eight."

I nodded and headed down the hall to Bella's room. Bella sat on her bed with her laptop open and a big smile on her face. I hated to ruin her mood by bringing up Renetta, but I had to see if she knew more about Ren's concerns the day she called.

"Hi, mom." She smiled at the boy she was Facetiming and said, "Gotta go. Mom's home and dinner smells delish."

He laughed and told her he'd call later.

She shut down her computer. "How're things going?" she asked, the smile still playing around her lips.

I sat down next to her on the bed and put my arm around her. "I hate to bring this up, honey, especially when you look so happy, but I need to talk to you about Renetta."

It was as though a cloud passed over her face. She went from smiling and happy to frowning and sad. "Okay." Her tone was hesitant, but she leaned closer to me, and I hugged her.

"Tell me everything you can remember about the last few days before Renetta died. Did you talk more than that one time?"

Bella pulled a pillow onto her lap, putting her arms around it. She closed her eyes, concentrating on remembering. "We talked right after you and I got back from Europe."

"What about?"

She shrugged. "About the trip and what she was doing." Bella stared at the pillow for a couple seconds. Then she looked up. "She told me about a dentist who kept asking her out. She said she wasn't comfortable around him."

"Did he harass her?"

"I don't think so. He didn't want to take no for an answer, but she said he finally gave up and left her alone. She thought someone told him that she was underage."

I watched as she stared at her pillow. "She seemed fine. Then she called and left the message wanting your phone number. She sounded so scared." Bella burst into tears. "I tried to call her back, but it went to voicemail. I should've tried again instead of hanging out with Ben. She might still be alive." She leaned into me and put her head on my shoulder.

"You can't know that, honey." I kissed the top of her head, my heart aching for my girl. "If you remember anything that might help us find out who did this to her, let me know, okay?"

She nodded and wiped her eyes with the sleeve of her sweatshirt. "I will. Have you talked to Brad?"

"Brad Thomas?" My heartbeat quickened. "You know him?"

"No, but Renetta told me he claimed he was her brother. She asked Lilly if he was, but Lilly would never say one way or the other."

That wasn't surprising. Lilly always clammed up when she didn't want to talk about something. "Did Renetta ever mention that Lilly's family had a lot of money?"

Bella laughed and sat up. "Lilly? You're kidding, right?"

"No, she's apparently the daughter and only heir to the Portland Abbott's fortune. They own furniture stores all over the Northwest."

"Lilly?" Bella gave me an incredulous look. A frown formed between her eyes. "She lives on the streets."

"I know, it's crazy, and she says she's giving all the money to charity." I still didn't get why Lilly didn't keep enough to make her life a little easier. What had happened between her and her father that made her leave the safety and security of her family and become homeless?

Bella stared at me for a couple seconds. "Someone killed Ren because they thought she would inherit the money if Lilly was dead."

"But Lilly is still alive."

"Because she's outrun them so far." Bella put her pillow back on the top of the bed. "Mom, Lilly is next. You need to keep an eye on Brad Thomas. He probably killed Ren and now he's after Lilly so he can get the money."

What she said made sense, but what about Willow? How did she fit in? None of it made sense. It was giving me a headache. I needed to think about something else for a while.

I stood up. "Travis has dinner ready; we'd better go eat."

Bella unwound her long legs and moved off the bed. "Thank God for Travis. If he wasn't here, we'd be eating popcorn, wouldn't we?"

"Probably." I reached out and gave her a hug. "But it would be super buttery popcorn."

Bella laughed and led the way into the kitchen.

Over dinner, Travis and Bella bantered back and forth over whether Oregon State or Washington State, where Travis went to school, had the best football teams. I tuned them out and let everything I knew about Lilly and Renetta run through my mind.

It made sense that someone had killed Renetta because they knew she'd inherit Lilly's family money if she outlived Lilly. So, was the plan to kill Renetta first and then Lilly? Did Brad Thomas, do it? But what about Willow and the children's jewelry left at both crime scenes? Was Brad smart enough to set us up to think there was a serial killer when he was the killer? I didn't get that impression, but maybe I wasn't giving him enough credit. Maybe he was smarter than I realized. Or maybe he had help.

Bella cut into my thoughts. "Mom, tell Travis that OSU is the best school in the Northwest."

I smiled at her. "We have to forgive Travis for going out of state to school. He must not have had good info at the time."

Travis raised his eyebrows, grabbed the fettuccini and stood. "No seconds for you two until you agree with me." He held the food over the table.

"Don't take the food. That's mean," Bella said, laughing at him and reaching for the dish.

Travis sat down. "Well, I don't want to be mean, so I guess you can have seconds. But no more talk about how great OSU is, okay? It's bad for my digestion."

Bella and I laughed. We finished dinner and Bella and I had just started dishes when my phone rang. It was Mitch. "I'm sorry, I need to take this." I grabbed my phone and went into the living room.

"Hello?"

"Liz, we've got another body."

My heart sank. "Oh no. Do you know who it is?"

"Yeah, it's Lilly."

Chapter 43

C hapter 43

Lilly. So that's why we hadn't been able to find her. I hated the thought that we'd let her down. We should've been able to keep her safe.

I left Bella with Travis after explaining what was going on and headed to town to meet with the team. Lilly had been found sitting in a chair in the middle of Jackson Park. Her body was frozen, just like Renetta's.

I pulled up and parked beside Enrique's SUV and got out. It was slow going in the deep snow. The roads were being plowed, but the park had at least three feet of snow. "Who found her?" I asked as I got closer.

Enrique looked up from where he'd been examining the area around Lilly. "Some kids sledding down that little incline saw someone sitting in the chair. They thought it was funny until they made their way over here and found Lilly dead."

I scrunched down in front of her and looked at her face. Her eyelashes were frozen, and her jaw hung down on her chest. If she hadn't had frost on her skin and eyelashes, she would've looked like she sat down to rest and fell asleep. "How long do you think she's been here?"

"It's hard to tell. It's only been dark for a few hours. It would be hard to bring her here in the broad daylight without someone seeing you."

Lilly wore the same coat she'd worn the other times I'd seen her recently. I looked her over for stab wounds or needle marks. When I moved her hair away from her ear with my gloved finger I said to Enrique, "Look at this."

He was taking pictures of the scene around us but turned back towards the chair when I spoke. "What is it?"

"Looks like a needle mark." I showed him the small puncture wound. "I haven't found any other wounds. I wonder if someone shot her up with a drug that killed her."

"We'll have to wait and see what Doc finds. She's on her way." Enrique shook his head. "We've got to get this guy. Why is he trying to kill off Lilly's family? We'd better make sure Brad has a guard on him."

"Yeah, we need to go talk to him again. I have so many questions for him."

Enrique moved around Lilly taking pictures of her, the chair she sat on and finally the wound. "Has anyone talked to him lately?"

"Yes, but he's refusing to talk. He should be getting out of the hospital soon. We can take him in for questioning and see if he'll tell us what's going on."

Enrique nodded and continued looking at Lilly. "I don't see blood anywhere, so either we're right and she died of an overdose, or she was killed somewhere else and had stopped bleeding by the time they moved her."

Other deputies were milling about putting up yellow crime scene tape. Jackson Park included almost three acres, so it would take them awhile. Mitch pulled up while we were looking at Lilly and he came through the crowd with a scowl on his face.

"What the hell…" He stopped and shook his head. "Why can't we find this guy? Have you walked the perimeter of the park? We need to walk around and see if we can tell which direction she was brought in."

"We just got here," Enrique said. "Look at this." He pushed Lilly's hair back and showed Mitch the needle wound.

"Crap. I want this place gone over with a fine-tooth comb even if it takes all night." He looked around. "Liz, grab Garcia and talk to every homeowner up and down that street." He motioned to 13th Street. "See if anyone saw anything."

"Mitch," I lowered my voice and walked closer to him. "I'm thinking Brad Thomas did this." I lifted my hands at the shake of his head. "Not that he did it himself, but he could've hired someone to kill them. If he's Lilly's only surviving heir, he's going to be a very rich man. And what better way to have an alibi, being in the hospital?"

Mitch stared at me for a second. "Wouldn't it be something if he inherited all of Kenneth Abbotts's money? The old man would probably turn over in his grave. I talked to the Abbott family lawyer earlier. He said Lilly left home because she was pregnant with Brad and the old man refused to let her marry his father."

"The guy in the newspaper picture we saw?" I thought about the picture I'd seen of the man. He'd looked so familiar, but where had I seen him?

"Yup. He managed one of Abbott's stores and he and Lilly met at a Christmas party. They fell in love and wanted to get married, but the old man thought he was marrying Lilly for her money. He said if she married him, he'd cut her out of the Will. She told him she didn't want his dirty money, but Brad's father had other ideas."

"He wanted money?" Of course he did.

"Yeah, Abbott paid him off to stay away from Lilly. When Lilly found out she went crazy and told her dad off and left."

"She must've been pregnant with Brad when she left." I felt convinced it was Brad behind the killings. Unless it was his father. "We haven't really thought about Brad's father. Would he inherit if Brad doesn't?"

Mitch rubbed the back of his head. "That's a good question. Let's see what Garcia finds out. In the meantime, why don't you go try and talk to Brad again? Maybe he'll open up when he hears that Lilly is dead."

"Okay. Have you seen Garcia?" I pulled my phone from my pocket and called the hospital. I'd called so many times, I didn't have to look up the number.

"She's over talking to the deputies putting the crime scene tape around the perimeter of the park." He motioned for Enrique to follow him. "Rodriguez, come with me."

"Where are you going?" I asked.

"We're going to put up the biggest lights we can find. I want this park to be lit up so it looks like daylight around here. I don't want anyone leaving until we've gone over every inch. If we leave it until morning, you know someone will be in here screwing around."

He was probably right. I put the phone up to my ear and when the receptionist answered, I asked for a nurse. It took a couple minutes but soon someone answered. "This is Detective Liz Ellisen; we need to talk to Brad Thomas. Is he up to having a conversation?"

"I don't think so, Detective. He hasn't talked to anyone. Even the mayor came in to see him and Brad refused to talk to him."

"The mayor? What did he want?"

"I have no idea. He was in the room with Brad for quite a while. He didn't say anything when he came out."

I was sure Brad was involved somehow. I just didn't know how deep his involvement was. I went in search of Garcia, thinking we probably wouldn't find anything useful in our canvas of the neighborhood, but we needed to do it anyway. She was helping unroll the crime scene tape. "Hey Anna, can you come with me?"

"Sure." She tossed the roll of tape to one of the other deputies and headed my way. "Where are we going?"

"Mitch wants us to go to every house that is remotely close to the park to see if anyone saw anything." I trudged through the deep snow with Anna doing her best to keep up with me.

"Did you have time to check into Brad Thomas's father? Is he even alive?"

She shook her head. "I haven't found him. I'll keep looking."

It was pushing eight o'clock and almost everyone was home for the evening. We knocked on every door on the East side of 13th Street until we got to the top where it flattened off and homes turned into businesses. We turned right on Taylor Avenue and went to every house along the top of the park. No one saw anything. No one heard anything.

Garcia and I made our way back to the park and found Mitch and Enrique. They had set up enough lights so that the whole park looked like daytime. "Find out anything?" Mitch asked as we walked up.

I shook my head. "Nope. Nobody saw or heard anything."

He looked up from the light he was trying to get to come on. "We need to talk to Brad Thomas, Liz."

"Okay, we'll head over to the hospital and talk to him. Maybe something we say will get through the fog in his brain. I feel sure he had something to do with the murders. The only thing I don't understand is Willow."

"And the little girl's jewelry."

"Yeah." I looked out over the park. Deputies and Hood River City Police Officers were scouring the grounds looking for clues. It looked like something from a horror movie. Soft voices came to us across the park, but most were moving silently around, like zombies from the apocalypse.

I noticed something shiny on the ground several feet away from where Mitch and Enrique stood talking. Garcia had moved a few feet away looking around the base of a tree. I went in the other direction to see what had caught the light.

I was deep in thought when I heard the Police Chief's voice cut through the frozen air. Chief Pauley was intimidating in size, standing well over six foot five and he had a booming voice to go with his stature. Even if you weren't breaking the law, you worried when he came around. No one wanted an altercation with the Chief.

I found what looked like a broken mirror and bent over to pick it up when what he said penetrated my mind.

"Hey Mitch, too bad about old Lil' huh? Remember the time you invited her to the poker party?" He guffawed, and spit tobacco. "She was on you like honey on toast. None of the rest of us had a chance with her that night."

Everyone went quiet. I stood up, the broken mirror in my hand, and stared at Mitch. He'd turned stone white, and his eyes were huge when he stared back at me. Sweat formed on his forehead. I looked around expecting the guys to laugh it off, but no one laughed. It was then that I realized that Mitch had invited Lilly for sex.

"You stinking piece of garbage," I said, moving towards them, my voice low and husky. "You were fooling around with Lilly? And coming home to me?"

"Liz..." Mitch held his hand out.

"Liz!" The chief exclaimed. "I thought you were still in Europe." He looked wildly around, like he was hoping someone would bail him out of the mess he'd made, but no one said a word.

"No, I came home," my voice was still quiet, but deadly. I marched up to Mitch. My dad hated swearing. He'd taught my sister and I not to, but I'd been around cops most of my adult life and I'd learned a lot of words through the years. I used everyone I could think of on Mitch, finishing with, "You lying piece of shit. When this case is over, you'll have my resignation." I turned and stomped off.

"Hey, sorry buddy," I heard Chief Pauley say. "I really thought she was still on leave. Hey Liz, it was just that one time."

I didn't hear Mitch's reply. I was almost to the hospital before I realized Garcia and Enrique were with me. I'd put everything out of my mind to concentrate on the job. Later I would probably vomit, but for now I held it together, barely. My stomach was tied in knots and my skin burned like I'd been in a fire.

"Liz, I'm so sorry," Garcia said, catching up with me.

"Did you know?" I stared at her.

"No. I wasn't invited to the poker games."

I turned to Enrique who held up his hands. "No, I'd heard there was some bad things going on at those games, but I didn't go either. Jo would've had my head."

I nodded. I was too enraged to say anything.

"Do you want me to try and talk to Brad Thomas? You don't have to do this." Garcia caught up with me and reached out a hand to stop me.

"Let us handle this. You go spend time with Jolene," Enrique said. "She'll listen and you know she cares about you."

I stopped in my tracks and looked at Garcia and then Enrique. I was beginning to realize how lucky I was to have them in my life. "No,

I need to do this. If I don't keep my mind off that man slut, I'll take my gun and shoot him." My fingers itched to do just that. The nasty scumbag. I hated him with every fiber of my being. "But thank you both. I really mean that."

Enrique threw his arm around me. "We've got your back, Liz. Whatever you need."

Garcia nodded and I smiled through a sudden mist in my eyes. "I know." I started walking again. "I love you both, but I need to do this. After we solve this case, I'll deal with the sheriff." I'd tried to be civil for Bella's sake, but I didn't want that filthy worm near my daughter. The gloves were off, and Mitchel Ellisen was going to find out what I was made of.

Chapter 44

Chapter 44

Brad Thomas was asleep. The three of us stood just inside the door to his room. The lights were off, and he was restless.

I didn't get it. I was sure he was the killer, but how could he kill Lilly when he was still in the hospital? "He must have a partner," I said.

"But who?" Garcia asked.

"I don't know." I reached over and shook Brad's arm. He woke up and groaned, holding his head in his hand.

"Go away. I'm not talking to you."

"Brad, Lilly is dead."

He stared at me. His eyes were wide with fear. He glanced around the room. "Lil's dead? You've got to protect me. If he killed Lil, I'm next."

"Who? Who killed Lilly?"

Brad shook his head. "If I tell you, I'm dead."

I tried several times to convince him to talk, but he refused. I turned to the nurse who had stepped into the room with us. "Has anyone been in to see him?"

"Just the other deputy." She moved to the computer by Brad's bed and looked at his chart.

"What deputy?" I asked. I hadn't heard that anyone but me had been in to check on him. I would have heard if Mitch sent someone. Or was he deliberately keeping things from me?

The nurse looked at me. "I didn't get her name. She's tall, with blonde hair and wears glasses."

"Sounds like Connolly," Enrique said. "I thought she had a heart attack."

"So did I." I turned to the nurse. "Can you check and see if she's still a patient here?"

"I don't think she is." She went to the computer and typed in Connolly's name. "It looks like she had an anxiety attack. She checked herself out late last night."

What did she want from Brad? Did she know something about him that we didn't know? "I think we need to visit Connolly." I thanked the nurse and started to the door. Enrique and Garcia fell in behind me.

"You think she knows something?" Garcia asked.

"Yup." I strode down the hall to the main door. It was everything I could do to keep it together and do my job and not let angry tears fall. But I would not cry over that man again. I'd used up all my tears when I found out he'd been having an affair with my best friend. I crammed the despair to the back of my mind. I'd deal with it later. "I'll go find her. You two head back to the crime scene."

They nodded and we walked across the street. I stopped by my Jeep. "Let me know if you find out anything," I said to Garcia. Enrique had hurried over to where the other deputies were huddled around Lilly's body.

The ambulance pulled up, followed by Dr. King. I nodded at Garcia and got into my Jeep. On the way to Connolly's house, I called Travis to check on Bella. Luckily, I'd calmed down a little and could talk without spitting fire through my nose.

Travis answered. "She's asleep still. Where are you?"

I told him what I knew then said, "Keep a close eye on her, Travis. I was sure Brad Thomas was our killer, but he's still in the hospital and won't talk to me. He's afraid of someone but he won't say who."

"Be careful, Liz," Travis's deep voice soothed my cranked-up nerves a little.

"I will. Thank you for watching out for my girl."

He chuckled. "She's easy to watch. She's been asleep all night."

While I might never trust another man after everything Mitch had pulled on me, Travis was my friend. You thought Mitch was your friend, too, a tiny voice said in my head. You really screwed up with him.

I shoved the voice away and headed my Jeep towards Connolly's.

Chapter 45

Chapter 45—Connolly

Megan Connolly came awake with a start. Someone was shining a light in her eyes. She tried to push it away but couldn't reach it. "Sweetie?" She hadn't seen him for days, but who else would be in the house with her?

Then her heart started to pound as she remembered the break-in the day before and being shot at. She'd made sure the doors were locked and bolted. The alarm was turned on. How had he gotten into her home? She sat up trying to find her glasses, but they weren't on the bedside table where she'd left them. She started to slide out of bed and a deep voice startled her. She screamed.

"Shut up." It was a man's voice she didn't recognize, and horror shot through her. "You need to get up."

"Who are you? What do you want?" She put her hand under the pillow where she'd left her gun. She felt around, but it wasn't there. Where was it? Had he taken it? She fumbled for the light next to the bed. It was so dark in her room. She switched it on, and a weak light flooded the room.

"Looking for this?" The man held up her .38 revolver. He laughed. "Not very original leaving it under your pillow."

Connolly groaned. She didn't recognize him. Who was he? Why was he after her? What had she done? Her side felt like someone had stuck a knife in it. She put her hand on the bandage. She needed her gun. Where was her boyfriend? Did he send someone to kill her? Why? She'd never tell anyone that he knifed her. It was an accident, she was sure. Her voice shook. "Who are you?"

He wore a black face mask. He pulled it off, but Connolly didn't recognize him. She knew it wasn't good that he was letting her see his face. "Should I know you?"

"Nope, but you will." He hauled her to her feet. The pain in her side was so intense she almost fainted. A groan ripped from her throat.

"I promise I won't tell anyone. Just go away, please." She tried to focus on him, but it was hard in the dim light and without her glasses.

"No, you won't tell." He dragged her out of her bedroom and into the living room. "Where is the gun?"

Connolly struggled to see him. His voice wasn't familiar. Who was he? "What gun? You took my gun, remember?"

He laughed, a nasty sounding bark. "You know what gun I'm talking about. The one you took from Brad Thomas."

Connolly thought fast. She remembered taking the gun from Brad Thomas the day he went into the hospital. She'd put it in the evidence room, hadn't she? She couldn't remember. So much had happened since then. "I don't have it. I placed it in evidence."

He shook her shoulder, leaning down, his breath in her face. Funny, she smelled mint toothpaste. She'd expected his breath to smell foul just like he was. "You did not. I checked."

She narrowed her eyes. How would he be able to check unless one of the deputies was feeding him information? That must be it because she didn't recognize his voice. Unless maybe he was city police? "Are you a cop?"

"Just give me the gun." He tightened his grip on her arm and Connolly groaned.

"I don't have it." Connolly wished her boyfriend would show up. She'd called him several times and he hadn't returned her calls. Where was he?

The man drew back his fist. "Don't make me hit you."

Connolly reached up and grabbed his fist. "You can go to jail for hitting a law enforcement officer."

He shook his hand, trying to get free from her, but she had it in a death grip. They struggled and he got away long enough to pull back and slug her on her right temple. Connolly saw stars. She lunged for him, and they ended up on the floor, rolling around on her carpet. His fists rained down on her shoulders.

Connolly said, "Stop!"

A pounding on the door got their attention. Connolly's first thought was it must be her boyfriend. She tried to get up and head for the door, but the man grabbed her legs and held on. "Get rid of them," he hissed.

Not on your life, she thought, but she nodded and felt him loosen his grip. She struggled to her feet, her head swimming, and made her way to the door. The pounding had gotten louder.

"Connolly! It's Liz. Let me in."

Liz! What was she doing there? Connolly needed help, but not from Liz. She opened the door and lunged at Liz, taking them both down into a snowbank.

"What the..." Liz gasped. She pushed Connolly away, but Connolly got on top of her and grabbed her gun. She felt her side tear open again and the warm flow of blood drip through her nightgown. Liz grabbed her hands and held them away from her body.

"Stop! What are you doing? Have you gone nuts?" she hissed.

"Just give me your gun and get out of here. I'll explain later," Connolly growled, fumbling for the gun she knew Liz wore on her hip.

"Get off of me now," Liz commanded in a harsh voice. "What is wrong with you?"

Connolly felt like she'd lost her mind. What made her think Liz would give up her gun? That was the last thing she'd do.

They both looked up when the door banged open. A man, dressed head to toe in black, held a gun on them. "Both of you get up. Now."

Connolly rolled to her side and Liz grabbed for her gun. "Put your gun down," she shouted towards the intruder.

"Nice try," he growled. "Now get up slow and easy or I'll shoot you. I'm not kidding around, Detective Ellisen."

He knew who Liz was? That wasn't good. Connolly watched as Liz slowly crawled to her feet. She glanced down at Connolly who was clutching her side, her hands slick with blood. She shook her head, a worried look in her eyes. How was she going to get them out of this? Connolly didn't think she had a chance.

"Who are you?" Liz yelled at the man.

"It doesn't matter. I'm the guy with a .38 pointed at your head." He beckoned her inside. "Get up slowly and put your gun on the ground next to you."

Liz did as he asked.

"Now, move it towards me with your foot. Easy or I'll shoot."

Again, Connolly watched as the detective did as he asked.

When the gun slid to a stop next to him, he reached down and picked it up, putting it in his coat pocket. "Get in here before you wake up the neighbors." He motioned them both inside.

The detective reached down to help Connolly up. "You need to get her an ambulance." She nodded towards Connolly. "She's bleeding."

He laughed. "As if I care." He motioned inside the house. "Help her up and get her inside."

Liz did as he asked, helping Connolly to her feet, putting an arm around her and leading her inside. Connolly gripped her side, feeling blood soak through her fingers. It wasn't good. She felt weak and knew she was losing too much blood.

When they got into the living room, he switched on a lamp. "What happened to her? Did you knife her while you two were rolling around in the snow?" He chuckled and Connolly wanted to deck him. If she could've gotten away from the detective, she would've gone after him. She didn't care about the consequences.

Chapter 46

I put my arm around Connolly and helped her into the house. I felt her getting heavier and wondered if she was going to pass out. How was I going to get us out of this mess without someone getting killed? I had to think of something quick. "Why are you here? What do you want?"

He motioned to Connolly with his gun. "She has something belonging to me."

"What?"

Connolly stirred. She looked at me and whispered, "He's looking for the gun I took from Brad at the warming shelter, but I don't have it."

I stared at the man. Was this Brad's accomplice? My heartbeat tripled. Why else would he be looking for Brad's gun? "Who are you?"

"It doesn't matter who I am. You and your friend need to get me that gun." He pointed the gun at Connolly again and I could tell he was shaking. Was he hopped up on drugs? Probably.

"If it has been entered into evidence, there's nothing we can do." I knew trying to reason with him wouldn't get me anywhere, but I had to try.

"Sure, there is. All the cops in town are at the park. You can go in and get it out of evidence."

Connolly groaned and grabbed her side.

"I've got to get her some help. I think she's going into shock." I didn't know what to think about Connolly's knife wound. Who gave it to her, and why? What was she into? There were a lot of possibilities floating around my brain. Was Connolly involved with criminals? That was really the only thing that made sense.

"She'll be in more shock if she doesn't do what I ask."

I could tell he was trying to sound mean, but he wasn't a hardened criminal. Who was he and why was he so determined to get the gun from Connolly? What was the gun used for? To kill Renetta and Willow? They'd both been shot, but Lilly hadn't been. It looked like Lilly had been given a drug and left out in the freezing cold to die.

I led Connolly to the sofa and pulled a throw from the chair next to it and put it over her. Then I turned to the man. "What do you want?"

Sweat dripped off his nose and he swiped at it with the hand that held the gun. I watched him. What was his problem with Connolly? "Listen, let's talk about this. If Connolly has something you need, maybe I can get her to give it to you."

He croaked out a laugh. My radio crackled and Enrique's voice came across asking where I was. I reached up and clicked the radio a couple of times and the man screamed. "Turn it off right now."

"I'm trying," I said, doing my best to keep my voice calm when I wanted to scream back at him. I clicked the mic again and shut the radio down, hoping Enrique would realize Connolly and I were in trouble and come find us. "You do understand if I don't check in the sheriff will send someone to find me." Anyway, I hoped he would. Who knew what Mitch would do anymore? Apparently, I never really knew the man. My heart hurt thinking about all he'd done while we were married. It sickened me and I knew I'd never be able to look at him the same way again.

He laughed. "I think he's a little busy."

Did he know about Lilly's murder? I frowned and kept my eyes on him, wishing I could see him better. Who was he? I didn't recognize him as someone who had been arrested before. "Did you kill Lilly?"

Connolly moved, trying to sit up. "Lilly's dead?" Then her eyes rolled back in her head, and she passed out.

"I've got to get her some help. Tell me what you need, and I'll do what I can to help you. But if you let Connolly die, there isn't much I can do."

He sat on the recliner, the gun pointed at the floor. He rubbed his forehead. "You don't understand."

"Let me get something to staunch the bleeding and then you can tell me what I don't understand." I had pressed my hand against Connolly's nightgown, trying to stop the blood from flowing, but I could feel it seeping through my fingers.

"Stay there." He went into the kitchen and came back with a towel and threw it at me. "Here, hold that against her side."

I grabbed the towel, rolled it up and pressed it against Connolly's wound, keeping pressure on it. "Please let me call for an ambulance. I'll stay here with you, but we've got to get her some help."

He looked up at me through bleary eyes and shook his head. "You don't get it do you? It doesn't matter if I live or die. I've got nothing left to lose."

I felt my heart stop, then pound. My nerve endings flamed. "What do you mean? Did you kill Lilly?" If he did, he probably killed Willow and Renetta too.

He shook his head. "No, that wasn't me. I didn't kill anyone."

"Then do you know who did?" Come on, tell me what you know, I silently urged him.

To my surprise, he nodded. "Yes, I tried to stop her, but she…" he stopped and shook his head.

"Who?" I asked, hoping he'd tell me. Afraid he wouldn't.

He sighed. "You'll know when this is over."

"What does that mean?" I could feel his longing to spill his guts. He'd come to some kind of decision. I could see resignation in his face. "Can't you tell me?"

His eyes filled with tears. "I never should've let her talk me into it." He swiped at the tears. "She always kept me so torn up inside, you know? And if the cops have the gun, they'll never believe I didn't have anything to do with it. My fingerprints are all over it."

I nodded, wanting desperately to know who she was. "Tell me who. What did she want you to do?"

"Help her."

The room was dead quiet. I couldn't hear Connolly breathing and feared she wasn't going to recover from this. I kept my attention firmly on him. "Help her what?" I asked, gently.

"She killed the babies." His eyes were wild. His voice so low I could barely hear him. "She said we had to kill her."

I jumped up. "What babies? Who killed the babies? Who did you kill?"

He shook his head and put the gun to his mouth. Tears streamed down his face.

"Tell me," I yelled. I hadn't heard of any babies being killed. What was he talking about? I had to get it out of him. "Please, for the babies' sake, tell me what happened." I moved towards him, but he turned the gun on me.

"Stay back."

I stopped. "What babies?"

"Mine." Then he put the gun back into his mouth and pulled the trigger.

Chapter 47

Chapter 47—Mitch

If he could've gotten his hands around Chief Pauley's neck, Mitch knew he would've happily killed him. The Chief knew Liz was home. Mitch had told him so himself. But he'd opened his trap and said things that would end any hope Mitch had of rebuilding his relationship with Liz.

All around him, his people were staring at him. No one spoke. The chief stood in front of him, his mouth open as Liz screamed at him and walked away, her strides long and purposeful. With every step, Mitch felt her walking out of his life.

"Hey, man, I'm sorry. I didn't mean to make things worse for you."

Right. Mitch held up his hand and turned away. He was afraid he'd deck the chief if he didn't.

For the first time since he'd become Sheriff, he didn't know what to say to his people. He wanted to run after Liz. Tell her that it was all lies, but she'd see right through him.

Mitch drew himself up to his full height and glared at those around him brave enough to look him in the eye. "Let's get this place cordoned off and I want you going over it with a fine-tooth comb. I want to know who killed Lilly Larson and I want to know now."

He picked up the light he'd dropped when the chief opened his big fat mouth and held it up. "Clues, people. There must be clues."

No one said a word. As one, they all went back to their jobs. Mitch breathed a sigh of relief. He was a shit-poor husband, but he was a good sheriff. He'd find out what happened to Lilly and then he'd talk to Liz.

Nausea built up inside him. He felt in his gut that it was over between them. If she'd had any desire to make up after she'd found out about his affair with Jenn, finding out he'd been with Lilly would end all that.

He hated the thought of losing Liz, but even more than that he hated the disgust he knew he'd see in his daughter's eyes. She'd looked at him that way when she found out he'd cheated on her mom with Jenn. It would be worse now.

He shook his head and tried to reign in his mind. Think only about the job. That was the only way he'd get through the next few days.

He avoided the Chief and went back to work. At first, he could feel his people giving him looks, but soon they were more involved in the job at hand than they were in his life.

About an hour later, Enrique walked up to him. "Hey Sheriff."

Mitch looked up from the area of the park he was combing through. "Rodriguez. What did you find out from Brad Thomas?"

"He's afraid of someone, but he wouldn't tell us who it is. He didn't seem surprised about Lilly, just worried that the killer would come after him."

"Where are Liz and Garcia?" Mitch looked around for the two women. It was hard to see anyone, even though they'd put lights up, the surrounding area was in total darkness, and it obliterated the faces of anyone if they were far from him.

"Garcia is over there." Rodriguez pointed towards a group of deputies who were working close to the public bathrooms. "They think they may have found Lilly's phone."

"That's great. Have the techs see what they can get off it." Mitch glanced around. "Where's Liz?"

"She sent us back here and went to talk to Connolly. Brad Thomas' nurse said Connolly insisted on seeing him before she left the hospital."

Mitch frowned. "Why?"

Rodriguez shrugged. "No idea, he's not talking. Liz said as soon as he's released, we can take him to the office and see if we can get it out of him."

Rodriguez walked off and Mitch thought about what he'd said. What was Megan up to? She'd been secretive and someone had hurt her. Was Brad in on that? How could he be? He'd been in the hospital for the past few days. He needed to talk to Connolly. Maybe he should head over there and talk to her. If his team had found Lilly's phone, they probably weren't going to find anything else tonight.

He called them all over to his pickup. "What have you found?"

Garcia held up a phone. "It's Lilly's. There's no password to get in, but either she's erased all the calls she got the last few days, or she didn't get any. I checked out her texts. She got one from Brad Thomas a few days ago. It said, Talk to Deputy Connolly. She knows who killed Renetta."

Mitch frowned. "Okay, put things away for the rest of the night. CSI will be out here tomorrow. I'm heading over to talk to Connolly."

Chapter 48

Chapter 48—Liz

"Noooo!" My scream filled the air seeming to go on forever. Standing in Connolly's living room, screaming at the top of my lungs. As soon as I could get a little control, I ran to him, but I knew he was gone.

I felt for a pulse, anyway, not surprised when I didn't find one. Then I grabbed my phone and called it in and rushed back to Connolly.

She was still out, but she had a steady pulse when I put my fingers under her jaw to feel for one. Thank God. I didn't think I could handle two deaths on top of each other. I was holding the blood-soaked towel to her side when the paramedics came in.

They took over and I went through the deceased man's pockets and found his wallet. I needed to know his name. I pulled the wallet out and looked at his driver's license. He was Colin Derrick Symons. Where had I heard his name before? I rubbed my temple trying to bring back the memory. Then it hit me. He was Amy Bryne's ex.

Enrique and Garcia came through the door, and I ran to them, explaining what I'd learned. "He said someone killed his babies?" Enrique asked, his face white as the snow outside. He looked like he'd been sucker-punched, and I knew it would hit him hard because of his new baby.

"That's what he said. Can you clean up this mess and make sure Connolly gets to the hospital? I'm going to talk to Amy." I didn't wait for them to agree, I just booked it out to my Jeep and climbed in.

When I pulled into Amy's driveway, Willow's car was still there, but the house was dark. I pounded on the door, but no one answered. I tried looking in the window, but it was so dark I couldn't see anything. Would she have gone to her sister's? Maybe. I took out my phone and scrolled through my calls. I knew I'd called the sister the day I'd informed Amy of Willow's death. What was her name? Oh yeah, Jill.

Jill answered on the first ring. I told her who I was and asked if she knew where Amy was.

"She's not home?"

"No, I'm at her house and no one answers the door." I looked around for any sign of life but didn't see anything.

"Hmm, maybe she went to work. She cleans for that enviro-friendly cleaning company in town, Sudsy Suds."

"Do you have a number for them?" They couldn't come up with a better name? Where were their marketing people? Figuring they probably didn't know anything about marketing, I shrugged.

"No, sorry."

"No problem, I can find them. If you hear from Amy, please have her call me."

"Okay. What's up? Is something wrong?" She sounded nervous and I wondered what she knew.

"Colin Symons killed himself."

"Colin? That's horrible." I could hear her muffled cries. "Why would he do that?"

"I don't know. I need to find Amy. Does her mother-in-law still have the children?" I was hoping with all my heart that she did. If she didn't, I feared for their lives.

"I think so. Amy said she did and she's in Gresham, so she wouldn't have been able to bring them home in this weather."

"Okay." I drew a breath of relief and ended the call. Maybe Colin was wrong, and the children were still alive. *Please let them be alive.* Then I looked up Sudsy Suds on my phone and called them.

"This is Sonni with Sudsy Suds. How can I help you?"

I introduced myself and asked if Amy was working today. She said Amy had called in sick the day before and they hadn't heard from her that morning. I gave her my number and asked her to have Amy call if she checked in.

Now I was getting worried. Where was Amy? Had Colin killed her, then when he realized he was going to be implicated in the other murders, killed himself? I turned back to Amy's house knowing I needed to go in.

I called it in as a wellness check. Then I tried the door. It was open. "Amy!" I called out. "Are you home?" Silence.

I walked in and flipped on the light. "Amy! This is Detective Liz Ellisen with the Hood River Sheriff's Department." I took my gun out and walked down the short hallway wondering if I'd find Amy's body in the kitchen or living room. The hair on the back of my neck stood up. I felt like there was someone there, but if they were, they weren't making themselves known.

"Amy!" Still nothing. "If there's someone here, you need to come out with your hands up."

I held my .45 out in front of me as I entered the kitchen. There was no one there. To the left was a small bathroom, also empty. That left two bedrooms. Both doors were closed. What would I find when I opened them?

I announced myself and opened the first door. It must've been the girl's bedroom. It was painted pink and had two small beds with white bedframes. A small white dresser sat across the room with a little girl's jewelry box on top. I walked over to the dresser. Pulling a pen out of my vest, I eased open the jewelry box. Small trinkets, tiny bracelets and necklaces were stuffed inside. I thought of the tiny jewelry that had been found next to Renetta and Willow. It was similar, but the killer had taken them from Britney Fraizer's daughter, Kennedy.

On the floor were boxes of toys and clothes. Was Amy packing everything so they could move?

Things were starting to come together in my mind, and I didn't like the pictures I created. Had Willow killed Amy and Colin's children, so they killed Willow like Colin said. But what about Renetta and Lilly? I could kind of understand why they'd kill Willow, but not the other two. I was still missing a piece of the puzzle.

I turned towards the other bedroom. Would I find the missing piece in there? Just as I reached out to open the bedroom door, another door banged open. I turned back towards the hall. A figure stepped into my line of view, and I pointed my weapon. Seconds before I pulled the trigger, I realized it was Mitch.

Chapter 49

Chapter 49

"What are you doing?" I asked in a harsh whisper, my hands shaking. I gripped the gun tighter. "I could've killed you." The thought flitted through my head that it would've been manslaughter, not murder, and I should've pulled the trigger. No one would've blamed me after what I'd learned from the Chief of Police that day. *Except Bella.*

"Looking for you. Rodriguez said you were coming to talk to Amy Bryne because her ex-husband claimed he'd helped her murder their kids." His face was pasty looking and he wore a black cap with earmuffs that looked ridiculous on him. "I didn't want you to talk to her alone."

"Why not? I'm quite capable of talking to her."

Mitch motioned me back down the hall towards the kitchen where we could keep an eye on Amy's bedroom door, but whoever was inside couldn't hear us.

"Tell me what happened," he said in a low voice.

I filled him in on what Colin had told me. "But that still doesn't mean they killed Renetta and Lilly."

"Too bad Colin didn't tell you more. He just said he'd let Amy talk him into killing Willow because she killed their babies?"

I nodded, feeling sick.

Mitch rubbed the back of his neck. "Why would she want to kill them?"

"The only thing I can think of is she was in love with Amy, but she didn't want the kids. Maybe Amy was a part of it. She may have thought the only way she could be with her lover was if the children were out of the way."

Mitch nodded. "It's happened before."

It had happened many times before. "But that doesn't explain why she or Colin killed Renetta or Lilly."

"Or if they did," Mitch said. He looked back down the hall. "You looked all through the house?"

I stopped and let my pounding heart calm down. "All except for the bedroom on the left. I was just about to go in there when you showed up."

We walked back down the hall, and I rapped on the door. "Sheriff's Office, open up."

Nothing. I reached out and turned the doorknob. It was locked. I motioned to Mitch, not wanting to say anything more in case Amy was behind the door listening to us.

He whispered, "Stay here in case she comes out. I'm going outside to try and look in the window."

I nodded and watched him walk away. Then lightning fast, the door behind me opened and before I could react, an arm snaked around my neck pulling me into the bedroom. I tried to hit the person with my elbow, but they danced back out of my way. The lights were off, and the door banged shut. The lock clicked.

I did my best to get away. I couldn't believe it was Amy, we were similar in size, but I knew I was stronger. Whoever had their arm around my neck seemed bigger and stronger. Who else had Amy talked into helping her kill people?

Then a man's voice spoke in my ear, "Stay still or I'll blow you in two." He tightened his chokehold on me, and I could barely breathe. He grabbed my right arm and twisted it behind my back so I couldn't get my gun up to stop him. What felt like a gun was pressed into my side. "I have a .45 pointed at you. If you move or call out, I'll use it. Understand?"

I nodded and he eased the hold he had on my neck, letting me breathe. Then he backed me into the room and sat me on a chair. He kept my arm behind my back and tied me to the chair. Then he turned on the night light. I blinked. I couldn't believe my eyes. Mayor Clifford Long was standing over me with a gun. "Mayor?"

"Is Mitch out there?" He swung his gun towards the bedroom door. "I'm sure I heard his voice."

"He's calling for backup." Anyway, I hoped he was. The mayor snorted and I looked closer at his face and gasped. I hadn't realized it before, but he looked like the man in the old newspaper with Lilly. "Who are you?"

"Don't be stupid. You know who I am."

"You're Brad's father. You killed Renetta and Lilly so you and Brad would inherit the Abbott family money." It was all beginning to make sense now.

"Brad shouldn't have made it. I gave him enough Oxy to kill an elephant."

"You tried to kill your own son?" What kind of monster was he? My heartbeat tripled and my hands were sweating. I had to figure out a way to get out of there before he killed me or Mitch.

I looked around the small bedroom and noticed Amy Bryne cowered in a corner. "Amy?"

The mayor swung his gun in her direction, and she squeaked. "Keep your mouth shut or you'll be next."

"What are you going to do?" I asked. I hoped Mitch was listening to our conversation and would help us.

He laughed. "I'm going to kill you and the sheriff and make it look like little Amy did it."

She squeaked again.

"Then I'm going to take care of Brad." He shook his head. "Poor kid, has such an addiction problem, you know."

"And you think you'll get away with it? Did you kill Willow too?"

"I didn't kill Willow or Renetta. Amy took care of that."

A noise sounded outside, and light flashed in the window. "Damn. Amy, get over here and keep a gun on Detective Ellisen while I go take care of the sheriff."

Amy stood slowly and walked over, taking the gun he handed her. "Don't let her get away." He eased open the door and walked out.

"Colin is dead," I whispered, hoping to get her to talk so Mitch had time to figure out what was going on.

I felt her grow still next to me. "What did you say?" She ground the gun into my side.

"Colin is dead. He ate his gun."

"Noooo!" She cried out. "He can't be. Why did he do that?" She bent from her waist, clutching her stomach.

Was she putting on a show for my benefit? "I hoped you could tell me. He said something about helping you kill Willow because she killed your children. Or did you kill them?"

Amy sank down onto the carpet, but she kept the gun pointed at me. "I didn't. I swear. It was Willow. That's why I had to kill her. She killed my babies." Tears ran unchecked down her face. "My poor little babies. I didn't want them to die. I just wanted them to live with Colin or his mom so I could live with Willow."

"Who killed Renetta and Lilly?"

Amy didn't say anything. She sat so still I could barely feel her breathing next to me.

"Amy," I asked softly. "Did you kill Renetta and Lilly?"

She shook her head. Her eyes looked off in the distance and I wondered what she was seeing in her mind. Was she out of it enough that I could get her gun with one hand tied behind me? I'd have to try. But first, I wanted answers.

"Amy, who killed Renetta and Lilly?" I raised my voice.

Amy blinked. "I didn't want to hurt Renetta." She still had the faraway look in her eyes.

"Why did you?"

"She saw us."

Was I going to get a confession? My heart sped up. "Saw you? What were you doing?"

"Willow gave them some Tylenol to make them sleep before she took them down to the bridge. Then she threw them over. I tried to stop her, but she locked me in the car." She stopped talking and sobbed. "My little babies. I can't believe she killed them."

"Did Colin help you kill Willow?"

She blinked. "When he found out, he killed her. He was so mad, but I tried to get him to take the kids and he wouldn't." She stared at the gun barrel. "I didn't know what to do. I asked his mom if she'd take them and she said, no. Willow said she knew what to do." Big fat tears slid down her face. "Then Colin said she couldn't live because she killed our babies." She got up and picked up a pink fluffy baby blanket with the hand not holding the gun and held it against her. She looked at me with glazed eyes. "Have you found their bodies?"

"I just found out. We'll have to search for them. They may show up down the river somewhere." Poor little ones. My heart hurt at what had happened to them. "Why did you kill Lilly?"

"Brad saw us leave with Willow. He told Cliff. Did you know the mayor is his dad? Anyway, the mayor said he wouldn't go to the police if we got rid of Lilly for him." She shook her head and held the blanket closer. Tears poured down her face. "Colin said no one would miss her."

And Brad and Cliff Long would be filthy rich. Or the mayor would if his plan worked to have Brad overdose again. "Whose idea was it to put Lilly on a chair and leave her in the middle of Jackson Park?"

Amy's eyes brightened. "That was mine. She was so easy to drug. We gave her a little extra and she went out like a light."

"You had to know she'd be found in the park."

"I didn't think she'd be found until morning. Colin and I had a great plan. We'd kill Lilly, then take her money and leave town. Did you know she was some kind of heiress? A lawyer came by and left her a huge check. She wanted to give it back, but we talked her into cashing it, so she'd have enough money for her drugs."

She stood up. "That's enough talk. You know I can't let you leave this house, right? It's not going to be the same without Colin, but I'm taking the money Lilly left and I'm heading out of town. After I kill you, the mayor and the sheriff. I heard the freeway opened. I'm sorry to have to shoot you, Detective Ellisen, but I don't have any other choice."

"Wait a minute." I raised my free hand, wanting to keep her talking until Mitch could get back in the house. Did she really think she could get away with killing more people? "Who left the children's jewelry at each scene?"

"Don't you think that was smart? I watched a movie about a serial killer, and he took something from each person he killed. I told Colin it would confuse you if we left something."

It was scary how close she was to being right. I looked up into her face and realized she'd lost all touch with reality. She was wearing a silly grin. Had telling me her story made her snap? Or had she snapped the night Willow killed her babies? "That was pretty smart of you." I wanted to keep her talking. "The only people who know you're guilty are Brad and his father. And if you stall long enough, the mayor will probably kill Brad for you."

Amy shook her head. "You're trying to confuse me." She pointed the gun at me again and a light showed through the window. Amy turned towards it, and I threw myself at her, chair and all.

We tumbled to the floor, and I heard something fall and skitter off. Hoping it was the gun, I grabbed at her hand with my free one. I half expected the gun to go off and blow me away, but instead, Amy screamed.

The door flew open, a light came on and Mitch slammed into the room. "Stop. Sheriff." He had his gun pointed at us. Amy tried to wiggle out of my grip, but I wasn't going to let her.

Mitch hurried over and grabbed her, putting her hands behind her back and cuffing them together. He pushed her to her feet.

I scrambled to my feet. "It's about time you showed up. I was doing my best to keep her talking, but we were running out of things to discuss, and she was thinking seriously about shooting me." I looked past him. "Where's the mayor?"

Chapter 50

Mitch leaned down and helped me up. He untied the rope Cliff had used to keep me in the chair. "He wasn't as good a shot as he thought he was."

"Is he dead?"

"No, but he's not going to be able to walk for a while. I got him in the thigh when he tried to jump me. Idiot." He shook his head. "I cuffed him and he's in the back of my car." He motioned to Amy, who sobbed into her hands. "Let's get her out of here."

We headed to the office. Once we got there, Mitch turned both Amy and Clifford Long over to a deputy to book and called in all the deputies who'd been working on the case. We talked the case through, with me telling them everything Amy had told me.

"Man, Brad Thomas will be filthy rich if he ever wakes up," Williams said.

Mitch shook his head. "If Amy's right and he asked them to kill Lilly, he won't be able to enjoy his millions where he's going."

After we finished, I went to my office and picked up my phone to call Bella. A glance at the clock on the wall showed we'd worked through the night. It was nine o'clock in the morning. Before I hit the button for the call, Mitch knocked on the door and came in.

"Good work tonight."

I nodded and waited for whatever else he wanted to say. There was no way I was going to make it easy for him. I crossed my arms.

He rubbed the back of his neck. "Listen, I know the chief said some vile things tonight."

"Are you going to tell me it isn't true?" I tapped my fingers against my arms. There was no way I'd buy that.

Mitch must've realized that. He shook his head. "No, I can't deny it. I just want you to know that I'm sorry." He looked at me and I could tell that he was sorry. Sorry that he did it or sorry that he got caught? Probably the latter.

I nodded. It sure made filing for divorce easier. "I don't want you around Bella for a while."

"What? Why not?"

I narrowed my eyes. "I think you know why not. Don't make me spell it out. You can pretend to be busy. Just until this blows over. I'll tell her before she goes back to school that we are filing for divorce."

"Are you sure, Liz?"

I laughed. It wasn't a sarcastic laugh; it was just a laugh. "Oh yeah, I'm sure. I don't think we can work together either. I can't trust you and I have no respect for you. You'll have my resignation on your desk tomorrow."

He shook his head and looked at the floor. Then he looked back up at me. "What are you going to do?"

I shrugged. "I don't know. I haven't had time to really think about it. I may apply to the State Police. I may go do something else. I don't know." The elections were coming up. Maybe I'd run against him. I didn't say that out loud, though. I didn't want to give him any warning if I decided to run.

"This is not how I saw things turning out." He looked sad. Maybe he was, but I knew his feelings weren't my concern any longer.

"How did you think things would turn out?"

"I hoped…"

A knock on the door interrupted him. He turned to look when Rodriguez stepped in. "Hey, sorry to interrupt, but Wells just picked up Blake Peters."

"The dentist?" I asked.

"Yeah, he beat up a gal who works at Trillium." He named one of the bars in town. "Apparently, she told Wells that he's the one who knifed Connolly."

"Did she say why?"

Enrique's cheeks turned red. "Apparently, it was a kinky sex thing that went bad."

I covered my ears. "TMI! TMI!"

Enrique laughed. "I know, right? Anyway, he's in custody. Connolly's back in the hospital being stitched up again. Do you want to go talk to her?" He looked at Mitch.

Mitch shook his head. "Tomorrow. Connolly needs to rest."

"Okay, just thought you guys should know."

My phone buzzed as he walked out of the office. I looked down. "It's Bella." I picked it up and held it to my ear. "Mom, you've got to come home. Travis caught some old lady trying to break into the house."

"You're kidding me. Was she planning to rob us? Tell Travis I'll send a deputy."

"You might want to come yourself. She says the house belongs to her."

I was too tired to play games. She sounded as delusional as Lilly. Did Lilly have a sister? "Let me talk to Travis, honey."

"Okay." I could hear her speak to him and then his voice on the phone. "Hey, we heard you had an eventful night." His voice was soft and soothing, and I wanted to feel him there, holding me.

"How did you hear that?"

"Instagram. We've been following what was going on since early morning. Are you okay?"

I chuckled. "I'll fill you in when I get home."

"About that. Bella is right. This woman walked in, said she's the owner and you are squatting on her property."

I glanced up at Mitch and saw guilt written all over his face. "Who is she?" Instantly, I was worried. Not that she could waltz in and claim my dad's property. Unless there was something he hadn't told me.

"She says she's Missy Scott. Your mother."

"My what?" My heart pounded. My hands began to shake. Nausea roiled around my stomach. Mitch looked sick. I glared at him. He knew she was in town.

"I checked her identification. The name is Melanie Scott. Do you know her?" Travis asked. I could hear Missy's voice, a voice I recognized after all the years, talking to Bella. And I heard Bella respond. Not like she was upset, but like she was excited to meet the woman.

Did I know her? Oh yes. Missy Scott. The woman who had walked out of my life forty years ago. The woman who broke my dad's and sister's hearts. The woman I had no desire to ever see again. My mind flew to the break-ins at my house in the last few days. "It must've been her walking through the snow, leaving doors open, *stealing my dad's checkbook.*" Had she tried to steal my dad's pickup? I looked up at Mitch, grinding my teeth, barely able to spit the words out. "What have you done?"

The End

Also by

The Truth Will Set You Free – A stand-alone mystery

My Sister's Keeper – Book 1 in The Hood River Valley Mystery/Crime

Series

Acknowledgement

A huge thank-you to Shelley Goss for coming up with the title for this book! I love it!

Special thanks to my first readers, Mary Birk and Sarah K. Fox, who not only read through the book, but painstakingly looked for mistakes and made sure the story flowed. They both put a lot of work in on this project, and I can't thank them enough.

To my dear friend, Beverly Shackow, who has encouraged me from the first time I told her I wanted to write a book. Bev has been one of my first readers from the beginning, and we share a love of mysteries and crime stories.

Special thanks to Ricki Swearingen for her expertise copy editing.

Thank-you to Andrea Fox, 911 operator, Ricardo Castaneta, Hood River County Deputy, retired, Ange' Goodwin, Weiser, ID Police Department, and Mike Goss, Jefferson County Volunteer Deputy Sheriff, retired, for answering all of my questions. Any mistakes in procedure are mine, not theirs.

Special thanks to my sons, who helped with techy stuff that their mom isn't great at! And to my daughter-in-law, Sarah J. Fox for helping promote my book.

Book cover credit: 99 Designs, Razvan Nitoi (frankkko), designer

Author photograph: Kristin Fox

Website design and maintenance: Bob Fox

And to all of you, my dear readers, who have enjoyed the books and asked for more! I can't tell you how much it means to have you ask when the next book is coming out or tell me how much you enjoyed reading the ones that are already out. I write with you in mind. And if this is the first book of mine that you have read, thank you!

About the author

Lana M. Fox is a mystery author who lives in Hood River, Oregon, where she and her family own cherry and pear orchards. When she isn't writing, Lana loves to read, travel and spend time with her family.

Please go to www.lanamfox.com and sign up for emails to learn more about her books, and when the next one will be coming out.

You can also connect with Lana on social media.

A note from the author: I would love to hear from you. Please leave a message on my website.

Lana M. Fox June, 2024

Blurbs

Reader reviews for The Truth Will Set You Free

5-star review "Excellent book. Suspense around every corner. Picked it up to read and didn't put it down until finished."

5-star review "You'll Never Guess Who. Loved the story. It grabs you and doesn't let go. Tightly woven together with history of a generation a small town and its characters. The author has crafted an ending that takes you flying to the last suspenseful sentence. I'm waiting patiently for her next book."

5-star review "Couldn't put it down! A true thriller. Totally enjoyed this book. Every other page was an OMG moment. Plot twists, suspicious characters with a lovely damsel in distress."

Reader reviews for My Sister's Keeper

5-star review "Great story! Absolutely loved this book! Can't wait for the next one! This is definitely a MUST read! I give it 100 stars! "

5-star review "Great Book, It's a Must Read. This is a great book. If you read her first one you will love this one also. Will keep you reading until the very end."

5-star review "The ending is not exactly what you expect! I took My Sister's Keeper to read during a recent trip to Mexico where I was addicted to turning pages to find out "who done it" as well as "why, when and how." Then, there was also the subplot of what was going on in the private lives of the chief investigators! I recommend the book and, yes, the ending will surprise you!"